A CADGER'S CURSE

DIANE GILBERT MADSEN

THORNDIKE
CHIVERS

This Large Print edition is published by Thorndike Press, Waterville, Maine, USA and by BBC Audiobooks Ltd, Bath, England.
Thorndike Press, a part of Gale, Cengage Learning.
Copyright © 2009 by Diane Gilbert Madsen.
The moral right of the author has been asserted.

LIBRARY OF CONGRESS CATALOGING-IN-PUBLICATION DATA

Madsen, Diane Gilbert.
    A cadger's curse : a DD McGill literati mystery / by Diane Gilbert Madsen.
        p. cm. — (Thorndike press large print mystery)
    ISBN-13: 978-1-4104-2328-3 (alk. paper)
    ISBN-10: 1-4104-2328-X (alk. paper)
    1. Insurance investigators—Fiction. 2. Counterfeits and counterfeiting—Fiction. 3. Rare books—Fiction. 4. Murder—Fiction. 5. Chicago—Fiction. 6. Large type books. I. Title.
PS3613.A289C87 2010
813'.6—dc22   2009042433

BRITISH LIBRARY CATALOGUING-IN-PUBLICATION DATA AVAILABLE

Published in 2010 in the U.S. by arrangement with Midnight Ink, an imprint of Llewellyn Publications, Woodbury, MN 55125-2989 USA.
Published in 2010 in the U.K. by arrangement with Llewellyn Worldwide Ltd.

U.K. Hardcover: 978 1 408 47806 6 (Chivers Large Print)
U.K. Softcover: 978 1 408 47807 3 (Camden Large Print)

Printed in the United States of America
1 2 3 4 5 6 7 14 13 12 11 10

A Cadger's Curse

This book is dedicated to the memory
of
Alta Crohn Sumner,
college roommate, dear friend, and the
keeper of The Contract.
Thanks for helping me remember and
helping me forget
the infamous Mr. Bailey.

Let Kings and courtiers rise and fall,
This world has many turns,
But brightly beams, abin them all,
The Star O Robbie Burns.

"The Star O Robbie Burns," a simple
ballad, regularly sung in his memory
and which pays great tribute to him,
from World Burns Club.

PROLOGUE

Robert Burns, revered by current-day Scots and the author of such standards as *Auld Lang Syne* and *A Red Red Rose,* was twenty-eight when he stood before a window at the Golden Lion Inn in Stirling, Scotland.

It was October, 1787, forty-one years after the Battle of Culloden, where the exiled Stuart king, Bonnie Prince Charlie, had led an army of Scots in an attempt to reclaim the British Crown from the House of Hanover. The failure of this revolt had resulted in severely repressive measures being taken by the Hanoverians against suspected Stuart supporters, Jacobites, and all Scots. Despite it being deemed treason by the English, Jacobite feelings grew and persisted, hanging like a black cloud over the Hanoverian Throne.

Burns contemplated the verse scratched into the windowpane:

Here Stuarts once in triumph reign'd;
And laws for Scotland's weal ordain'd;
But now unroof'd their palace stands,
Their sceptre's fall'n to other hands;
Fallen indeed, and to the earth,
Whence grovelling reptiles take their birth.
The injur'd Stuart line are gone,
A Race outlandish fill their throne;
An idiot race, to honor lost;
Who know them best despise them most.

The verse was Jacobite propaganda. It was treasonous. It was being attributed to Robert Burns.

ONE

"There's good and there's bad," John Wayne drawled laconically in some movie or another. "And you're either doing one or the other." This morning I was definitely doing bad, and I was hoping I wouldn't get caught.

My hands were sweaty as I pulled the lock-shooter from my purse. I'm not a burglar by trade, though Lord knows why I'm not. There are thirty burglaries committed every second, but only 2 percent of professional burglars ever get caught. Great odds, considering those who do get caught mostly get charged with Misdemeanor Trespass.

Believe me, breaking and entering is not my usual *modus operandi.* I usually play it straight, and I knew it was risky for me to be here this morning. I'm an insurance investigator, and I free-lance out of a tiny office in the Loop. My name is DD McGil, and don't ask me what the DD stands for.

I'm female, thirty-eight, and, they tell me, not bad to look at. I've been doing interesting investigations ever since I had an awful experience in the academic world a few years ago. Back then I was an Assistant Professor of English, and I wrestled with words and concepts. Now I make my money duking it out in the business world of frauds and fakes. I'm happy to be as far away from the university as I can be, and I clutch at statistics the way an auto mechanic grabs his wrenches.

I turned to the task, stuck the business end of the shooter into the lock, and pulled the trigger, hoping the damn thing would work. It did, just as promised in the TV commercial. I'd enrolled in the Locksmith Training Class, and this handy gadget had arrived in the mail along with the mid-term test.

I swung open the front door, entered and looked around. I had to quickly find the location of the alarm box — the one big unknown in my risky excursion today. Alarm companies almost always put the box in the master bedroom closet, so I headed to where I thought the master bedroom would be. I prayed today wouldn't be an exception. I'd already faced one hurdle earlier when a nosy neighbor outside had prevented me from disconnecting the phone line, which would have made my job so much easier.

I'd guessed right and easily found the master bedroom closet. Voila, the alarm box, just as statistics predicted. And the key was in the lock — again which I'd counted on. Owners almost never remove the key because they're afraid to lose it.

I unlocked the alarm box door and opened it. There wasn't much time left to find the power switch before the alarm went off. I could have disabled the alarm with some household spray foam, but I didn't want to leave any evidence of my break-in. I pride myself on my business ethics. This lapse was not strictly ethical, but it was necessary. More sweat beaded on my forehead at the thought of what I was doing.

I bit my lip and refocused, looking for a little slide thing with a red light above it. I spotted it in the lower left-hand corner, flicked it, and thankfully the red light went off. I could now breathe again. I'm only thirty-eight, but I'm getting way too old for this stuff.

I closed the metal door, locked it and left the key in just as before. With luck, he'd never know anyone had been here. Statistics were, after all, in my favor as the perpetrator. In a burglary, nothing's in the victim's favor. And for once, Mr. Eric Daniels, Head Comptroller of Mooney Investments, was going to be the victim, not the perp. As for today's perp, I couldn't let myself think about that right now.

My cell phone vibrated, and I damn near peed in my pants. I hesitated, then snatched it from my pocket. "Who is this?" I hissed.

"DD, why are you whispering?"

It was Phil Richy, one of the attorneys who gives me work.

"Not now, Phil."

"Listen, this is urgent. You . . ."

"I'll call you right back." I hung up and disabled the vibrate option. My nerves were jangled, but I steadied myself by thinking of Mr. Eric Daniels. Mr. helpful, cooperative, efficient Eric Daniels. He'd managed to convince everyone else on the insurance investigation team that he was pure as the driven snow. I didn't agree. Our client, Mooney Investments, Inc. was being robbed blind, and I suspected he was responsible. Unfortunately my opinion wasn't based on any hard evidence. I'd noticed his eyes shifted to the left too often, his hands kept shielding his face, and his smile was as shallow as a fashion model's. My gut told me he was a liar — a very good liar. I had tried to convince a few of the guys on the team to see him the way I did, but all they gave me was a ribbing about "female intuition." So while Eric was busy testifying this morning before the Securities and Exchange Commission, I was busy breaking and entering, hoping to find some evidence to back up my intuition.

I was already frazzled because I'd gotten out of bed way too early to get here before Eric left his house. I'd missed breakfast and my usual morning crossword puzzle. Like the other sixteen million Americans who do crosswords every week, I get testy when I miss. But this morning I couldn't afford any distractions. I had to concentrate on Eric Daniels and nothing else. Mooney Investments was relying on our investigation team, but we'd hit a brick wall. My money was on Eric Daniels, and I was pissed that the rest of the team thought I was hallucinating. I had to find out one way or the other. I didn't like breaking and entering, and I knew if I was caught I would lose my license and worse. But it was my only option.

I'd parked and studied his house carefully before he left. I could have advised Eric that if he wanted his house burglar-proofed, he should have double-glazed his windows and installed a video camera. Lucky for me he hadn't asked my advice, and I knew I'd be able to get in relatively easily.

As soon as Eric drove away, I'd called his home phone to be sure no one else was there. There shouldn't have been — according to his file he lived alone — but I couldn't afford to run into the unexpected. It's always the unexpected that trips you up.

With the alarm safely off, I took another deep breath and surveyed Eric's pad. He certainly had good cover. Most thieves give themselves away by spending the loot, but Eric Daniels drove a plain Honda Accord, and the interior of his house was as nondescript as his car. I pegged him as a double lifer — like the prominent, civic-minded investment banker who embezzles funds then disappears to Vegas and spends it all on showgirls. I had no doubt Eric Daniels had embezzled the funds from Mooney Investment. But he hadn't fled yet to Vegas, and he was living modestly and not spending wildly. So where was he keeping the loot? My mission today, right or wrong, was to look for the answer.

His lap top computer was on a highboy dresser in the bedroom. Usually he carried it with him everywhere, but I'd counted on him leaving it behind this morning when he testified.

I turned it on. I had a hunch, and I was hunting for evidence of off-shore accounts.

Damn. The whole computer was password protected. I couldn't get in. I was afraid this might happen. I'd never guess his password. But I'd come prepared with a Line-based thumb drive, the would-be computer hacker's best friend. I inserted it and typed in the system command. It displayed a snapshot of everything running on the machine. Next I invoked the system monitor, looked for the password process and with a few more clicks Microsoft security let me in, just like magic.

I pulled up Eric's address book and started with "B" for "bank," and was prepared to go next to "C" for "credit." Ha! I didn't have to. Right there under the "Bs" was a listing for Bank of the Cayman Islands. Mr. Daniels might be money-smart, but he lacked imagination.

I opened his e-mails and sorted by sender. The resident encryption program kicked in, conveniently deciphering all the gibberish into a neat little row of sixteen acknowledgements of deposits, along with the account numbers. A quick perusal showed me they added up to over $4.5 million. Got you, Mr. Daniels!

I copied down the information, re-sorted

the e-mails by date, and shut down the computer before it really had time to warm up.

I hurried out, glad to be in the clear. John Wayne should have said, "There's good and there's bad, and sometimes you can be doing one while you're doing the other."

Two

I drove away quickly, anxious to get out of Eric's neighborhood before I called Phil. Even though the B & E had gone well, my forehead was still clammy, and I was breathing rapidly. Statistically speaking, I'm in the prime of life and should be out there having fun, but that wasn't how it felt today. My mother says I should stop dealing in probabilities and deal with reality, but in this job, statistics are my reality. At least today the odds had been in my favor.

The day was cold and gray — usual weather for Chicago. The traffic was stop and go — also usual for Chicago. The date was Wednesday, December twenty-third, almost Christmas. First of all, I don't trust Wednesdays. And ever since Frank died, damn him, I don't trust Christmas either. My Aunt Elizabeth, the Scottish Dragon as I call her, doesn't see it that way. She adores holidays and insists on flying across the pond to celebrate even the little ones. In fact, I was on my way now to pick her up at O'Hare airport. Auntie's visits always spell trouble. She calls me her favorite niece, but she behaves more like a five-star general than a doting aunt. La Dragon reveres anything Scottish, especially the Bard o' Scotland, Robert Burns. She believes being Scottish is more than a place of origin, it's a state of mind. Her favorite book, next to anything by Robert Burns, is Arthur Herman's *How the Scots Invented the Modern World.* Right now she's feverishly working to get me married to a bank president — must be a Scot of course — so the dirtiest thing I'd have to deal with is money.

As soon as I paid the toll on I-294, I pulled over and phoned Phil.

"What took you so long?" he demanded. "I've been calling and calling but you didn't answer. And what's with the whispering?"

I wasn't about to let him in on my unorthodox visit to Mr. Eric Daniels. Worst case he'd have had a heart attack, and best case I'd be in for a long lecture on standard ethics of an insurance investigator. Instead I equivocated. "I'll fill you in later. What do you need?"

"You've got to hustle your buns over to HI-Data Corporation and check out some

20

new employees for me."

"Okay. First thing Monday."

"Nix, DD. Right now. This is urgent, like I said. HI-Data wants a full-report on some new employees — three guys and a girl — and they need it by the first of the year. Since HI-Data is Universal Insurance's biggest client, it's axiomatic that what they want is what they get."

"Axiomatic, huh? This must be important. Why the big rush?"

"Apparently the new employees can't work with the company's top secret technology until official clearance comes through. HI-Data's in the middle of some top-secret project. I told them you could do it."

"Phil, that's only a week away, with Christmas in between."

"Jingle your bells, DD. Universal Insurance has opened up its pocketbook. There's a big fat bonus in it for you. Just be sure their employment records contain 'the truth, the whole truth,' and you know the rest."

I knew exactly. Employers today, especially those in high tech, do very little investigation of their employees on their own. They pass this task on to the resources of a bonding company, and the bonding company hires some independent investigator, like me, to do a comprehensive check on the employee. This way the employer is safe-guarded against the usual liability losses as well as against any fraud an employee might commit — either against the company, against a client, or both — while employed.

"Phil, I can't do it. It's impossible."

"What do you mean, impossible?"

"I'm on my way to O'Hare to pick up my Aunt Elizabeth."

"But the file's already waiting for you in Personnel. I promised them you'd show up first thing this morning. My reputation's on the line here, DD."

"Sorry, but I can't leave my aunt sitting at the gate." I didn't bother to explain that La Dragon considers it her due to be greeted with six heralds, two bishops, and twelve men at arms, like the Queen.

Phil made some noises in his throat that sounded like he was choking. "All right, all right. Get right over to HI-Data. I'll go pick up your aunt myself."

"Okay. Her name's Elizabeth Foster. She's arriving on British Air at the International terminal." I detailed the flight number and arrival time and assured him he wouldn't have any trouble recognizing her. "She's sixty-three, five foot nine, slim build with hazel eyes and silver-tipped hair." I purposely omitted describing her ruby red lipstick and voice loud enough to summon mastodons to lunch. Phil would notice those things himself.

"And she'll be dressed to the nines," I added, knowing Auntie would be wearing her flashy diamonds, even though I'd told her not to and had explained the concept of Risk Management to her at least a hundred times.

"Wait a second. Is this that eccentric aunt of yours who's always causing trouble?"

"I'm off to HI-Data. Talk to you later." I hung up before he could say another word. Statistically speaking, I'd gotten the better end of this deal. Briefly I felt sorry for Phil who was about to be pulled into Auntie's force field. Nobody's ever figured out Auntie. She's a study in contradictions that could keep an analyst busy till the next ice age. She's jaunty yet extremely disciplined, shrewd yet unfailingly generous, and once met, never forgotten. Her biggest anomaly is that she tends to live more in the past than the present. To her, a current event is the Hanovers stealing the British crown from the Stuarts in 1714. And she's not shy about sharing her views. In fact, she relentlessly tries to enlist all and sundry in her efforts to restore the Stuart descendants to their rightful place on the throne. And may the heavens defend you if by happenstance you should mention the name Oliver Cromwell. La Dragon turns positively icy and mutters unintelligible things in pidgin Scots about Puritans. All of which and more I'd forgotten to warn Phil about.

The next exit on I-294 was Lake Street. I was headed in the wrong direction for HI-Data, so I took the turn off, carefully avoiding the ice on the exit ramp from yesterday's snow.

Chicago winters are hard on people and on cars, too. I hate this weather, and so does my car, a green two-seater Miata convertible. I'm never sure she's up to coping, but I needn't have worried. She hummed along in third gear, the new Michelin tires rooster-tailing the slush and scattering a clump of sparrows feeding at a roadside ditch. Even though the speed limit was twenty-five, I took the tight curve at forty. Frankly, ever since I read a University of Iowa study about men driving an average of six miles an hour faster than women on freeway ramps, I've been doing my personal best to equalize the differential.

I did a quick turn-around in a truck terminal on Lake Street and merged back on 294, this time heading south. Naturally I had to pay another toll. A few minutes later at Oak Brook, the sign for the Reagan Memorial Tollway entrance appeared. I changed lanes, paid that toll, and headed west to Naperville. This job was already costing me a lot of money and effort.

No time now to do the usual background check for this client. Instead I grabbed my phone again and hit the speed dial for Tom Joyce. Tom and I have enjoyed a long-standing friendship fueled by our joint curiosity. On top of which we're both competitive. We strive to amuse each other and to top one another, but most importantly, we always watch each other's back. Tom's a well-known antiquarian bookseller, and we'd met in his bookshop when I was a first-year student at the university. He appreciates my flair for statistics and literature, whereas I envy his uncanny ability to deliver facts, figures, and arcane trivia on demand. Fun to us is challenging each other often and unmercifully.

"Caller ID says this is the fair DD," Tom answered. " 'Tis true, 'tis you?"

"Dammit, Tom, I hate that caller ID. It takes all the surprise out of life. For once I'd like to disguise my voice and pretend I'm from Barnes and Noble looking to buy your bookstore."

"I'd never sell to Plebeianism at its finest," he laughed.

"Tom, I'd make an offer you couldn't refuse."

"If I did sell, they'd have to take me along with the books. We can't be parted, like Romeo and Juliet, Hamlet and Ophelia, Tristan and Isolde . . ."

"Yeah, but doesn't it strike you as odd they all died young?"

"Stop being so damned literal, DD. The simile was meant to be romantic, not suicidal. Anyway, you can't expect too much of me this early. I'm still in my jammies, having coffee. What's up?"

"I need a favor. You know how I hate to walk into the jaws of a new client without knowing if it spits fire, has twelve eyes, or eats virgins."

"I'm not commenting on that."

"This is serious, Tom. I need you to find out whatever you can about a high-tech company called HI-Data. Its world headquarters is located in Naperville. I'm on the way there now, and I need to know everything A.S.A.P."

"I thought you were picking up the Aunt from Hell this morning at O'Hare. What happened?"

"Rush job offer I couldn't refuse. Someone else is fetching her. Lucky me."

"Oh, so this is another one of those awful jobs from your attorney friend, Phil? Do you have Attorney Insurance, DD? Sometimes I think he likes making your life miserable with some of these crazy jobs. He's . . ."

"Tom, could you just do your magic stuff however you do it and get back to me in the next twenty minutes?"

"Okay. Forget about Phil for the nonce. I'll see what I can do. You'll owe me big for this. Adios."

I hung up, confident he'd unearth any big issues at HI-Data. Tom's resentment toward Phil dates back to Frank's suicide. Tom believed then and believes now that I'd function better if I were still in academia, doing research and writing books. He never believed I could be happy in insurance investigation. But Phil had saved the day for me in that dark period after Frank's death, and I'll always be grateful to him for that. True, most insurance investigation work is strictly routine, but when there is action, I enjoy it. The only action in academia is back-stabbing, and I'd had enough of that to last me several lifetimes.

For the rest of the trip, I enjoyed the ride and tried not to think about the Christmas season. Holidays haven't been a lot of fun since Frank died, damn him. It had been different when he was alive. Lots of things had been different.

I'd been teaching one class in English lit and doing post-grad research at the university, working on a compendium of Restoration materials when I'd met Frank. He was a much-admired Dean at the University of Chicago, as popular with the faculty as with the students. Even Aunt Elizabeth liked him, though she complained I was too young for him and accused me of falling in love with him only because he looked like Sherlock Holmes. Practically every able-bodied female on campus flocked to his lively lectures on the history of the English Civil War. As part of my research on the seventeenth century, I'd enjoyed attending these lectures. He was not just interesting, he was fascinating. The English Civil War and the Restoration period came alive under his spell. I was as taken with him as were the others, and when he asked me to dinner, I was surprised but willing. When we began our affair, I was more than willing. And when he asked me to marry him, I was terrifically happy. Or so I thought. And then . . .

I'm no hermit, but after Frank's suicide, I was so hurt and angry, I couldn't face much of anything. I left the university and began doing insurance investigations work for some attorney friends. True, it's a completely different field than English lit, but that's exactly what I like about it. Anything connected with English lit or the university opens painful wounds. Truthfully, I'm not really back on my feet yet. I'm still paying off the last of Frank's debts, and I'm still not over what happened. Maybe I'll never be. A few months ago, I met a handsome brown-eyed guy named Scotty Stuart. Our romance has been going well, probably because his job keeps him away so much. Right now Scotty was in London, trouble-shooting for a conglomerate. He'd asked me to join him there for the holidays, but I like paying my own way and couldn't afford the airfare. I wasn't sure yet how things were going to turn out with Scotty. I only knew that after we met, a tiny kernel of happiness had settled in one corner of my heart that had been so empty for so long, and I wanted to hold onto it.

In my reverie, I damn near missed my exit. I braked hard, downshifted and exited the Tollway onto a long, winding access road just as the winter sun broke through thinning clouds. The HI-Data building came into view — twelve stories of white exterior with blue windows and a chrome sign, one of the biggest computer science palaces lining the Tollway's high-tech corridor about thirty miles west of the Loop. This is Chicago's version of Silicon Valley. The company's mega-bytes had earned mega-billions, and HI-Data had dumped a ton of it into their facility, including two retention ponds stocked with geese and the *de rigueur* formless art statue at the main entrance.

The phone rang as I parked. I hoped it was Tom getting back to me.

"I found out a few things that may be of interest," Tom said without preamble. "But first, I'm curious, DD. Usually you ask for information on esoterics like the Carolingian minuscule, not on pedestrian topics like technology palaces. You don't even believe in electricity. Just what are you up to over there?"

"I'm going to be their grammar police."

"Yeah, sure, for their technical manuals. Seriously, I hope you're not out of your depth on this one."

"Don't worry. They've got me vetting some new employees. What'd you dig up?"

"HI-Data is one of those privately owned companies that's grown fast and furiously. Principal owner of record is Jeffrey Fere, rhymes with 'dear'. A Ph.D. in Computer

Science from MIT, a Diploma in Informatics from the Swiss Federal Institute of Technology, and a knack for industrial utilization of cutting-edge technology. The company's carrying more debt than it should be, but it's also well known for its Research and Development successes, and it's rumored that's where they put all the bucks. It's also rumored that their investment's going to pay off with something really big anytime now."

"What is it?"

"It's so top secret, I haven't found out yet."

"Let me know as soon as you do. Anything else?"

"Nothing specific. Just watch your step. And be careful about asking too many questions about the 'something big.' Industrial espionage is big in CS, and . . ."

"CS?"

He laughed. "Oops. Sometimes I can't help myself from falling into their lingo. CS is Computer Science."

"Thanks. I should have guessed that. And by the way, exactly what *can* you tell me about the Carolingian minuscule?"

"Ha. You never let me off the hook, but luckily I know everything. The short version is that it's a script style of historic writing with round, clear letters where words are separated rather than running all together as in early Merovingian script . . . it was developed at the Abbey of Corbie and in use from 900 through 1150, then later revived during the Renaissance and has survived today as our lowercase letters."

"One of these days I'm going to stump you, you know."

"I doubt it. Au revoir."

Three

I locked the Miata and hurried to HI-Data's entrance, fighting the bitter west wind we Chicagoans call the Hawk. The glass doors reflected my jeans, black turtleneck, Bandera leather jacket and low-heeled boots. I was dressed more for sport than for success, but this was a rush job, and I wasn't out to impress anyone.

The splendor of HI-Data's marble and granite lobby made me feel like a supplicant at Versailles. A gold Christmas tree surrounded by white poinsettias in the center atrium did nothing to add warmth or cheer. There was no building directory. The place was deserted. I hit the button in a recessed bank of elevators, intending to do a random search for Personnel. Nothing happened. I punched it harder, and a loud, shrill alarm echoed off the marble walls.

"What the hell are you doing?" shouted an overweight security guard bursting out of a nearby stairwell.

"I'm looking for Personnel," I yelled over the alarm.

He was holding a mini-computer. He typed something on its keyboard and the alarm shut off in a jolt of silence.

"You have to sign in. This here's linked to our central computer, and if your name ain't on today's guest list, you gotta leave. No, don't use that." He grabbed my pen. "Use this."

He handed me an electronic stylus. I'd sat through a demo on this new security system a couple months ago at a classified seminar hosted by the insurance industry. Much of that seminar remains a blur because I was checking out the nice-looking buns of the male instructor. Yes I do believe in electricity, but I'm continually amazed at some of the new developments in the sophisticated paraphernalia that's coming on the market. I heartily recommend these new options to my clients, but silently I wonder where it's all going. We're already light years away from the yin and yang of the seventeenth century and into a new interconnectivity with the forces of the universe.

DD McGil, I scratched on the opaque swatch. *Universal Insurance Co.*

The guard wiped his sweaty brow. "Only

ways I missed you is I been checking the stairwells." He scowled at my scrawl. "What's that say? DB?"

I wasn't about to elaborate and tell him that my real name is Daphne December, hence DD, the result of an unfortunate power struggle between my parents and Aunt Elizabeth, the outcome of which made nobody happy, especially me. After getting tagged with the nickname Daffy, the family formally agreed I was to be known as DD. Only my mother reverts occasionally if she's really piqued. So I just smiled and said, "DD. Two capital Ds."

His eyes narrowed, but he didn't pursue it further. Instead he said, "Let's see, we got to get some details here about your person. Uh, what color eyes?"

"Blue."

"You're . . . what, five foot eight?"

"Five-eight and a half."

"Okay. And let's see, blonde. Right?"

I hoped he wasn't going to make any blonde jokes. I get them all the time. In the looks department, I'm used to being type-cast as the dumb blonde, and it doesn't bother me — much. My mother's biggest lament is that I inherited all the Mason good looks, but got the McGil tempera-ment. Physically, I guess I do resemble my

35

great-grandmother Mason, who was a tall, slim, easygoing beauty in her day. I've got her blue eyes and good legs, but I'm not what you'd call easy-going. Any canny Buchanan on my father's side would instantly recognize me as one of the clan. I've always had trouble straightening out people over what I do for a living. Especially after Frank died, when no one at the university wanted to publish my historical compendium titled *Restoration Scandals.* "Too populist," they claimed. They questioned its relevance to the university and scorned it for being too much like a pop culture best-seller. I wasn't about to straighten them out. That's when I left the university, and that why I'm in insurance investigations today.

I smiled and nodded in agreement, and he handed me the ID smart-card that slid out from the little computer. "Okay, you're on the list. But you're clear only for Personnel on the third floor. I gotta go back on my rounds. Return that card in the slot over there when you leave."

I remembered from the seminar demonstration that these smart-cards look like ordinary credit cards, but carry a heap of information in their micro-electronic circuitry, including my height and the color of my eyes and hair. Even if I didn't return it, it was undoubtedly date-encoded and wouldn't be good after today. Technology is always edging into science fiction, and in the back of my mind I heard George Orwell whisper "Big Brother Is Watching." I shivered, not from the cold.

The card activated the elevator and the doors sprang open. After a few seconds, they opened again and a clipped, mechanical voice intoned, "Third floor." I stepped into the corridor.

The guard hadn't given me Personnel's suite number, and none of the offices was marked. I didn't know which way to turn.

"Left," I said to myself out of habit and flashed the card at the electronic entry panel outside each door. The first two I wandered into were executive offices, but not a creature was stirring, not even a mouse. Must have all gone home early for an extended holiday weekend.

The next office had two eyelash windows at the top. I stretched, peeked in, and saw someone hunched over a computer. My entry card worked. As the door opened, I knocked lightly.

"Excuse me," I said and coughed discreetly.

Nothing broke his self-absorption. I didn't like being ignored. I walked across the room and tapped him on the shoulder. "I'm try-ing to find Personnel."

The man did a slow pirouette in his chair, toppled to one side and hit the floor. The computer keyboard landed on top of him with a hollow thump.

FOUR

The man's face was bluish-purple, and he wasn't breathing. In the next instant I recognized him. It was Ken Gordon, Frank's half brother. I hadn't seen him in years. I wondered what he was doing here and more to the point why he was dead.

I looked at him carefully. No wound was evident. His clothing was in perfect condition. He must have had a massive heart attack. He was perhaps more gray around the temples but otherwise looked much as I'd last seen him in Frank's lawyer's office. He and I had had a big blow up, and I'd never forgiven him for refusing to come to Frank's funeral — and for a lot of other things.

I touched his face. It was cool and hard, like granite. This was the only time I'd seen his eyes look unambitious. I was certain he was dead. I reached for the phone to call the paramedics, mentally calculating the odds of me finding his corpse. The cops could calculate those odds just as easily, and with my past history with Ken and Frank, I had a sickening feeling they'd throw the book at me. My little inner voice told me to drop the phone, put Ken Gordon back into his chair and get the hell out.

I grabbed the lapels of his expensive suit and pulled him up onto the chair, trying not to think of the phrase "dead weight." I was sweating from both exertion and nerves. At least he wasn't overweight — six foot one and a trim hundred sixty-five with all his clothes on. Just like Frank.

I retrieved the keyboard and noticed a few melted, discolored keys. Then I spied burnt patches on Ken's fingers, especially near his ring, a family ring just like the one Frank had always worn. Suddenly conscious of a burning odor, I jumped back and bumped into somebody. I froze.

"Who are you?" a man's voice shouted. "What are you doing here?"

I turned. The guy I'd collided with was short but trim. He looked to be in his late forties and he wore a pair of horn-rimmed glasses.

He removed his glasses and gave my casual clothes a long look. "This is a restricted area." He waved the horned rims at me. "I'm in charge, and I didn't authorize any visitors today."

I knew I must look guilty because I felt guilty. "I was looking for Personnel," I answered as casually as I could.

"Personnel's nowhere near here. Who let you in?"

Shooing me to one side, he grabbed the back of the swivel chair on which Ken's body was delicately balanced. Gravity did the rest. Ken Gordon swerved off the chair and hit the floor again with a thud.

"What . . . ? Ken?" He put his glasses back on, knelt down and lifted one dead arm. I stood mute.

"Jesus," he said and looked up at me.

The burnt flesh odor had expanded, filling the room. I could barely keep my stomach under control. This was no heart attack. I wondered how long this guy had been standing behind me and how much he'd seen. I wondered, too, what I should or shouldn't say about knowing the corpse.

"You better not touch anything," I cautioned.

"I'll handle this." He dropped Ken's arm, stood up and grabbed the desk phone, punching in what I suspected was the building's three-digit security code. Then he rapidly entered another series of numbers. He took off the horned rims again and

41

said, "Margaret, Norman here. Get an ambulance to room 322R at once." His eyes flicked over to Ken's purple face, then back to me. "Never mind details, just do as I tell you."

He banged down the receiver. His expensive gray suit hugged his well-muscled body as he steadfastly stared at me. "You've got some explaining to do. Ken is a partner here, and I'm not going to get my ass in a sling for you. Understand? What's the story? You one of his chippies?"

So Ken was a partner here at HI-Data. Was I having a fit of subjective memory? Did I forget he worked here? No. I never knew where he worked. He and Frank weren't very close. But I don't like co-incidence, and I didn't like the smell of this.

The strong scent of Norman's aftershave was now competing with the burning odor, and my stomach did another flip.

I stepped toward him. He took a big step backward and put on his glasses. He was a few inches shorter than me, and I find in general that short men are awful cowards. I explained who I was and showed him the smart card the guard had given me.

"He was sitting there when I came in. That's all I know." I didn't mention the burns on Ken's fingers or the fact that I knew him.

"By the way," I asked innocently, "what's a chippie?"

Before he could answer, the security guard opened the door.

The guard looked at me and asked, "What're you doing here? You're supposed to be in Personnel." Then he saw Norman. "What's wrong, Mr. Norman?"

"That's what's wrong." Norman pointed to the corpse sprawled on the carpet.

The guard looked at Ken's body, then at me.

"Get the police," Norman shouted.

"Yessir, Mr. Norman. Right away."

As he hurried out, I fervently wished I could follow. Right now, even Aunt Elizabeth would be welcome company.

"We'll wait here," Norman ordered.

Ken's corpse gazed unblinkingly up at me. I had hated his guts while he was alive, and I couldn't pretend to be sorry he was dead. I stood there calculating the odds of coincidence and the Laws of Statistics. Maybe I could convince the Naperville cops that I didn't know about Ken working at HI-Data by invoking the Law of Truly Large Numbers. Considering their law enforcement experience, they might be receptive to this particular law that says that the chance of any outrageous thing happening is more likely than unlikely, if you have a large enough sample size. But in my heart, I knew the sample size wasn't large enough, and I knew the cops were going to give me a rough time.

FIVE

Things don't happen very fast in a police station, but they happen inexorably. As soon as the Naperville cops found out I knew the victim, they questioned and re-questioned me about finding the body and anything else they felt like asking. I spent the rest of the day explaining to four different cops with four different ranks that I hadn't seen Ken since Frank died. Through it all, I tried to conceal my true feelings about Ken the Rat.

Detective Morton shifted position in a chair clearly too small for his athletic frame and said, "Frankly, Miss McGil, something doesn't play here."

I didn't say anything. I knew what was coming. My stomach was struggling with the grease from a chocolate donut one of the cops had offered me earlier. All in all, I was feeling awful.

Morton continued. "We know that Ken Gordon personally requested you to do the

HI-Data trainee investigations. What we don't know is why."

Ken Gordon would have been the last person in the world to hire me! We'd parted bitter enemies. He hated my guts as much as I hated his. None of which I was about to tell these cops.

"If Ken did ask for me on this job, I didn't know about it. I took this job from the law firm that works for HI-Data's insurer."

"All right then, let's go over your story again. Start with Frank's death."

It was still difficult for me to talk about that.

I took a deep breath. "Frank and I were going to be married in two months' time. We were very happy. Things were fine as far as I knew. One evening I arrived at our Lake Shore Drive apartment to find cop cars, an ambulance, and a crowd of people. Somebody had just jumped from a balcony. They said it was Frank."

Morton picked up the story. "So Frank was diagnosed with prostate cancer, and he told Ken he was worried he'd be impotent? Didn't he know about Viagra?"

I studied Morton's face and wondered if he was enjoying this.

"The coroner ruled his death was suicide," I said. It was a struggle to keep the emotion out of my voice.

"No suicide note?"

"No note was ever found," I said. The questions of why Frank jumped and why he left no explanation were ones I still wrestled with daily. I would never understand. Statistically, Frank's death didn't fit the numbers. I didn't tell them that, either. The recovery rate for prostate cancer is extremely high, 9 in 10, and Frank knew it. On top of that, 95 percent of the 24,000 men that commit suicide in the United States every year use a gun or poison or hang themselves. They don't jump out of windows. But the investigation into his death turned up no evidence to suggest it was anything other than suicide, and the bleak reality of that had dumped me into a black hole.

The detective peered at me across the table. His lips were smiling but his eyes weren't.

"Help me out here," he said. "Was there some kind of feud between you and Ken about Frank's money?"

"No. There wasn't any feud about money. I didn't care about the money."

"But it's true that Ken inherited everything, right? You got nothing?"

"Frank and I hadn't gotten around to drawing up new wills yet."

"That sounds like a feud to me. And it

sounds like a motive, too. First you don't get any of the money, then you end up paying all of Frank's bills. Tell us, why'd you pay 'em? Legally you didn't have to."

It was cool in the police station. Detective Morton's shirt was fresh and unwrinkled, but I felt wilted both inside and out. I didn't want to go on, but I took a deep breath and continued.

"Ken blamed me for Frank's death. He refused to pay any of Frank's debts. He wouldn't come to the funeral." I swallowed, still tasting the bitterness of that day. "He wrote nasty letters about me to the newspapers, the university, credit card companies, God knows who else. Like I told you, Frank had added my name on all his credit cards. We'd run up some bills buying a lot of nice things for the apartment and for the wedding."

"It says here that Frank paid all his medical bills by credit card," Detective Morton observed. "An established guy like that. Didn't he have insurance?"

"Frank didn't want the university to find out about the prostate cancer, so he didn't file any claims."

I paused at the uncomfortable realization I was digging myself in deeper. The cops hadn't understood Frank's desire for privacy then, and they weren't going to understand it any better now. And they didn't seem to believe that I had no idea Ken had asked for me on this job.

"Go on," Detective Morton urged.

"Money was never an issue between us. Frank was happy to pay for everything. He'd always had his mother's family money, so it was nothing to him. When his father died a few years ago, Frank inherited a large estate on top of what he already had."

"Tell me, did Ken have the same mother as Frank or the same father?"

"Same father. And to answer your next question, yes, they shared their father's inheritance equally."

"And the last time you saw Ken was in Frank's lawyer's office when he told you he wasn't gonna pay one dime of Frank's debts from the estate?" Morton asked, checking his notes.

"And his attorney informed me that since my name was jointly on all Frank's credit cards, Ken was fully within his rights not to pay."

"That would've made me pretty damn mad. I still don't get why you paid 'em off."

"I wasn't about to have Frank's name involved in lawsuits. Or mine, for that matter."

"An' you're sure you haven't seen Ken or talked to him since that day?"

"Positive."

These Naperville cops acted friendly, but they were tough cookies, like most suburban cops. They felt they were always competing with the big city boys, and they had a reputation of making things even more complicated than the city cops, just to show their muscle. When they finally completed the requisite paperwork, it was after two in the morning. It was clear they still didn't want to, but they had absolutely no evidence against me, and finally had to kick me loose. Too tired to get my car from the parking lot at HI-Data, and despite the pricey fare, I took a cab back to my apartment. When I unlocked the door, my Ragdoll cat, Cavalier, rushed at me and meowed, his way of scolding me for leaving him all day without companionship, as if I'd done it deliberately. Sometimes I don't know what goes on in those little kitty brains.

My answering machine was full of messages — one from Phil, one from Tom, and four from Auntie ordering me to call immediately. Unable to face anybody or anything, I crawled directly into bed. Sleep came at once, but it was fitful, haunted by visions of Ken's unblinking eyes, and the remains of that chocolate donut the well-meaning cop had offered me and I'd been foolish enough to eat.

SIX

At seven the next morning Cavalier and I were both awake but not rested. I fed him while I brewed coffee. He doesn't like it if I eat first, which doesn't bother me because breakfast isn't my favorite meal. I keep forgetting which of the food groups you're supposed to have when. All of which brings on the guilty realization that I don't live right, and it's all my own fault. I enjoyed a cup of Chicory coffee and worked the crossword while I finished the Shrimp Diablo leftover from Ina's restaurant where Tom Joyce and I had had dinner a couple days ago. That seemed like a few years ago.

Today I chose a beige suit and heels, a contrast to yesterday's jeans. I refused to wear black, but stopped myself from picking red. They say it's healthy to forgive and forget, but Auntie says that doesn't apply to us Scots. I couldn't forgive Ken. Not yet and maybe never. The cops determined he'd been electrocuted. When I left, they weren't sure whether his death was the result of a freak accident or foul play. Either way, they were reluctant to stop focusing on me as the prime suspect.

It was Christmas Eve today. Despite Ken's death, I was going to have to make up for the lost day on the trainee investigations, that is if I was still employed. Before I confirmed that, I had to return Aunt Elizabeth's calls, dread it though I might. I reached for the receiver and the phone rang. I picked it up gingerly, envisioning Auntie on the other end, ready to unleash one of her frontal assaults.

"What the hell happened at HI-Data yesterday?" Phil asked without preamble.

"Thanks for asking how I'm doing."

"Sorry, DD. Knowing you, I just assumed you'd be okay. So, uh, how are you?"

"I seem to be the subject of a police inquiry, whether it's for murder, accidental death, or witchcraft, I'm not sure. I don't know why they're considering me a suspect. Tell me Phil, can a computer electrocute you?"

"When are you finally gonna sign up for that course in Applied Electricity? I told you a million times that Universal Insurance would pay for it. You need to keep up with all the advanced electrical spy equipment that's out on the market. And from what the cops say, you're not a suspect. They had to give up that idea when I told them about assigning you to the job yesterday morning. They know you didn't have enough time to rig that computer. But listen, DD. What I'm hearing is that you knew the victim. True?"

"Yeah. He was Frank's half-brother. The cops said he specially asked for me on this HI-Data job. True?"

"You were mentioned, yeah."

"Why didn't you tell me?"

"I didn't think it was important. The contact came through Universal Insurance from HI-Data with a notation requesting you as the contact investigator. In retrospect, I guess maybe I should have said something, but it's not that unusual for clients to ask for you. You do have a reputation, you know. So why did he want you on this?"

"Phil, I haven't a clue."

"Where are we with the investigation?"

"I was just going to ask you the same thing. Do they still want me out there? Some Vice President named Norman really had a burr under his saddle."

"I already talked to Personnel. The

trainees'll be there today, even with the holiday."

"Good. I haven't even met them yet. I was at the police station until two last night."

"Well, how soon can you get to HI-Data?"

"I'll leave right now. I had to go there anyway to pick up my car."

"So on Dasher, on Vixen, and report back to me right away if there's any more trouble. By the way, did I mention you are forever in my debt?"

"For what?"

"For picking up that aunt of yours yesterday. It was a near-death experience. Getting Attila-the-Scot through customs was like steering a dreadnought into harbor. That jewelry she was wearing cost more than the gross national product of Scotland. I told her having all that stuff on her person when traveling wasn't risk-averse, but all she did was pooh-pooh me. And she's got some crazy notion that she's got hold of, as she put it, 'a wee Robert Burns treasure.' Look, I gave her what legal advice I could, and for free. She's determined you'll sort it out. And I'm not even going to mention how she's still pulling for Bonnie Prince Charlie and the Stuarts. My God, DD, she reminds me of you."

"I knew you'd like her," I declared and

hung up.

I took out my notes from yesterday's breaking and entering at Eric Daniels place. I was about to do something I didn't like because I despise anonymous notes, but there was no other choice. The information I'd gotten at his house would never be admissible as evidence, and I certainly couldn't reveal how I'd gotten it. That would remain forever my secret. However, a staggering number of cases are solved through anonymous tips, and I knew the team — including me — would jump fast to investigate. So I block-printed an anonymous note to Mr. Ed Mooney, President of Mooney Investments, telling him about Mr. Eric Daniels and some numbered off-shore accounts. It would be enough for a search warrant. I sealed the envelope with a wet paper towel, put on a pre-sticked stamp, and dumped it into my purse to mail. Then I called Tom Joyce's cell phone. It was too early for him to be at the bookshop.

"I heard about yesterday," Tom said as soon as he picked up. "Makes you wonder about probability theory and random events."

"Tell me about it. The odds of writing a *New York Times* best seller are 220 to 1, and my finding Ken's body is even more unlikely. The cops think so too."

"Let me know if there's anything you need. I'm doing an appraisal for the Chicago Public Library today, so use my cell. I'll switch it to vibrate mode. I love that. Merry Christmas Eve. Over and out."

I screwed up my nerve and called my mother. Immediately after saying hello she transferred the phone to Aunt Elizabeth. I took a deep breath, bracing myself.

"Who was that handsome, canny man who fetched me from the airport yesterday?" the Dragon inquired sweetly. "His automobile was verra big and comfy, not like that little toy convertible model you drive. Is he Scots? And he told me he's an attorney, but of course I did not believe him. As I said to your mother, whatever would a lawyer be doing fetching me in the middle of the day? By the bye, where were you yesterday?"

"Didn't Phil explain I was called away on urgent business?"

"What does this Phil really do?"

"Just what he said. He's a lawyer. And he told me he gave you some free advice about risk management that corresponds exactly to what I've been telling you for years."

"Never mind about that. There's something much more important. You must hie yourself over here immediately. I've been offered a rare Robert Burns manuscript, and I'm convinced it's the real thing. You must authenticate it for me."

"There are firms that specialize in document verification, Auntie. Hire one of them."

"No, no. No need for that. This is unique. I have faith in you. You're the investigator. And you're an English major expert, too. After all, you've had experience in this sort of thing."

"I haven't done anything like this, Auntie. I . . ."

"Nonsense. We must needs keep this in the family. Here's your mother."

"Aunt Elizabeth, please, I . . ."

"DD, this is Mother. Elizabeth feels you should at least take a peek at her find. That's not too much to ask, is it?"

Because of La Dragon's lifelong passion for anything Robert Burns, I knew a lot about him and his writings through osmosis. "Mother," I responded, "everything Robert Burns wrote was catalogued extensively. Most of it is housed in well-known collections in the National Library of Scotland or the Mitchell Library. Experts would easily be able to authenticate whatever she's got. Believe me, I know some things, but I don't have that kind of training or specialized knowledge. You're putting me in a bad position."

"You don't understand, DD. Just come and take a look. That's all I ask. Please?"

I relented finally. She knew I would. "Okay. She's won again. Put her back on the line."

"Thank you, DD," Aunt Elizabeth cooed, dripping sweetness like a Venus flytrap digesting prey.

"What do you want me to do?" I asked.

"I canna tell you over the phone. Come here and see for yourself. You'll be excited, I give you my word on it."

"You have it with you?"

No seller would allow a putative buyer, even a putative buyer named Aunt Elizabeth, to take a Burns manuscript from Scotland to America purely "on spec."

There was a long silence.

"Auntie? Dammit. You've already bought the whateveritis, haven't you?"

"Aye, so I did," she declared forcefully. I could visualize her chin jutting at the phone. " 'Twas a one-time offer. I could not *not* take advantage of something so unique."

Whenever the Scottish Dragon employs the double negative, it's pointless to argue. I asked instead, "What happens when you get proof it's a fake?"

"That's not possible. You must prove it's genuine. You'll see when you get here."

I explained I'd be there later than originally planned because I hadn't taken care of all my business yesterday. Naturally she demanded to know why. After I related the day's events, she said, "Everything to do with Frank was a disaster. Your mother and I told you he was too old for you. An' I won't say I'm sorry about Ken. He was a conniver and a turncoat. This job of yours is awful. An' your office is a hovel. You must give it up and get something respectable. No one in our family has ever been in jail."

"I wasn't exactly in jail, Auntie. I was only at the station for questioning." I hung up, exasperated. When — correction if — Aunt Elizabeth ever dies and ends up in Heaven, she'll tell God what to do. If she ends up in Hell, God help the Devil.

SEVEN

I hailed a cab and gave directions to HI-Data. Before we hit the expressway, I told him to make a detour to the main downtown Chicago post office. Correction, the new main downtown Chicago post office. I couldn't get used to the city fathers' decision to abandon the former post office, a massive Art Deco structure that straddled Congress Parkway and now sits nearly unused with one small sign directing patrons to the new undistinguished facility facing it across Harrison Street. I dropped the anonymous note into one of the mailboxes at curbside and, as the cab lurched back into traffic, I wished Mr. Eric Daniels a very Merry Christmas and a Happy New Year.

The cab took me to HI-Data's main front entrance. I paid another pricey fare and hurried into the building, chased by a gaggle of bold, belligerent geese nipping at my ankles. "You could be somebody's Christmas dinner," I yelled at the feistiest one as it pecked at the closing door.

"Hey! You got to report in here."

Startled, I turned to see a young, uniformed guard with a 9mm Smith & Wesson strapped at his slim hip.

"I'm looking for Personnel. My name's DD McGil, Universal Insurance."

His black eyes cased me. "Oh, you're the one they told me to watch out for. I got to escort you directly to Personnel and not let you out of my sight. Follow me."

The bloodless elevator voice announced the third floor. Today we exited and turned right.

"Page me when you're ready to leave so's I can escort you out of the building," he said. "You can't go nowhere in HI-Data without a card, and I ain't givin' you one."

When we reached Personnel, he repeated his instructions to the receptionist, making me feel like a high-school truant. The nameplate on the receptionist's desk read "Sparky Groh, Personnel." Her deep reddish-black hair surrounded her thin face like a dark halo. She sported a leopard pin on her black suit, and I approved the hint of citrus from her Michael Kors Hawaii perfume.

She turned her sharp gaze on me and said

matter-of-factly, "You're the one who found Ken's body yesterday."

"Yes."

"Norman called a special staff meeting this morning. He threw a fit about you. Imagine — a staff meeting on Christmas Eve. When he couldn't get you canned, he gave strict orders you're not to be left on your own for one second."

"Usually when a company is paying me to do a job, they don't treat me like an industrial spy. I guess finding a body falls outside the usual personnel regulations."

"Sorry about that." Sparky's red lips curled into a small smile. She stood, and we shook hands. She had long, shapely legs and topped six feet in her spike heels. She carried herself with panache and made it clear she was in charge of Personnel, not merely a receptionist.

"Everybody's in an uproar over Ken's death, especially Norman," she said.

"Why is he convinced I'm involved?"

"Because he believes Ken's death wasn't an accident. After all, computers don't just up and electrocute you. We'd have to shut down shop if they did."

She was right. I'd looked up the statistics and the odds of being killed by lightning were 2,320,000 to 1. The odds of computer electrocution were even higher. In fact, they were so high the insurance adjusters hadn't yet calculated them. Instead, I asked if Ken had any enemies at HI-Data.

"Everybody has enemies in this business," Sparky replied. "Norman's sure you're involved because Ken requested you to do the investigations. That's why you make a good suspect. He's having fits because he couldn't convince the police to arrest you."

"Well, my name was still on the roster today, so I'd better get on with the job."

She smiled. "Don't mind Norman. It's nothing personal. He's a real company man. He'd probably sacrifice his wife if he thought it was for the company good."

Sparky kept her eyes on mine. "Why did Ken want you in particular to do the trainee investigations?"

"I was hoping you could tell me."

After a pause, she said, "I almost forgot. Our President, Mr. Fere, wants to see you before you meet the trainees."

She led; I followed.

"What's the big rush getting these four trainees vetted?" I was subtly trying to get some information on Tom's "something big" at HI-Data while trying to match her brusque pace through the maze of HI-Data's empty corridors. "I'm being pushed hard to get my reports in by the first of the year."

"All four of these new employees were hand selected by Ken and Norman to work on a special project vital to HI-Data," she explained, slowing down. "Each has a special skill they bring together to complement the others for the short-term success of the project and the long-term growth of HI-Data."

"Why are we just getting to this now?"

"It's Norman. At first, he didn't feel that these new guys had to be put through the bonding process. Then he changed his mind. That's why you're here."

"Tell me a little about the company."

"Don't you have any idea what goes on here at HI-Data?" she asked as we turned down another deserted corridor.

"You mean high-tech research?"

"No, I mean soap opera stuff." She glanced down the corridor and lowered her voice to a loud whisper. "It's all one big power struggle here. Everybody's busy backstabbing everybody else. You've got to watch over your shoulder every second because someone's right behind you with a knife. Only reason I'm safe, nobody wants my job."

"Every company has office politics, but

murder?"

"Listen, on any given day, HI-Data's drama can out-do anything on TV. It's a high-stakes game. Your career can go in the dumpster in a second. Take my word for it."

HI-Data had a corporate culture from hell, I concluded, remembering Norman questioning if I was one of Ken's chippies.

Sparky flashed her ID card at an elevator panel. "This takes us directly to the executive suite." The doors opened, and I followed the trail of her soft perfume.

"Oh, be sure to address him as Mr. Fere. And don't smoke. We have a total ban on smoking in HI-Data."

The executive suite was plush and subdued, a throwback to the formalities of another time. The glass and chrome, laid-back casual of competing computer palaces was conspicuously absent here. The reception area was lined with impressive rosewood doors polished to a gleaming red-bronze. The only concessions to the holiday season were the ornate gold wreaths hung on each door and a small gold tree on the corner of the receptionist's desk.

A door to our left was marked "Ralph Trout, Sales." One on the right read "Ken Gordon, Treasurer," and someone had draped black crepe over the gold wreath under his name.

The door directly in front of us was marked "Jeffrey Fere, CEO," and an adjacent door's nameplate read "Norman Richtor, Vice President."

"April, tell Jennifer I've delivered Ms. McGil from Universal Insurance." The receptionist, April Nimicz, had beautiful long fingernails polished an eye-catching pink. She picked up the phone and drew her lips together in what might have been either a smile or a scowl.

Jeffrey Fere's door opened, and a trim, middle-aged woman wearing a dark brown suit with her graying hair piled high in a bun came toward us. I assumed this was Jennifer, his secretary.

"He'll see you now," she announced with a thin smile.

As she led me toward the inner office, I heard Sparky tell the receptionist to call her after the interview and she would introduce me to the trainees.

EIGHT

The spacious office had floor to ceiling windows offering a panoramic view of HI-Data's fields and retention ponds to the west and south. From up here, the straggling geese and blanket of snow looked cleaner and more picturesque than they really were.

Jeffrey Fere was silhouetted against the long windows, swinging a golf club. He putted a ball into a cup on a patch of raised artificial turf. We all waited and watched the putt sink.

"Great shot," he announced. His fitted Savile Row suit and blue silk tie masked a slight paunch, but he moved with a grace that wasted no energy. He dismissed his secretary, removed his granny glasses and extended his hand.

The room's rosewood wainscoting, leather furniture, and rich fabrics created the effect of a comfortable gentlemen's club. There was no clutter denoting work except a fancy flip chart against one wall reading "OFFENSE" in red letters with subheadings of "Frontal Attacks, Flanking Attacks, Envelopment, and Isolation." Big business was definitely war around here.

Motioning to a sofa across the room, he said, "Miss McGil, please take a seat." I thought his slight accent might be Irish or Welsh.

We settled in, facing each other along a rich expanse of Italian leather. He replaced his gold-rimmed granny glasses and focused his sharp eyes on me.

"I asked to see you this morning to impress upon you the importance of getting these new trainees mainstreamed into our top-secret project as quickly as possible. I realize what happened yesterday makes your job even more difficult. However, it is essential we have their final clearances by the first of the year. Do you believe you can deliver on time?"

"I think so, barring any other unforeseen circumstances."

"I understand it was you who found Ken's body," he said.

I wondered what Norman had told him. "Yes, I'm sorry to say I did."

"I understand Ken had requested you

69

personally, Miss McGil, to investigate these trainees. Why?"

"People keep asking me that. I don't know. Didn't he tell you?" I asked.

"I was unaware Ken knew you when he hired you, but it doesn't surprise me. He often did things to help out friends."

I didn't bother telling him I wasn't a friend and Ken would never have done anything to help me out.

"Now that we've lost a key person," Jeffrey Fere continued, "getting the trainees on board immediately is even more critical."

I sat quietly, wondering if he was going to ask anything more about Ken and me and Frank. I felt certain HI-Data knew everything I'd told the cops.

"The police now believe Ken was deliberately electrocuted. I would like to find out exactly what did happen. Perhaps, as a trained investigator, you might have seen something that could help us."

"Mr. Fere, if it was no accident, then somebody rigged that computer. Whoever sat down and turned it on, in this case Ken, became part of a conducting path between two terminals of a high voltage source. I'm sure the police have already or will soon identify whatever path was used. Tell me, did Ken use both hands to type on his keyboard?"

"I would have no idea," he responded, looking puzzled. "But a secretary or our Personnel Administrator might be able to tell you."

"Why does Norman think I'm involved?"

"For that, Ms. McGil, I apologize. I have already spoken to Norman about his over-zealousness. I assure you he will not pursue the matter any further. But I'd like to know exactly what you saw and what you think."

"I really can't tell you anymore than I told the police, Mr. Fere."

"I'm hoping you might recall some little detail that could assist us. Ken was a tremendous asset to HI-Data."

"I wish I could help, but I don't know anything else. Maybe Ken wasn't the target."

He looked up at the ceiling and was silent a long moment. Then he smiled at me warmly. "You see, Miss McGil, this is my company. I started it from nothing except brains and luck, and it bears my indelible imprint. It's my child, and every employee here is like a member of my family. For Ken's sake, as well as for everybody else at HI-Data, this has to be cleared up. And if Ken wasn't the target, we need to find that out, too. Please, if you think of anything else, get in touch with me personally."

I nodded. "I'll let you know."

He rose, signaling the end of our interview, and walked to his massive desk, all the more impressive because it was free of clutter. Not even a computer was in sight, although I did spy a tap-detector plugged into his gold phone. Today, even that precaution is no guarantee against spying from the newest high-impedance monitoring devices.

He block printed a phone number on an embossed card with a gold pen out of a fancy penholder in the center of his desk. "You can reach me anytime at this private number," he said, handing me the card. "I'll look forward to receiving those reports on the trainees as soon as possible. Happy Holidays."

A door opened without warning on the far side of Jeffrey's office, and Norman popped in like a jack-in-the-box. He must have been eavesdropping from his office on the other side of the adjoining door.

Norman ushered me out past the receptionist, and when the elevator doors slid closed, he hissed, "You made me look bad in front of my CEO. Nobody does that to me."

"Norman, I'm here to do a job. The

quicker I do it, the quicker I'm gone, and we'll both be happy."

"HI-Data is a good luck company because Jeff is lucky. He's a genius, and I'm proud that he's my CEO. But you're bad luck, you're going to wreck everything. I can smell it."

The elevator voice announced the third floor and the doors opened.

"You really believe in bad luck?" I asked.

"You bet I do. Luck is everything. And you're a jinx."

Not even an autographed Miss Manners book was going to help Norman, so I said, "Just stay out of my way, and I'll be gone by the first of the year."

Neither of us spoke the rest of the way to Personnel. I remembered that the odds of a meteor landing on my apartment were 182 trillion to one, and I realized the odds of my ever having a good thought about Norman were even greater.

"Ready for the trainees?" Sparky asked.

I nodded.

"Follow me. They're in room 333T, doing an introductory R&D tutorial."

"How do you know where you're going around here?" I asked. "It's so confusing. Nothing's marked."

"That's done on purpose," she explained.

"HI-Data's like England during WW II when all the signposts were removed. Once you're here a month or two, you get used to it. Until then, you just have to leave trails of bread crumbs." She laughed. "It's a good security device. If somebody looks like they don't know where they're going, we automatically stop them for questioning. Nine times out of ten, they're just lost and not snooping, but still, they're where they're not supposed to be. It's a small security technique that seems to work."

"Speaking of security, I see there are cameras everywhere in HI-Data. I asked the cops for a look at the surveillance tapes when they were grilling me, but they told me there weren't any. What happened?"

"A few days ago, Ken had everything disconnected except for the entry level. All the cameras feed into one system, and they're very high resolution. Ken was worried that the cameras might be hacked into and used by competitors to find out details of SAFECRACKER and other HI-Data secrets. Norman disagreed, but Ken was a partner and Norman isn't. That's one of the reasons you're here."

Sparky used her electronic access card in the double door panel of Room 333T to gain entry. We each pushed opened a door and entered the semi-dark training room.

Ken Gordon was in the front of the room, speaking to the trainees.

NINE

We were looking at a Power Point presentation at the front of the lecture room. Ken was up there on a giant screen, his animated, smiling face and white-wing sideburns engaging the audience. He was in his element — selling.

"HI-Data's SAFECRACKER program," Ken's webcast voice was saying, "is our brand-new, state-of-the-art proprietary disassembler program. Our version one point oh-two has the unique ability to easily allow a user to reverse engineer ANY computer program. SAFECRACKER represents a breakthrough on several fronts. First, it allows HI-Data R&D to examine the source code of ANY software application. Second, it allows HI-Data to select, modify, and mix-and-match the best from each application to create a superior application with perfect, non-buggy code. This makes HI-Data competitive with anyone. If we can get a competitor's beta version, we can beat them to market with a superior version of the application."

The webcast image of Ken smiled broadly. I watched in fascination as a close-up revealed a dab of spittle at the corner of his lips. "And so," he continued, "I don't need to tell you the enormous value of this SAFECRACKER software to HI-Data. Distribution and access to this software is VERY tightly controlled to prevent it from falling into the wrong hands. Creation of the software involved a completely different starting point and some good fortune on our part and I doubt our competitors could recreate it without long delays and ruinous costs."

"Sparky," I whispered, "should these trainees be seeing this before the full investigation?"

"It won't be a problem," she whispered back. "This is a sales presentation Ken put together to attract other investors. It doesn't contain anything that's program specific."

Fine, I thought to myself, but I knew Scotty, my computer-expert lover, would have given a lot to be in this room. Their new program sounded like a tremendous breakthrough. To me, it also sounded like it should be illegal, but business ethics was not what I was investigating.

Somebody switched on the lights and killed the webcast, and Ken's image disappeared.

Sparky called the names of the four trainees and told them to accompany us. Then she gave the command to resume the R&D tutorial.

One of the trainees loudly complained about having to leave the tutorial and miss a crucial concept.

Sparky bristled and stopped in her tracks. She pointed at the offender, but included the whole group in her admonition.

"Mister Olson, I'm not going to debate you. If you fail to pass muster from Ms. McGil on the comprehensive background check, you're out of HI-Data. Technically, we stretched a point to let you see this presentation before you were fully cleared. Now let's get going and stop wasting company time."

We single-filed out after her like goslings following our imprint. We had to. She was our Ariadne, the only one who knew where we were going.

TEN

I generally start a comprehensive background check by talking with the object of my investigation. It's unorthodox, I know. Most investigators never meet their subject and don't want to. I'm different. I look at the subject as raw data. Everything else confirms or denies.

Sparky had put us in a small conference room — me, the four trainees, and a pile of paper that constituted their confidential personnel files, all together in the Palaestra. Let the games begin.

"All right, it's now 10:22 a.m., December 24." I opened one personnel file as a visual aid. "As of now, none of you has any secrets."

I smiled broadly and, I hoped, somewhat evilly. The group got restless which made me happy. I like to scare the pants off my subjects right from the start so they tell me their sins. It's the nearest I get to being

James Bond, and considering human nature, the technique's generally a success. In my experience, nobody ever tells the whole truth. In one out of every three investigations I run, somebody quits the job the next day. This way, I figure, we're all happy. Nobody gets caught, nobody gets embarrassed, and I get paid the full amount by doing only half the work. It's my version of increased productivity, and it's one reason I like my job. And I was as far as I could get from studies of English literature and those dark days after Frank's death.

The four trainees nervously drank their sodas and their waters while I told them that having their personnel files would make doing their background checks a breeze. With their vital stats at my fingertips, all I had to prove was that something wasn't kosher, and they'd be in deep trouble at HI-Data. Each of them was more computer literate than I, so I didn't have to explain further. They listened attentively though as I reminded them how easy it was to zero in on hundreds of national databases through IQUEST, such as ORBIT and NEXIS and LEXIS. What I didn't tell them was that I'd recently downloaded the newest version of "Online Detective" onto my computer. With its ninety-five thousand databases, I was now privy to what brand of underwear each of them preferred.

Despite the fact the trainees had already signed a consent form for HI-Data agreeing to have their records searched, I always followed Phil's advice to get a release of my own signed.

"The best way to check information, though," I informed them as I handed out my form, "isn't through any database. It's through the people trail, the live bodies you've all come in contact with since you were born. It's my favorite part of this job. You might not think so, but people love to talk to me."

As I collected their signed forms, I hoped they were feeling naked, unable to hide as much as a birthmark. They were all eyeing me with contempt and disgust, convinced I was totally obnoxious. Well, I hadn't been hired to be Mother Theresa. Their discomfort meant I was doing everything right so far.

"And last but not least, let's not forget routine credit reporting, and parallel, indirect and operative backgrounding, where we check out everything you've ever been involved in, including your alumni associations, magazine subscriptions and religious affiliations."

Although it was cool in the conference room, my four trainees were sweating. Everybody has something to hide, even if it's something stupid rather than illegal.

"Now I'm going to pass your personnel files out to you."

I handed the Marcie Ann Kent file to the only girl in the group. She reminded me of Mariska Hargitay on *Law & Order SVU*. She had shiny chestnut hair cut very straight and chic, a great figure and a soft voice. She was like one of my girlfriends in high school — also smart in math and really attractive. All the guys were after her. I used to think she had it all. I tried not to be envious.

"And you are Mr. Joe Tanaka?" I asked, handing a file to the very handsome Japanese man in his mid-20s.

"Thanks, I think," he said with a wink and a grin. His dark eyes, dark hair, and white button-down shirt open at the neck accentuated his good looks.

"And who is Mr. John Olson?" I held up his file. It was taken by the trainee who'd complained about missing the remainder of Ken's video. He was in his thirties, with thinning brown hair and tinted, wire-rimmed glasses. His tailored sport jacket and pants were right out of an Eddie Bauer catalog. I noticed he was wearing a Rolex and wondered if it was a knock-off.

The last file I handed to a smiling, black-haired man with a trim beard. "Mr. Ron Rivers, I presume?" I smiled. He, like Joe Tanaka, was in his late twenties. He wore a light blue suit and red tie. Behind his glasses, his eyes seemed wary.

"We'll be meeting individually in the adjoining office," I announced. "In the meantime, why don't you all take a minute to decide if there's anything you want to change or add to your files."

John Olson asked to be excused to use the facilities. He ducked into the corridor so fast, I wondered if he was going to make it in time.

The room was silent as the others reviewed their files. I decided to interview Olson first and made a note to check the e-chat on HI-Data's computer system. E-chat tells you what's really going on in a company. Nine out of ten employees don't realize it can be read by others. If they did, I guarantee they wouldn't write what they do.

I was ready to begin, but Olson still hadn't returned. I checked my watch. He'd been gone for ten minutes. I remembered with a jolt that he'd run out with his file.

I rushed down the corridor and burst into the men's room. A young guy was at a sink washing his hands.

"Hey, lady, this isn't unisex."

I ignored him and shouted, "Olson, come out right now if you're in here."

There was only silence. A sign on the wall next to the mirrors read "At the feast of ego, everyone leaves hungry." The young guy eyed me with amusement. His lashes were so long, if I wasn't angry I would have been jealous.

I pushed open all the stall doors asking, "Anybody else in here?" Nothing and no one. I headed for the door.

"See you tomorrow, same time?" the kid cracked as I left in a huff.

I immediately phoned Sparky and informed her Mr. John Olson had failed the first phase of the comprehensive check. "You might want to have him debriefed and recover his Smart card and personnel file," I advised.

"Debriefed," Sparky chuckled. "I like that. I'll see to it right away, assuming he's still in the building. Confidentially, Olson's been a pain in the ass from day one of his arrival. Have you got some special shit detector or something? Anyway, good luck with the rest of them." She rang off, and I faced the remaining trainees.

ELEVEN

Only three trainees were left. Technically my job at this point was done concerning John Olson. But that curious gene most Scots have was acting up like a bad tooth. I couldn't stop wondering what Olson was hiding and whether it had anything to do with Ken Gordon's death.

As I walked into the adjoining office where I'd be conducting the interviews, I casually picked up the Diet Coke can Mr. Olson had left on the table. I had a plan, and I'd have to ask for Phil's help.

By now, the trainees' looks of loathing had been replaced by ones of unease. Joe Tanaka, Ron Rivers, and Marcie Ann Kent all had one thing in common. They were smart cookies. Smart in the ways of thermonuclear dynamics, quantum calculus, advanced engineering this and advanced engineering that. Especially Ms. Kent. Looking at her academic performance at MIT made me feel like my own cerebral cortex was a mere speck of dirt in the universe. Here she was at the tender age of twenty-two garnering all sorts of honors and awards for Expanding Boolean Search Paradigms. In this lifetime I was never going to understand Expanding Boolean Search Paradigms. Don't get me wrong. I wasn't jealous of Marcie Ann's theoretical and technical abilities. Instead, deep in my bones, I was proud and impressed by a woman who could beat the boys at what once had been considered their own game.

I switched on my trusty little Sony 256 MB digital voice recorder with up to ninety hours of recording time. I often wonder how Sam Spade and Mike Hammer did it — they never even wrote anything down.

I called in Joe Tanaka first, then Marcie Ann Kent and lastly Ron Rivers. The interviews extended late into the day. It was a Christmas Eve they'd all remember. I asked a lot of questions for clarification and amplification. My subjects flesh out and take on dimension during these interviews. That's why I do them. I make it a rule to try not to like or dislike a subject. That gets in the way of objectivity. But you can't completely avoid first impressions.

I liked Ron Rivers. He joked throughout

the interview, which is what I might have done if our roles were reversed. Marcie was extremely bright, but wound very tight and not very forthcoming. She was a bundle of brains and breeding tied up with a red ribbon of ambition. She knew how smart she was, and I wasn't sure how ruthless she was or to what extent she might go to succeed. Joe was one of those naturally math-smart kids. He'd gone through life without working very hard and was now a twenty-seven-year-old conman. He even tried to con me during our interview by spouting technological double-speak. Then he tried to date me.

I would have liked to know more about the scope of each of their jobs at HI-Data, but frankly the complexity was beyond my understanding, and anyway that wasn't what I was getting paid for. I carefully placed John Olson's Coke can into one of the paper bags I always carry, picked up the Sony and my notes, and went to Sparky's office. It was six o'clock on Christmas Eve, and I could see why nobody wanted her job. She dialed security and notified the guard I was ready to leave.

"That was some job you did on Mister Olson," Sparky said as we waited. "I'm impressed. Did you get what you needed from the other recruits?"

"You never know from the first session," I said.

"Did Marcie tell you how Ken was hitting on her? Because if she didn't, somebody should."

"How do you know about that?" I asked in my best investigator's voice, as if I already knew. The only fact Marcie had given me was that she'd met Ken once since she started her training.

"Hey, my office is Gossip Central. I usually get to know everything. I'm telling you so that uppity bitch doesn't pull the wool over your eyes. When these new trainees started, I warned them they'd be living their lives in a petri dish. But do they listen? No. The little snots always think they know everything."

I couldn't tell if she was lying, so I stayed quiet. Sometimes that's the best response of all.

"I'm not saying Ken was an angel. He wasn't. Ken was like that with every skirt at HI-Data. He was our resident Don Juan. But I don't want Miss-High-and-Mighty Marcie thinking she can lie about it. Frankly, I'd like to see her squirm."

Sparky took a key from her center drawer and unlocked a beige filing cabinet against the far wall. She extracted a file from the bottom drawer and returned to her desk.

"Let me guess. You don't like Marcie," I said.

Sparky tossed the manila file she'd taken from the cabinet onto her desk with a flourish. "She could at least be civil. I'm not just some secretary. I happen to know a lot of things." She opened the file and pointed at a page. "For instance —"

The office door banged open, and the young guard burst in.

"Let's go," he said, hiking up his shoulders. He looked ready to handcuff and drag me out by my hair. Norman had probably told him to be sure to personally escort me out or he'd lose his job. I didn't want another scene, so I thanked Sparky and left quietly. I'd have to come back another time to find out what was in that file.

The guard escorted me all the way to my car and didn't re-enter HI-Data until I'd cleared the farthest perimeter of the property. I drove slowly, hoping he'd freeze.

TWELVE

Heading back to the city, I thought about what Sparky had said. Computers don't just zap you to death. Somebody with special knowledge had gone through a lot of trouble to rig that computer and had counted on Ken using it, assuming Ken was the intended victim. That somebody was undoubtedly from HI-Data, no matter what the CEO might think. But who? And I was determined to find out why John Olson had walked out of HI-Data before the interview even started. Was he involved somehow in Ken's death? Was he an industrial spy for a company competing with HI-Data?

Suddenly I was snapped brutally back to the present. I'd sped up on the entrance ramp to merge into the heavy traffic on the tollway. I was now traveling faster than the traffic. I hit the brakes. Nothing happened.

There was no way I could merge at this speed. I braked again. The pedal sank to the floor, but the car didn't slow down.

My heart raced, but everything else went into slow motion. To my left was a stream of unfriendly, fast-moving vehicles. To my right was a three-foot wall of ice, the built-up residue of snow plows. My only choice was to go straight ahead down the shoulder, which was rutted with ice and looked as inhospitable as the Antarctic.

I braked again, this time very gently. The Miata's rear end started to fishtail into the moving traffic. I was trapped. I drove straight ahead along the shoulder. It was as bad as it looked. The Miata twitched left toward the streaming cars, then right toward the ice wall. With each lurch, I held my breath, expecting to crash. The car and I were both taking a pounding.

The steering wheel suddenly spun in my hands and the right front tire blew. Traffic to my left was now going faster than I was. The car was slowing, but I had no control over it. I prayed I wasn't going to veer into the now faster-moving traffic or hit the wall.

Miraculously, the car came to a stop along the shoulder. A wall of ice hugged her right fender and a steady stream of traffic whizzed past on her left. I sat still, too drained to even have the shakes. My fingers still clutched the steering wheel and both feet were still pushing down the brake pedal. Another five feet and the car and I would have smashed against the ice wall. A statistic from a recent insurance seminar flashed into my consciousness. There had been over thirty-seven thousand vehicle-related fatalities last year, and twenty-five thousand of those were the drivers. My heart rate slowed down just a little as I realized I wasn't squashed to death and I wasn't going to become one of this year's traffic statistics. At least not today.

The flashing red lights on the Illinois State Trooper's car behind me got my attention. I shut off the engine and waited, knowing he'd first check my license plate for wanteds or stolens and get all the information from my registration. I'd recently seen a video on the Automated License Plate Recognition program that could tell a cop everything in the universe about you and your car faster than it would take Superman to beat a speeding bullet. It was an expensive new toy, so I wasn't sure if the state troopers had it installed yet.

"What's the matter with you?" the trooper scolded as I rolled down my window. "You could have caused a hell of a pile-up. Let's see your license. I'm going to have to give you a ticket for reckless driving."

He didn't even get my story before he decided to peg me as the villain. I hate that, even though statistically they're right 99 percent of the time. I was trying to feel good about still being alive, so as he took my license, I calmly explained how my brakes had given out without warning and how I'd been trapped between Scylla and Charybdis.

"You mean there's other cars involved?" He stomped his feet to shake off the snow and scanned the horizon.

"No. No other cars were involved. I meant like Ulysses in *The Odyssey.*"

"Oh," he grunted and reached for his ticket book.

I capitulated to the reality that most cops don't read Homer and tried a cogent explanation, still hoping to avoid being ticketed. "You see, Officer, I just missed being either squashed like a bug by the flow of traffic or slammed into smithereens by the ice wall."

"Have you been drinking?" the trooper asked, sniffing my breath.

"No. I haven't, Officer. I've had no alcohol. Nothing."

"I should be giving you a sobriety test, but I'm gonna believe you about that. But you shouldn't be driving a sports car like this in the middle of a Chicago winter," he advised. "Little foreign jobs like this just aren't reliable. Go get yourself something bigger. While you're at it, get something American."

Why bother to explain that my Miata was cherry and this was the first time anything like this had happened? I couldn't believe my brakes failed. They'd been checked last week when Dieter, my mechanic, put on the new Michelin tires. I felt sick and wondered if this was a new pattern I'd be having to cope with. I wasn't happy, but for once, I kept my mouth shut. Especially since he still had my license.

No sooner had he left than a tow truck appeared. Two young black guys jumped out, put on heavy gloves, and efficiently hooked up the car. They offered me a ride to the tow company, and I readily agreed, grabbing my purse, the Sony, my notes, and the can of Coke.

Once there, I called Dieter, my German mechanic. I squeezed the receiver as I told him the brakes had failed. I was ready for a lecture about not taking care of my car. Instead, Dieter confirmed my own fears.

"Dose brakes couldn't fail, Shatzy. Dey were in perfect order. Last week I went over dem when I installed the new tires. Something is definitely nicht right."

THIRTEEN

I wrapped presents, grabbed the cat, and left for Mother's. The Rent-A-Wreck I'd gotten didn't want to start, and the heater didn't work. Cavvy meowled the entire way, making it crystal clear he hated the loaner. Running late as usual, I braced for the consequences.

My mother lives in Andersonville, on the city's north side. It used to be a Swedish neighborhood; now the only vestige left is Ann Sather Restaurant, no longer owned by its namesake, but still serving Swedish meatballs and fresh cinnamon buns to die for. The area has remained vibrant and is now home to every imaginable ethnic and racial group. Mother still lives in the same neat bungalow she and my father had been happy in for so many years. I was glad she stayed on after his death — the house keeps him close for us both.

Cavalier's little cat breaths puffed into the

night air as I carted him and the presents from the car. The shrubs around the front porch were nestled in snow, but the walkway was completely clear. Mr. Poulakas, one of Mother's neighbors, likes driving his snow-plow and always clears the whole block.

Aunt Elizabeth met us at the door, the big diamonds in her Scottish thistle broach winking in the gloaming.

"Can you never be on time, even on Christmas Eve?" She pointed at the Rent-A-Wreck. "And whose car is that?"

Aside from La Dragon at the gate, the house was warm and welcoming with colored Christmas lights and smells of baked goodies. All the presents went under the little Scotch pine decorated with ornaments I remembered from childhood. Then Auntie Elizabeth kissed and fussed over Cavalier while I explained what had happened to me and the Miata.

"Honestly, it's amazing you're alive," my mother scolded, as if it had been my fault. Cavalier meowed in apparent agreement. He was enjoying Auntie's attentions, but still sulking about the Rent-A-Wreck.

"Time for the holiday toast," Auntie said, her bright eyes twinkling. I knew how she liked her toasts at Christmastime to the Stu-arts and to Scotland. She brought out the bottle of Glenlivet pure Scotch malt Whisky she never travels anywhere without and splashed some into three of mother's crystal tumblers.

"To the Tartan," she said solemnly, and we all managed tiny sips of the golden fire.

Mother held up her glass and said, "May every day find you safe and well."

Auntie said, "An' speaking of safe and well, oft and again I've wanted to buy a sturdy German car for you, DD. That is the safest. But stubborn you are, even as your grandmother. You'll ne'er let me help."

"And you need to meet the right man and get out of that business you're in," Mother added, heading for the kitchen, Cavalier at her heels. She'd be happy if I were the kind of daughter who kept a clean house and used the oven timer. I admire those women who do, but a timer is useless since I don't cook too often, and I never know when I'll get home. Jung explains the unexplainable as a mother-daughter cosmic thing where the daughter never measures up. Still, after Frank's suicide, when the blackness held me down in its depths, Mother had come through. She'd coaxed me into eating enough to stay alive. Now she'd like to see me get on with life — at least life as she saw it.

Before I could change the subject, Auntie put down her glass and said, "It's nigh time you peek at my wee Robert Burns surprise. Wait here." She headed for the guest bedroom Mother always keeps ready for her.

Auntie was excited, and she was beginning to lapse into Pidgin Scots, as Mother terms it. A few wisps of hair had by now fallen from her usually elegant upsweep, and she was in overdrive. My hopes to forestall the Burns affair till after dinner were dashed. I suspected her wee surprise would be a no-win situation for me. Despite the baking aromas, I lost my appetite.

She emerged carrying a red leather case the size of three or four volumes of the *Oxford English Dictionary.*

"Attend," she announced and placed it with great care on the marquetry table Mother uses to play poker. Auntie has a flair for the dramatic.

Even the most incompetent burglar could have popped the lock on the case in a nanosecond. I decided not to mention this. Mother came in, and we both watched while Auntie fumbled with the pathetic lock.

Finally I intervened. "I don't mean to point out the obvious Auntie, but this lock is broken." At a gentle touch from me, the lock popped.

"T'wasn't locked; t'was stuck," Auntie said. "The key went agley, an' it had to be broke open."

She lifted the lid. The box was lined in a deep red velvet, worn around the edges but nonetheless still beautiful. Inside was nestled an ornate Ormolu casket, inset with the initials "K. B."

"Come help me with this, DD."

"I thought you said you purchased a manuscript."

"Well, I did and I didn't," she replied in her usual Scots manner.

"What does the 'K. B.' stand for?" I asked.

"I don't know yet. That's one of the things you must find out."

We removed the resplendent casket. It too had a useless lock hanging by one hasp. As Cavalier pranced in, tail up and curious, Auntie ordered me to open it. I lifted the lid. The casket was lined in dark blue satin. Inside was a double sheet of letter paper, no envelope. Under the paper lay a leather pouch.

I reached for the pouch. "What's in here?"

Auntie grabbed my arm. "No," she yelled.

I froze and Cavalier retreated under the Christmas tree, hiding among the presents.

"Put these on." She handed me a pair of

surgical gloves from her purse. "You canna touch these precious things with your bare hands. I thought you knew about such things. Take out the paper first."

I obeyed instructions, put on the gloves, then gently removed the paper. A few grains of dark sand rattled in the crease. The paper was sturdy and had a crisp feel. The writing was penned in an old-fashioned flowing script, and it was with some difficulty that I read it.

Written by Somebody on the window of
    an inn at Stirling
On seeing the royal palace in ruins.

Here Stuarts once in triumph reign'd;
And laws for Scotland's weal ordain'd;
But now unroof'd their palace stands,
Their sceptre's fall'n to other hands;
Fallen indeed, and to the earth,
Whence grovelling reptiles take their birth.
The injur'd Stuart line are gone,
A Race outlandish fill their throne;
An idiot race, to honor lost;
Who know them best despise them most.

"Auntie." I faced her. "How much did you pay for this?"

"Well . . ."

Mother interjected. "Tell her Elizabeth."

"It was a verra special deal. Only one hundred thousand pounds."

"About a hundred fifty thousand dollars," I translated. "You are aware, Auntie, that this is probably a fake."

"Balderdash," Aunt Elizabeth said angrily. "How can you conclude that a'fore you even investigate?"

"Auntie . . ."

"Daffy, I ken it's real. Your job is to prove it," Auntie pronounced as she fingered the diamond pin. "I'm counting on you, as aye."

"Don't call me Daffy. And who sold this to you? Did you get any sort of provenance?"

Pulling another pair of gloves from her purse, Auntie drew them on and gently lifted the ancient looking leather pouch from the casket.

"Canna this be considered provenance?" One by one she removed five parcels from the worn pouch, each wrapped in yellowed, coarse fabric. Gently I unraveled the decaying fabric from each parcel and found myself staring at five pieces of thick glass with a greenish tint. The biggest piece caught my attention, and I held it up to the light. On it was etched the words:

Here Stuarts once in triump
And laws for Scotland
But now unroof
Their scept
Fallen in
Whence

"Oh this can't be," I said aloud as I examined the other pieces. Two of them had cracks along one end. When I placed all five pieces flat on the table and rearranged them around like puzzle pieces, they fit roughly together, resembling a rectangular jigsaw puzzle.

"Be careful," Auntie cautioned. "Dinna break any."

With the pieces together, the entire poem was now clearly readable. My heart jumped. I caught my breath and read the lines again. I have a vivid imagination, but was this possible? I swallowed hard and looked at Auntie. She raised her eyebrows but said nothing. That alone was earthshaking.

Her silence continued while I fetched mother's magnifying glass and examined the handwriting more closely. I was no Burns scholar, but Auntie's obsession had exposed me to a fair amount of his work. He was a fabulous poet who'd lived fast and hard and had died early. He was a lothario who'd had twelve children by three or four women, and he'd become an overnight celebrity, a rock star of the times, with the publication of his first book of poems. I knew he was a Jacobite, passionately in favor of a deposed Stuart king and passionately opposed to the Hanovers who'd taken over the throne — just like Auntie. And the incident where he scratched out this verse with a diamond-tipped pen on the window of an inn on a tour of Scotland was well documented.

"Auntie, is this supposed to be the glass from the Inn at Stirling?"

She nodded. "Aye. The Golden Lion Inn. Is it not thrilling?" she asked reverentially. "Something Rabbie himself touched. Look. It gives me the goose bumps."

"Auntie, if this were that same window pane, it would fetch a king's ransom." As I said it, goose bumps ran down my spine, and I could see the Inn, the window, and handsome Rabbie Burns thinking treason.

I braced Auntie. "Who sold this to you?"

Auntie looked stubborn and stayed silent.

"How can I investigate whether it's authentic if I don't know where you got it?"

"Elizabeth, if you want her to help, tell her," my mother insisted.

Aunt Elizabeth was my father's sister. She loved him dearly and used to take his advice. Since his death, she listens to no one. Except, occasionally, my mother.

"If I tell you," she said, relenting, "you must promise you'll not tell another soul."

"I promise," I said.

"All right," she yielded. "It all began with a phone call from George."

"George who?"

"You know. George Murray, my attorney. Of Murray and McSweeny in Edinburgh. He asked to come and see me. Verra important, he said, and also verra hush-hush confidential."

"He came to see you?" I asked.

"You don't understand, girl. Remember I told you how the moderns are pulling down all the beautiful old buildings in the city to erect high-rises? It's getting to be exactly like America. His firm has been in the selfsame building for almost three hundred years, but now the old grande dame is under the wrecking ball. It really makes me burn ta see so much auld architecture demolished. It's akin to the usurpers come back to set the country to wrack and ruin again."

"Get on with it, Auntie."

"Aye. Well, George knew I dinna like their new glass high rise, so he offered to come to me. And so he did, the very afternoon."

"What happened?"

"He brought that box along with him. That's the whole story," she said as she looked at me sidewise.

"Where did he get it from, Elizabeth?" Mother prodded. Even she wasn't satisfied with Auntie's bare-bones explanation.

"George told me the workers had found it during the demolition. He said it was found in a container wedged in a niche in one of the cellars of the old building. Only the name of the firm was on it. Nothing else."

"And who did it belong to?" I asked.

"They couldna trace an owner. According to George, the box had never been inventoried. He said there were no company files on it either. He assured me they looked into all their auld records."

"So why did George contact you about this, Auntie? Did he realize what it could be?"

"Oh, he ken it was Robert Burns. And o' course he knows my interest. He's accompanied me to the Immortal Memory Readings at the St. Andrew's Society and so forth, just as you have here in America. So it was only natural I'd be the first person he thought of."

"And he didn't offer it to anyone else? He came straight to you, and you bought it on sight. Auntie, had you been drinking any whiskys that day?"

"I already told you, DD, that I could not but buy it. You must see that now. As soon ever as I saw it, I recognized Rabbie's hand." She regarded me with the full force of her piercing blue eyes.

"An' by your leave, I had only a drop," she added defiantly.

"Auntie, I don't understand why your attorney wouldn't put this on the open market. It would have sold for a million dollars, if not more."

"All I know is George told me the firm was nae about to get itself embroiled in a lengthy dispute. Without proper records, they'd not be able to authenticate provenance. And George worried about lawsuits getting filed cock o'heap alleging the box and its contents belonged to every Jack 'n Jill that happened to be a client. They'd all say that the firm of Murray and McSweeney was . . ."

"Incompetent, irrelevant, and immaterial, to paraphrase Perry Mason." I finished the sentence.

"To say nothing of negligent," Mother added. "The firm would go bankrupt quicker than George could sing a chorus of 'For Auld Lang Syne.' "

"An' that's the whole kit 'n kaboodle,"

Auntie said. "And George explained I'm now established as the true legal owner. Besides, had I not agreed to the purchase, he was going to contact two American collectors of Burns memorabilia. They would have had a knock 'em down bidding war."

"Once again, Auntie, let me point out that George would have made a lot more money from them than he made selling it to you. So the question is, why would he sell it to you?"

Aunt Elizabeth was silent.

"What's the answer, Auntie?"

"Tell her Elizabeth," Mother ordered.

"All right. But you must never, never repeat this. George and I . . . we . . . how shall I put this, we are verra good friends."

"You're very good friends, and this is why he sold it to you?"

Mother glared at me and said, "DD, don't give your aunt a hard time. She's doing her best."

"All right, maybe more than verra good friends," Auntie admitted, studying the rug.

"Maybe what you mean is that you two are currently having a flaming affair. Ohmygod. That settles it. It's a sure bet that all this stuff is fake."

"You can't really think that, DD," Auntie protested. "The poem, the pieces of glass . . . they all seem so . . . so authentic. They make my heart race. Truth to say, doesn't yours race too, my girl?"

It had for a minute there, but I certainly wasn't going to admit anything to the Dragon.

"You must do the investigation for me," she pleaded.

"I can't, Auntie. I'm on a rush job with HI-Data. That's why I couldn't pick you up yesterday. I don't have any time for this right now. I'll give you the name of somebody who's an expert in . . ."

"But this is for family. This is for Scotland. Nothing else could be more important. Here. You take these precious objects and get on with the investigation." She replaced everything in the casket and handed it to me.

I was about to hand it back to her and tell her in no uncertain terms that I could not investigate anything, when I remembered seeing a similar casket on TV a few weeks ago on the "Antiques Road-show." That casket had held some surprises for the owner. Curious, I turned Auntie's box every which way and poked and prodded along the edges, just like I'd seen the dealer do on TV. I'd almost given up when all of a sudden a tiny drawer sprang open in the back.

"Look," Mother pointed.

"A secret compartment." Auntie clapped her hands. "Good gal." She patted my shoulder.

A folded paper was tucked in the small drawer. I used my fingernail to work it out, then carefully opened it. On it was the same "KB" crest that was on the front of the Ormolu casket.

"What does it say?" Auntie asked.

"It reads, *'Present'd Octob'r 1787 by the author.'*"

"Wow," I said. "That would be the right time frame for the incident at the Golden Lion Inn. I wonder what that 'KB' crest means?"

"See. I was right to trust only you, DD. No one else. I'm relying on you." She walked away and poured another wee dram. *"Hooi Uncdos,"* Auntie toasted and took a sip.

Mother and I eyed each other.

"She's into the auld toasts," Mother sighed. "I think that's the one meant to drive away strangers."

"I know what that one means, Mother. The Stuart-loving Jacobites used it as a toast to drive out the Hanoverians."

"Aye," Auntie said.

"If we don't soon eat," Mother interjected,

"the manglewurzels she brought with her will be ruined."

I lit the candles, put on the recording of Mendelssohn's Scottish Symphony, Auntie's favorite, and helped serve dinner. Usually we don't see manglewurzels until January 25th as part of the Burns Supper to honor him on his birthdate, but tonight the Scottish vegetable was on the menu along with a sherry trifle dessert called Typsy Laird. I stifled myself from making any comment whatsoever about the Tipsy Laird.

After dinner, the three of us settled around Mother's Christmas tree with Cavalier for the ritual opening of presents. Mother and I each had a small glass of port while Auntie finished her dram of Glenlivet. Of course we had to pass our drinks over a glass of water as Auntie made the Loyal Toast, "To the King Over the Water," a symbolic Jacobite toast drunk even to this day in honor of the exiled Stuarts across the water. Often when I'm with Auntie I wonder in what century I'm living. Existential differences aside, it turned out to be a nice holiday. Mother was pleased with the pink bathrobe and slippers I'd chosen, and I thanked her for the top drawer Borghese makeup case she gave me. I didn't tell her how handy it would be on domestic stakeouts.

Auntie handed me a beautifully wrapped parcel. Inside was a sterling silver pin engraved with the Buchanan crest and clan motto, *Clarior Hinc Honos,* which translates "I help the brave." The design was familiar. I remembered my father explaining that our crest contained a ducal cap held aloft which represented Sir Alexander Buchanan's killing of the Duke of Clarence and taking his coronet as a trophy at the Battle of Beauge in Normandy in March 1421.

"Auntie, this is . . ."

" 'Tis one of a kind," she nodded. "And quite expensive, girl. Dinna lose it."

I looked down at the pin. What I saw instead was the ring on Ken's dead hand, and I heard echoes of Frank telling me his family ring was "one of a kind and quite expensive."

I looked up. Mother had unwrapped a bottle of exotic perfume Auntie brought her from Paris, and thoughts of the ring got submerged in holiday spirit. We all tried a smidge of the perfume, just like girls-night-out. Meanwhile Cavalier gleefully unwrapped and played with a catnip mouse Mother had chosen specially for him. I kind of felt sorry for the mouse, but Cavvy adored being the center of attention.

"By the by, Auntie, Phil mentioned he

thought you were being followed on the way back from the airport. Did you notice anything?"

"When the Herons leave the tree, The Laird of Gight will landless be." Auntie recited the lines from the Scottish legend with verve. "Let's toast Scotland, the Stuarts, and Rabbie Burns," she said. "Where's the piper? Scots awa'."

"She'll never admit to looking behind her at anything, you know," Mother whispered to me. "You might as well give up the questions and enjoy yourself."

Later that evening Scotty phoned from London in spite of the inconvenient time difference to say how much he missed me. I thanked him again for the big box of Godiva chocolates he'd sent. I like my men to give me chocolate — good chocolate and lots of it. Then when he asked if I liked those new Michelin tires he'd given me for the Miata, I restrained myself from telling him what had happened to me and one of his tires today on the way home from HI-Data.

FOURTEEN

Early next morning, I drove from Mother's to my apartment building to pick up Glendy and Lucille, my twin-sister neighbors. They traditionally spend Christmas Day with us and adore Mother's Christmas goose with apple stuffing. But mostly they enjoy the after-dinner card-playing orgy where everyone gambles and gossips and cooks up crazy schemes to get me married and living happily ever after. I love them dearly, but I wish they'd mind their own collective business. And one day I'm going to say that — out loud — to their faces. I'm the lippyest person I know, but where my mother, my aunt, and the nosy twins are concerned, I'm hopeless.

Even though they're over eighty, the twins actively pursue new projects all the time. Right now it was bird watching, and they insisted on showing me the pair of cardinals at the bird feeder I'd helped them rig up on their little balcony.

"They mate for life, you know," Glendy explained as we watched the colorful birds in the sharp morning light.

"And they don't migrate south," Lucille added. "They stay here with us in Chicago all winter."

The handsome red male sat in the feeder while the brownish female jumped around the balcony floor, picking up fallen seeds with her bright orange beak. In between bites, they called to each other, but I didn't know if the communication was for security reasons or just casual conversation. Either way, it was a delightful beginning to the day.

Later, after Mother's excellent meal, Auntie played fourth hand at the card table, leaving me free to eat too many Frango Mints and think of happy times with Frank. Frank had liked playing Santa, and on our first Christmas together, he'd locked a little wrapped package behind the glass panel of our grandfather clock five days before Christmas. "Half the fun is in the waiting," he'd teased and tossed the key into his pocket. Of course, he'd been right, damn him, I thought, glancing down at the treasured gold bracelet. He'd died only a few years ago, but to me it felt more like a few centuries.

My cell phone rang, interrupting my memories. It was my best friend, Lauren, wishing me happy holidays.

"This year, I got a blue spruce and decorated it with all blue lights," she said. Her parents are Japanese, but Lauren married a WASP, and now cleverly incorporates holidays and religions from both sides, leaving nothing to chance.

"How's life with Auntie Attila?" she asked.

I lowered my voice so the quartet at the card table couldn't hear. "Can you believe this? She's sleeping with her lawyer, and he's running a con on her."

"Nobody cons your Aunt Elizabeth," Lauren declared.

"Except if it involves Robert Burns and/or Scottish nationalism. And in this case, it's both," I said. "I can't say more now. The twins are here too, and big ears are listening."

"Are you bringing Scotty to my New Year's Eve party?"

"I'd like to, but he's in London."

"Is that why you sound so low?"

"It's more than that. I stumbled over a dead body Wednesday. It turned out to be Ken Gordon, Frank's half-brother."

"Ohmygod, DD. What a horrible coincidence."

"That's what the cops said."

"I didn't mean . . ."

"I know. I'll be happy to see this year kick over, but I'm not in a festive mood."

"Well, if you change your mind, there'll be some interesting people."

I'd hardly hung up the phone when it rang again.

"Happy Christmas, Shatzy."

It was my German mechanic, Dieter. "Merry ho-ho-ho to you, too, Dieter. Why are you working on Christmas day?"

"I vanted to see what happened about dose brakes. And it is just as I thought. Nothing vas wrong. The problem is somebody does not like you too good. Dat right front brake line vas definitely slashed. This I found right away. It vas near to all the vay through."

I knew the brakes had failed, but I didn't want to believe it had been done deliberately.

"You are still there?" Dieter asked after a long silence.

I grunted something, and he continued.

"You must report this immediately to the authorities. You could have been really bad hurt. It is a miracle you and dat Miata are still breathing. The brake line is now repaired, and I put on your spare. So do not get into any more trouble until you have a new tire. You can pick her up whenever you want. I got to go home now or my wife vill murder me. Oh, I have put the bill onto your tab."

I was so shaken, I forgot to thank him. Somebody at HI-Data had cut my brake line. Who? John Olson? How would he know what car was mine? Norman? I couldn't figure out why Norman was so negative toward me. Maybe he needed cover because he had killed Ken. Whoever it was, I didn't like my odds in being someone's target.

On top of all this, Auntie was throwing me the Burns curve.

I decided to pick up my car at Dieter's and head for my office. It would be deserted today, allowing me to review the interview notes and tapes in peace and then move more quickly into the next phase of the investigations. Although there were only three subjects left, my tight timeframe had gotten even tighter with the day lost to Ken's death. I would try to carry on as usual with everything concerning HI-Data and act as if everything was normal. But it wasn't.

Before I left, I phoned Phil Richy's private number. I hoped he would answer, and he did. I told him what had happened with

John Olson skipping out of HI-Data.

"That's not so good, is it?" he said.

"That's why I need your help."

"Oh, shit. You always get me in trouble when you ask for my help."

"Never mind that. I need a referral to one of your erstwhile contacts who'll agree to get some prints run for me."

"Olson's prints?"

"Right in one."

"What's wrong with your sources?"

"I'm on the outs with everybody right now, okay? Don't ask. Can you get someone? Yes or no?"

"I'm thinking. Oh, yeah. There's somebody who'll do it for me. He's worked with me on two fraud cases involving homicides. But promise me you won't come on too strong. And above all, don't get him in any trouble. He's a pretty damn good detective. He's in the Cold Case squad. And DD, please try to remember that he's one of the good guys. Are you listening?"

"Yeah, yeah. So who is this peach?"

"Name's Morgan Fernandez. Lieutenant Fernandez to you. You know where Police Headquarters is, don't you?"

Phil gave me his number and promised he'd call Fernandez to tell him to expect my call.

The card sharks were in a dither as I was ready to leave. Aunt Elizabeth had been dealt the Nine of Diamonds. She immediately halted the game. To her, the Nine of Diamonds is known as the "Curse of Scotland." Legend has it the card was used to send a message ordering the Massacre of Glencoe on that fateful morning of February 13, 1692. Guests who had accepted their hospitality murdered thirty-seven members of Clan MacDonald, and the cold blood of that shameful incident is still remembered today by many Scots.

Normally Auntie doesn't make such a big fuss about the card. But today she threw down her hand and took me aside.

"It's an ill omen that Nine of Diamonds," she insisted as she tossed a hand-knit Glenshee cardigan over her shoulders and clipped it on with her thistle broach. "I do not like it. Are you taking the you-know-what with you to start investigating today?"

"No, Auntie. I was planning to work on the investigation for HI-Data. It's Christmas. Nobody else is going to be working. I won't be able to see anybody about the Burns stuff."

"But this is very important. This is for Scotland. Take it with you and do whatever you do on that Inter-Netty thing with your

120

computer."

Sometimes agreeing with Auntie is the better part of valor. At least it seemed so today. I started to remove the pouch and the papers from the box.

Auntie stopped me. "Dinna take them out. They've been safe in there for over two hundred years."

"Auntie, I'm not a stevedore, and I'm not walking around with something the size of a small steamer trunk. Your treasures will be safe with me."

I put them in a sturdy brown envelope, then into my briefcase.

"Oh, and bye the bye," Auntie called as I donned my coat. "Maybe that Nine of Diamonds has something to do with the wee flash I had this morning of you and the inside of your office closet."

"Auntie, you don't really believe that getting the Nine of Diamonds brings bad luck, do you?"

"Aye. Sometimes I do. An' don't make the mistake of thinking bad luck isn't real."

"Anyway Auntie, you've never even seen my office."

Her eyes held mine as she recited, "There's a coffee pot, one window right behind your desk, and a closet off to the left. Watch out for that closet. It's up to no good."

"What?" Icy fear gripped me. I really hate Auntie's visions. She's a bit fey, like my Scottish grandmother Buchanan. Granny had attributed her gift of special sight to her tortoiseshell cat. Scottish superstition holds that tortoiseshell cats can see into the future. Auntie Elizabeth didn't have a tortoiseshell cat, but nonetheless she has the damn sight. The worst thing is that Auntie's clues are never specific. All I know for certain is that they never bode well. She'd had one of them before Frank died. It's as if the fates aren't impersonal, and that scares the hell out of me.

"How could my own closet harm me, Auntie? The only things in it are a faded umbrella and my Rockports."

"Don't dilly-dally DD. And mind now what I told you," Auntie called as she sat back down with the "girls" and insisted on a re-deal. I noticed they knew better than to disagree. They were hunched over their cards, resuming play, as I walked out the door.

FIFTEEN

Thin gray clouds raced across the winter sky. It was even colder today than yesterday. I returned the loaner and found the Miata keys and car precisely where Dieter said they'd be.

It was great to drive my own car, and the trip to my office at the Consolidated Bank building went fast in the light traffic. Most people were still at home eating Christmas dinner, but tomorrow Chicago's Loop would be jammed with people returning presents they'd gotten from Santa.

Consolidated Bank was deserted too, and not just because it was Christmas Day. Nobody could miss the huge sign in front that read Drake Demolitions. The powers that be had decided to tear down this old structure and replace it with a bigger, shinier edifice. It was an odd feeling knowing that in a few weeks all this brick and glass and concrete and steel would be reduced to a pile of rubble. Buildings can die, just like people.

Over two months ago, we'd been notified to clear out. Most of the building had been vacated. I was the only tenant left in the tower wing. As usual I was procrastinating. Technically I was squatting. I really didn't want to move. This is where I'd started my climb back after Frank's death. Phil had found this tiny office for me and started giving me some insurance work. Maybe you had to use the Hubble space telescope to locate it, but enough people find my phone number in the book to pay the rent. I like it just as it is. I don't need more changes.

My landlord, George Vogel, keeps my rent down, which is good; but he's a compulsive neat-freak, which I am not. What's worse, he's forever staring at my chest. George had already offered me a comparable office at the same cheap rent in the new Consolidated Bank building, but I'd decided to look elsewhere and get out from under his stare.

My phone was ringing. I rushed to unlock the door, but by the time I got in, the other party had hung up and the line was dead.

I relocked the door. In my line of work, there aren't many visitors, and it keeps me feeling safe, even though the lock's not the greatest, which I keep telling George Vogel.

I dumped the Sony recorder and my notes from yesterday's interviews on my desk and rushed to the closet, yanking open the door, eager to confirm or deny Auntie's vision. The exposed lightbulb illuminated a folding umbrella, my spare pair of high heels, and the running shoes stuffed with dirty socks. Disgusting maybe, but definitely not threatening. It was a mystery what my closet had to do with anything. I pulled my coat tighter, trying to convince myself the sudden chill was from the lack of heat in the building.

Today the office was so cold, I suspected they must have pulled the plug on the heat. Thankfully the small electric heater I'd brought from home a few days ago made the place livable, but I knew it wouldn't be long before they cut off the electricity and the phone.

I turned on my ancient Mr. Coffee pot, hoping it wouldn't short out again. I'll have to buy a new one soon, but this one reminded me of Joe DiMaggio. Coffee is my designer drug, and I consume more than my share of the 140 billion cups Americans drink every year. While it brewed, the phone rang again. I picked it up on the first ring. There was a click and the sound of someone hanging up. I followed suit. Then I called the cell number Phil had given me for Lt. Fernandez.

"Hello," said a pleasant voice after I introduced myself. "Phil said you need some prints run."

"I do. Merry Christmas, by the way."

"And to you, too."

"Can you help me out?"

"Any friend of Phil's — you know the rest. I guess I'm stuck. So can you get over to the Main Headquarters at 35th and Michigan tomorrow at about two o'clock?"

"Absolutely. I really appreciate it. What'll you be wearing? I mean, how'll I recognize you?"

"Ha Ha. Phil said you had a good sense of humor. Just ask at the main desk. They'll page me. I'll be on the lookout for you. Phil described you down to your shoe size."

"Thanks. See you tomorrow then."

I hung up, hoping he'd be able to give me some answers about Mr. John Olson.

While Online Detective checked the three trainees' names for me, I reviewed and made notes on the recorded interviews. There were two more hang-up calls, and now I was more than annoyed, I was scared. Someone knew I was here today and might be stalking me. I unplugged the phone, hoping that would be enough to discourage whoever it was.

I next developed a PERT chart with "immediate" and "secondary" task categories and wrote up a timeline for the upcoming week, fitting each task into the timeline. Generally time and patience are on my side in a comprehensive background check. But on this job I only had a short week's window of opportunity, so I was going to have to hustle to meet the deadline.

I certainly didn't need and didn't want La Dragon's Robert Burns business. I had a feeling it was going to turn out badly — not just for Auntie, but for me, too. But I really had no choice. You couldn't say no to the Dragon. So I went on what Auntie calls the Inter-Netty and googled Robert Burns. A slew of sites popped up, including a Burns Encyclopedia, a biography, a family tree, and his complete works. Much of what they had to say about the Bard of Scotland I already knew because of Auntie. Burns was considered the superstar of his day, and his birthday — January 25, 1759 — is still celebrated the world over with a "Burns Supper." I'd accompanied Auntie to more than one of these celebrations where she repeatedly toasted the Bard in native tongue. I enjoyed it, really, and I like hearing the bagpipes. They always make my blood run hot, and confirm that no matter where I am or what I might want to be, I am Scots through and through, so don't cross me unless you are prepared for battle.

I continued surfing and uncovered a few interesting facts relating to Auntie's artifacts.

- On August 25, 1787, Burns and a traveling companion stopped in Stirling at the Golden Lion Inn on their way to Inverness.
- Auntie's verse was written by Burns the next day, after he'd seen the then ruined state of the former home of Scotland's kings, which aroused his Jacobite feelings. Burns took a diamond-tipped pen and scrawled the verse on the window of his room.
- Word of the verse, immediately attributed to Burns, spread quickly among travelers and was considered scandalous and treasonous by the current monarchy who had come to power after the overthrow of the Stuart kings.
- Burns worried about the rumors. He was being talked about as the author, and he feared being called a traitor. But more and more people talked, so a few months later, in October of 1787,

he returned to the Golden Lion Inn, accompanied by Dr. James McKittrick Adair. Sometime during this visit, he broke the windowpane with the butt end of his riding crop to eliminate the evidence.

- Burns and Adair stayed on for a few days at nearby Harvieston House because of bad weather. There they visited Mrs. Katherine Bruce of Clackmannan, a ninety-five-year-old woman descended from Robert the Bruce, the revered fourteenth-century Scottish ruler.

Mrs. Katherine Bruce, I reflected. Maybe that's the KB of the crest. I would do further research on her.

I found a site called Scotland.com and learned that the Golden Lion Hotel, which had opened in 1786, was still in operation today. On the Burns Federation site, I found out that there was a seventeenth-century inn in Dumfries, Scotland, called the Globe Inn, where Burns had also penned poems on their window panes. Like the Golden Lion, the Globe Inn still stands today. Two windows with Burns' poems still exist at the Globe Inn and are a great tourist attraction, along with the poet's favorite chair, which, if you sit in, you must quote some Burns or provide drinks for the house.

I was amazed at the amount of information on the Internet about Robert Burns' life and work. My research had provided a few things I could investigate immediately for Auntie, and I wanted to get Tom Joyce involved. He loves to sleuth, plus he'd have the resources to do a first-class authentication of the manuscript. I didn't know how familiar he was with Robert Burns, but I knew he'd love the challenge. I decided to stop and see him later. I planned also to stop at the university library to research where most of the Burns' manuscripts are housed. I wondered if the original of this poem was part of a current collection. Maybe Auntie's lover was dealing in stolen goods. Lastly I'd research Mrs. Katherine Bruce. Those initials, "KB," had immediately caught my attention. It was very possible that those were her initials on Auntie's box. At least this was a plan and would hopefully satisfy Auntie.

I turned off the computer, unplugged Mr. Coffee, and remembered to turn my phone back on. Then I switched off the heater, checked inside my closet one more time, turned off the lights, locked the door and scanned the corridor. It seemed deserted, but I heard sounds from other parts of the building. No doubt the Drake deconstruction crew was working overtime.

I made it safely to the parking lot and felt relieved as I merged into the evening traffic and headed to Mother's to pick up the twins and Cavvy.

Sixteen

I drove straight to Mother's, relieved that all I had left to do today was pick up the twins and Cavalier for the trip home.

As I opened the door, Cavalier approached, meowing loudly. Mother, Auntie, Glendy and Lucille quickly surrounded me, all talking at once. The words "armed robbery" and "Santa Claus" rang clearly through the clatter.

I shut the door and dumped my briefcase. "Hold on. One at a time."

"I was robbed," Auntie asserted.

Glendy chimed in, "I've never seen Santa wear sunglasses."

"I've never seen Santa pack a revolver," added Lucille.

"The cop who came said they were short-handed because of Christmas, so all he could do was file the report," Mother complained. "What kind of investigation is that?"

"Stop. One story at a time." I pointed. "Mother, you first. From the beginning."

"Let's see." She put her hands on her hips and looked at the ceiling. "After you left, we had cocktails. Then your Uncle Charles called, and we played another six or seven hands, and then the doorbell rang and . . ."

"We played eight hands," Auntie interjected. "You won the first two, Glendy and Lucille each won one, and I won the last four." She smiled broadly.

Glendy and Lucille both nodded and said in tandem, "Lizzy's right." Like Mother, they were in awe of Auntie's card playing prowess despite her aversion to the Nine of Diamonds.

"Fine. Eight." I waved my hands in frustration. "Who rang the bell?"

"Santa Claus," Mother said.

"Your mother opened the door," Aunt Elizabeth pounced accusingly.

"I thought it might be the carolers. They've come the last three Christmases," Mother defended herself.

"This Santa wore sunglasses. And his beard was definitely false," Lucille observed.

"And he was carrying an anti-personnel weapon," Glendy added.

"A revolver," Lucille clarified. "Definitely a revolver."

133

I noticed the two poinsettia plants that flanked Mother's front door were overturned, and dirt had spilled onto the carpet. I quickly cased the rest of the room for other damage, but none was apparent.

"Wait a minute. Let me get this straight. A Santa with a gun got in the house? Are you all okay?" I was suddenly chilled at the thought of what could have happened to them.

"We're okay, but I told you I was robbed," Auntie insisted, throwing her hands in the air.

"Did you call the cops?" I asked.

"First we tried to call you," Glendy said.

"You said you'd be at your office, but when we phoned, there was no answer," Lucille added accusingly.

Of course. I'd unplugged the phone because of the damn hang-up calls. I didn't want them to know about that.

"Where were you, DD?" Auntie demanded.

"I was there, but the phone wasn't working. I'll explain later. What did the police say?"

"That daft policeman who came was all higgledy-piggledy," Auntie said.

Whenever La Dragon invokes a reduplicated compound, a good auld story is sure to follow. I perceived I wasn't going to be disappointed as Auntie opened a new bottle of Glenlivet and poured out a wee bit for each of us. On this occasion, I approved and took a small swallow to steady my nerves.

"He said the whole horrible event was a joke. He dinna take us seriously," Auntie reported.

I imagined the cop confronting these four. I sighed, bit my lip, and commiserated with the cop.

"He kept insisting we probably knew this Santa," Glendy said.

Lucille added, "He told us the gun was probably rubber. But we know it wasn't."

Auntie pursed her lips together into what I call her Dragon pout. "He said he'd file a whatyamacallit report at once, but t'would be a few days afore they could follow up on it."

"So Phil was right." I took another tiny sip of the Glenlivet. It traversed from my throat to my toes in a burst of liquid heat, giving me the courage to add, "Somebody definitely noticed your jewelry Auntie and followed you from the airport, just like he said."

"Santa followed you from the airport, Lizzy?" Glendy asked.

"Don't be daft," Auntie protested. "Anyway, Santa didn't get away with any of my jewelry."

"What did he take?"

"Only the big red leather box with the Ormolu casket. When I explained the box and the casket were both empty, that daft policeman laughed. He said that definitely convinced him our so-called 'robbery' was a hoax."

"You mean nothing else was taken? No diamonds?"

"Hummph," Auntie snorted. "That policeman doesn't seem to realize those boxes alone are worth a boodle of money, not to mention their sentimental value."

"No diamonds are gone," Mother confirmed. "Everything's accounted for."

"You should have seen Cavalier." Lucille petted him on the head. "He was so brave."

"Heroic," Auntie pronounced, petting him fondly.

"He chased Santa out the door," Glendy explained, smiling at Cavvy.

"He really was wonderful." Mother offered him a cat treat, fussing over him. "He meowed and darted between Santa's legs, tripping him. I was afraid Santa would shoot him."

"But Cav slipped under the sofa before Santa had a chance." Glendy chuckled and proffered another treat that Cavvy snatched quicker than I could blink.

"That's why Santa left without cleaning out the place," Auntie explained.

"What did Santa say when you let him in?"

"I can't think," Mother said.

"Hmm," Auntie mused.

"I can't remember. Can you Lucille?" Glendy asked.

Lucille, eyes heavenward, inhaled deeply. "I don't think he said anything. Just kept waving that dang gun in our faces, herding us together like sheep into the closet."

I faced Auntie. "You realize what this means, don't you? This was no run of the mill robbery. Santa was after one particular thing."

"The you-know-what that 'twas in the box," Auntie whispered.

"What's the 'you-know-what'? " Lucille braced Auntie, demanding an answer.

"Face it, Auntie," I said. "Somebody knows you have the you-know-what. And that somebody wants it."

SEVENTEEN

Saturday morning dawned crisp and cloudy, a perfect day to curl up in front of a roaring fire and read a good book. For me however, it wasn't going to be a perfect day. I was juggling two jobs, both of which were causing me trouble. In the kind of work I do, a reasonable amount of trouble is routine. But nothing I was involved in today seemed reasonable or routine.

I squeezed two oranges for a dose of the real thing, fed Cav, and praised him again for being an Uber Cat last night. I quickly perused the Trib's crossword. The theme was "famous quotations," and it looked inviting, but I didn't have the time to work on it today. I needed to get to the office and make phone calls, and confirm or deny a bunch of stuff about the trainees.

Despite all the demolitions activity going on at Consolidated, the elevator still worked, and I still had electric. As soon as I unlocked my office door, I cleaned and plugged in trusty Mr. Coffee, then began calling. People generally offer you heaps of information over the telephone if you don't treat them like dirt. But it was Saturday and still part of the holiday weekend, so I didn't have much luck connecting with anybody live. I left a dozen messages, then pulled up PeopleFinders. They search over two billion records and cull all the information, so they're not only faster and cheaper than hiring a gaggle of operatives, they're also more likely to dig the dirt. Next I referred to the list I'd compiled yesterday of families, friends, and colleagues of my subjects. The list included everybody I wanted to see one-on-one, including, of course, my subjects themselves in their native habitat. Nothing tells more about a person than where he chooses to lay his head down at night. And because I'm nosy, checking out the environs is always my favorite part of a comprehensive.

I phoned Tom Joyce, not sure if he'd be at his bookstore today either. Tom is Chicago's antiquarian books guru. In addition to all his appraisals, he makes regular appearances on TV, and he puts in two days a week at the Chicago Rare Book Center. His professional credentials stretch from Lake Forest to Forest Park. He's also a long-standing member of Hugo's Companions Chicago, a group of Sherlock Holmes aficionados, all of which means he's good at thinking on his feet. I knew I could count on his curiosity to help me in this Robert Burns affair.

"Happy Holidays," I said cheerily when he answered on the first ring. He must have finished the job at the library yesterday.

"Good Yule, DD. I've got the wassail bowl here. Why don't you come on over."

"Are you kidding? I barely made it home last year after one teeny glass of that brew."

"Don't knock it," he laughed. "It took the Vikings across the waters."

"And it's your mother's own recipe. I know. You told me all that last year."

"How's your job going at HI-Data?"

"Interesting so far. You were right on two counts. One, there's definitely 'something big' going on; and two, scientific espionage is alive and well there. One of the trainees I was supposed to vet bailed out. He's on the run. The company suspects he was a spy, but nobody knows what he found out."

"Where's the Christmas spirit in today's business world?"

"I'm hoping you have more than your share because today I need another favor."

"What else is new?"

"How long you gonna be there?"

" 'Til seven. But I can't promise to be sober."

"Give it a try. I have something you'll want to see."

"What? Don't play evil games with my curiosity."

"It'll give you something to look forward to. I'll be there before seven. Cheers!"

After hanging up, I fished in my briefcase for the copy of the police complaint Mother and Auntie had filed last night on the home invasion burglary. I found the phone number listed and got connected with the female officer on duty. She rustled papers and put me on hold several times before she located the report. They were, she said, short-handed at the station because of the extended holiday and wouldn't be able to follow up on the report until January 4.

"That's next year," I protested. "No way. This was an armed robbery."

"According to this report," she replied curtly, "nothing was taken except two empty boxes. This does not constitute an emergency, Miss McPill." She hung up before I could argue the point further or correct her.

I printed out the reports from PeopleFinders and set up the computer to phone a few more of the larger data banks and query them about my subjects. As long as there was still electricity, this part of the job was easy. And if my phone was kept busy dialing out for the rest of the day, it might discourage whoever was the nuisance caller. I added the names of George Murray and Jack McSweeney, the partners in Auntie's law firm of Murray and McSweeney, to the list of subjects to be queried. Auntie might be "full o' certainty" that her main squeeze was on the up and up, but I was not.

I hadn't had any lunch, but it was almost two o'clock and I didn't want to be late for my meeting with Lt. Fernandez. I unearthed some Fig Newtons from a desk drawer, tucked them into my purse, grabbed the file box of HI-Data index cards and hurried out.

Today was windy as well as cold, and that first breath of frigid air was painful. A sign was posted across the street warning pedestrians to watch for falling ice. I glanced up, thinking of the incident a few years earlier when a passer-by had been killed by icicles falling from a high rise. Statistically speaking, that made me real nervous. In the spirit of caution, I opened the Miata's hood and checked her innards, then squatted down to peer at her undercarriage. After what had happened with my brakes, I was nervous every time I turned the key.

Chicago Police Headquarters was at 3510 South Michigan. There was bulletproof glass in its main door, and inside was a gauntlet of cameras, biometric scanners and monitors. This place had a lot more security than HI-Data — the benefit of having unlimited taxpayer funds. The only evidence of the Christmas season was a pair of shabby poinsettia plants on either side of the main door.

Cameras on the ceiling caught every angle as I slid a paper with my request to see Lt. Fernandez into a glass tray and spoke via microphone to a clerk sitting behind more bulletproof glass. She asked if I had any weapons. I told her no. She paged Lt. Fernandez, then told me to step aside.

In the waiting area, the only place to sit was on a cement bench. The décor was strictly utile, not even a hint of ambiance. There were doors for men's and women's restrooms. On both sides of the corridor were secure window banks with bulletproof Lexan. The two doors on each end were black metal with peepholes. Alongside each door was an X-ray machine. The doors were kept locked, and the clerk had to buzz you in. Fire sprinklers were everywhere and drains were visible around the floor. I suspected they could bring in a big hose and in a couple of minutes get rid of any blood or bodily fluid.

A side door opened and a vigorous man in plainclothes walked briskly up to me and made eye contact.

"DD McGil?"

"Lt. Fernandez? How'd you know it was me?"

"Here." He handed me a plastic identification card with today's date on it and a full color photo of me. It must have been taken by one of the cameras on the ceiling when I spoke to the clerk. I was impressed.

He grinned and said, "Clip this to your coat. We have to go through x-ray. Homeland Security paid for all this, but really I don't feel a hell of lot safer than the old days when anyone could just walk in."

"Really? Why?"

"Because half the cops are nutcases running around with guns," he whispered with a smile.

Fernandez was six one or six two, with dark hair, a tan complexion and a five o'clock shadow. He was wearing a light yellow golf shirt, tightly creased tan pants, and a .40 caliber Glock riding high on his right hip. The pants and shirt were kinda tight, forcing me to observe that he was all muscle. He wore his identification clipped on the point of his collar.

I dropped my purse onto the x-ray's conveyer belt and handed him the paper bag containing the Coke can with Olson's fingerprints.

He pointed at the conveyer belt. "Put it down there behind your purse and go through the magnetometer."

I did so without incident and when I was through, Fernandez laid his gun and car keys on the belt and followed suit.

When we got through the security door, the other end of the conveyer belt wasn't visible. There was a spring door that opened only if the examiner felt that everything passed muster.

While we waited, he looked me over and said, "Phil says you're all right."

"He said that about you, too."

"We were on a few cases together. He was good to do business with. How'd you meet him?"

"It's a long story," I said. "Maybe I'll know you well enough to tell you some day."

The door sprung open loudly, and we gathered up our stuff. He took the paper bag.

"We're going straight to the lab," he said. "I told them to expect us."

We went down a long series of corridors. I

admitted I was completely disoriented.

"Haven't you been in this new HQ before?" he asked.

"No. This is the first time. I remember the old headquarters at 11th and State. This place is so much bigger."

"Yep. It's three hundred thousand square feet of bureaucratic heaven." He waved his arms expansively. "They built it like a mini-fortress with all the comforts of home. We've got a running track and sauna on three north that rivals any downtown health club. No expense spared. Here's the lab. You'll see what I mean."

The lab was very Christmasy. Lights in the shape of Santas were strung along one wall, and there was a cute tree with flickering white lights flanked by two Frosty the Snowmen.

A friendly lab tech whom Fernandez greeted as Genevieve took the paper bag from him and said she'd lift the prints herself. I handed her a paper with all the information on John Olson from HI-Data, including his social security number.

We wished her good luck and trekked to Fernandez' office. On the way, he explained that he'd fallen out of grace with the brass at HQ, and that's why he was in Cold Case. "It's akin to putting me in the basement. If

I was a patrolman, they'd have assigned me somewhere out on Cottage Grove to write parking tickets. But I'm not bitter. I actually like this job. I have access to everything, everybody, every lab, every file, every jot and tittle with this job. And knowledge is power, as someone once said."

"Sounds like they don't know they've unleashed a monster," I said, and wondered what he'd done and who he'd pissed off.

On a wall in his office was a map of all the reported crimes in different neighborhoods. Fernandez showed me the little icons they use to categorize the crimes.

"See those little fists wearing brass knuckles? That's for simple assaults."

I looked closely and asked him about all the XXXs on the map.

"Oh, that's for crimes of prostitution. And see the little Zorro masks? They're for larceny."

In response to some of his questions, I told him about Insurance Investigations 101, but I could see he already knew it all. He related an incident back when he was doing traffic where he told the driver that his answer to one question would determine whether or not he was drunk.

"And the questions was?" I asked.

"Whether Mickey Mouse was a cat or a dog."

We were laughing when his phone rang. He picked it up at once, nodded, and gave me a thumbs up.

"She's got something," he said, hanging up the phone. "She's shooting the files up here right away."

"Great." I was again impressed at all the high tech in this place.

He put his elbows on the desk and cupped his face in his hands. "If we go on a date," he said, "we'd have to talk about something other than crime. Think you could do that?"

"A date? We're going on a date?"

"Well, you have to at least buy me lunch for running these prints for you."

"Technically, Genevieve down in the lab is running the prints. And isn't that a wedding ring you're wearing?"

"Oh, yeah, but we're separated."

"Oh, yeah, like every cop in the department is separated."

"No. I really am."

There was a rap on his door, it opened, and a uniformed cop dropped two folders on his desk without a word.

"Thanks, Harvey." Fernandez opened them and started reading.

After a moment he closed both folders

and looked across the desk at me. "This is interesting, Miss McGil. She sent up two folders. The name and the prints don't match up."

"Wow. I wasn't sure what to expect. Let me see."

"This is police property. I can't let you take these with you."

"But . . ."

"But if you promise to take me to lunch," he laughed, "I'll let you look at them and copy down anything you want."

"Give me those." I leaned across the desk, but he held them out of my reach. "Okay. Okay. Lunch next week. Now hand them over."

He did, and I opened them eagerly. The prints from the Coke can belonged to someone named Dan Karton with an address in Plymouth, Massachusetts. I pulled out the photo in the Dan Karton file. No doubt about it. It was John Olson. Online Detective had come out clean on the name of John Olson, and now I knew why. Dan Karton had been busted on a marijuana possession when he was sixteen — a good enough reason to want to change identities.

Jeff Fere was going to be very interested in this development. I was going to recommend that HI-Data check the employment roster of Steinmetz A.G. and any other competitors to confirm or deny whether Olson came to HI-Data as a spy. I'd also advise them to do an indepth investigation before, not after, an applicant was hired.

I copied down what I needed, and Fernandez and I shook hands.

"Remember, I'm looking forward to that lunch," he said. "Don't forget, or I'll tell Phil you got me in trouble."

EIGHTEEN

I gambled that the Miata was safe in the police lot with all the cops scurrying hither and yon. Even so, I was nervous starting it up, and let out a deep breath as the motor purred and the heater did its thing.

I was headed to Joe Tanaka's place on the north side of the Loop. All the trainees had been told that the time frame for the investigation was tight, so I was counting on them being cooperative, even though it was the day after Christmas. My plan was to drop in on Tanaka unannounced. If he was there, great. If not, I'd try again until I caught him. I never make appointments on a comprehensive unless it's with a public institution. No sense giving anybody a chance to straighten up, or say no.

A few years ago, this north Loop neighborhood had been populated by vacant factories, too old and run down to be cost-effectively renovated. A trend to convert the old printing companies into loft apartments had taken over, and now the area was booming again. For once, modern architecture was a good thing.

The clouds had parted and sun glinted brightly off the remaining snow as I parked in front of Joe's building. I rang his bell twice and waited. He wasn't exactly happy to see me. I walked in under his protests.

"I was out partying last night." He blinked his casual, bachelor eyes at me. "I lead a very active social life."

I took my time surveying his apartment. It was on the second floor, but too far inland for a view of the lake. The place was decorated like the inside of a Sharper Image catalog when there used to be a Sharper Image. Along with an overabundance of electronic gadgetry, there was a twenty-speed titanium Peugeot racing bike standing against some expensive weight lifting equipment. His small kitchen looked unused except for a couple of empty beer bottles on the counter, but his living room overflowed with computers. Three were on desks against the wall, and a sleek lap-top was on his coffee table in the center of the room.

I tried small talk before getting down to fact verification, but Joe was tight-lipped about everything personal. His file gave only the barest facts. Second generation Japanese-American. Mother: deceased; Father: inorganic chemist.

"Your father, Joe, Sr., lives in Chicago?"

"Yes, okay, but I don't see much of him anymore. He doesn't think Western," Joe said. "Why do you do this kind of work? You like nosing around other people's lives? With your looks, I don't see it. You should be investigating what's going on at HI-Data."

"What about HI-Data? You mean something to do with Ken's death?"

"That old guy? No. But there's rumors of a hostile takeover."

"Where did you find that out?"

"I'm just reading between the lines on some stuff I dug off the Web. You know, over one of my international computer link-up networks." Joe pointed at the various machines.

"Have you got any details?"

"Details, no. It's just a rumor. I don't know anything more. You told us you're the cracker-jack investigator. You should know all about this already."

When I asked him if he'd known John Olson before they met at HI-Data, he said, "Why do you ask that? Why not ask about my sex life? That's good news. It's real healthy. You know," he said, moving closer and running his fingers up my arm, "I'm going to be making a lot of money real soon. What about getting it on?"

I snapped my notebook shut and jammed my pen into my purse and gathered up my stuff to leave.

"Joe, you just made my job a lot easier. I'm going to abort your bonding investigation and notify HI-Data at once."

He jumped up and blocked the doorway. "No. You can't do that. I'll lose my job."

"Then answer my questions — all of them — and I'll reconsider." I sat down again, pulled out my paraphernalia, and clicked my cheap American Insurance ballpoint pen on and off a few times for effect.

Resignedly, he told me he'd never met John or the other trainees prior to being hired at HI-Data, nor was he familiar with their specific fields of study. He then hustled, if not willingly, at least efficiently about the apartment, collecting copies of his tax returns, lease, and other important papers that I enjoyed asking to see. On the surface, everything seemed to be in order, leading me to conclude that he was a jerk, but lacking evidence to the contrary, no worse. Naturally, I still had all the cross-checks going, which would verify everything

I now had. I smiled and thanked him as I left. I pride myself on my professionalism.

NINETEEN

The clouds had cleared, and the sky was now bright blue. I headed north on the Inner Drive to Marcie Ann's apartment. The sharp winter sun glinted off Lake Michigan's roiling waves — a beautiful sight, but in December, cold enough to kill on contact.

I rang the bell at Marcie's trendy near-north Lincoln Park apartment, then knocked. No answer. I immediately headed for Ron Rivers' place and would return here tomorrow.

Ron, his wife, and their baby daughter rented a two-bedroom apartment in a four-plus-one on Wellington and Sheridan. The living room was small, but tidy, and accommodated a playpen and a beautiful seven-branched holiday menorah. Baby Sara plopped against my knees and ran her chubby fingers up and down my legs, apparently fascinated by the feel of pantyhose. Good thing my mother, Aunt Elizabeth, and the twins couldn't see this domestic scene with me in the middle. I'd never hear the end of it.

Their modest status, Ron explained, was only temporary. They were about to pay off the last of his graduate school loans. His wife agreed that their "borrowed time" was coming to an end and the "good life" loomed on the horizon.

Mrs. Rivers hurried through the little apartment gathering the lease and tax returns, birth certificates, and diplomas while Sara continued her fascination with my legs. So far, everything looked clean on Ron. I asked about takeover rumors at HI-Data, but he claimed he hadn't heard anything about that or about Ken's death, either. I said good-bye after extricating myself from Sara's tiny hands. When the door closed behind me, I could hear them discussing what a takeover might mean to Ron's job security.

TWENTY

It was getting late. I wasn't sure if I'd make it to Joyce and Company before Tom closed up shop. Nevertheless, still jumpy, I again opened the Miata's hood and checked the undercarriage before turning the key.

Tom's eclectic bookshop was on the ground floor of a two-story building west of the loop near Oprah's Harpo Studios. The city fathers had turned Randolph Street into a boulevard along this stretch, and restaurants and trendy real estate have finally made Tom's investment of some years ago pay off. He had his own reserved parking spot directly outside the front door for loading and unloading books, which was a good thing because his street was usually parked up and you could cruise for an hour and still not find a parking spot. I parked in the pay lot across the street, took a ticket at the metal access gate, and hurried out.

True to his word, the "Open" sign still

hung on the door. A tiny bell tinkled as I entered. The mysterious and powerful smell of leather and old books engulfed me.

Tom glanced up from a book. His dark-rimmed glasses shaded tired but interested eyes.

"How does my good lady?" he asked in his best Shakespearean voice. "I've been waiting. I was half afraid your surprise was going to be Auntie Gorgon coming to meet me."

"No, but she is tangentially involved. I promise this will be worth it. Where's the wassail?"

"Alas, 'tis gone." He smiled through his tailored brown mustache. "A bunch of carolers came by, and needless to say, they were singing a lot more off key when they left." He chuckled heartily like Olde King Cole, and I could tell he was a bit fortified.

"You're higher than Everest," I quipped as I sloughed off my coat and headed for the massive oak library table at one end of the room.

"Mount Everest, I'll have you know DD, stands 8.85 kilometers above sea level, roughly the maximum height reached by international airplane flights, but much less than the 300 kilometers achieved by a space shuttle."

"Yeah, and the Statue at the Lincoln Memorial is made up of twenty-eight stones. We know we can trade trivia all evening, but this is really important . . . Can you clear a space here?"

Tom shifted piles of books from the table onto the maple floorboards. He watched closely as I set the briefcase on the table, drew on Auntie's gloves and gently removed the leather pouch with the glass fragments and the manuscript.

He rubbed his palms together. "Let's see what you've got here."

He watched intently as I carefully opened the pouch, unwrapped the glass pieces and laid them out on the table.

"Here you are, Tom. A little Christmas puzzle, as Sherlock Holmes would say."

Tom pulled out a pair of surgical gloves from an open box he always kept on top of his kidney-shaped desk. He put them on and lifted each piece of glass and slowly studied it as I outlined what Auntie had told me, along with the bits of investigation I'd gathered from the Internet.

When he'd finished examining the glass, he gingerly lifted the document.

"So this has to do with that Auntie Gorgon of yours. I'm assuming that she and you are telling me all the facts as you know

160

them. You wouldn't believe the number of people who bring things in and try to test me by withholding or making up data. So far, I've kept ahead of them."

"Artifacts 101," I joked.

Tom then slowly unfolded the document and examined it minutely. His forehead wrinkled as he scrutinized the etched lettering on the glass, bending forward for a closer look. He didn't appear tipsy anymore as he said, "Certainly looks like period handwriting."

"Supposedly," I related, "Burns visited Stirling in 1787 to tour the seat of the Scottish kings. You probably know that's where all the Scots Kings were crowned. I looked it up on the Internet. It's one hell of an imposing fortress. Made me think of William Wallace and all that."

"The castle rock at Stirling," Tom interjected, "has an interesting history with its Medieval great hall. It was built on a plain, 250 feet above an extinct volcano — and you're right, DD, a number of Scottish kings and queens were baptized, crowned, murdered, and were buried there since the days of Alexander the First and maybe even earlier."

Tom's knowledge on almost any subject was daunting. I was supposed to be the statistician, and we always traded facts and figures. But somehow, no matter how hard I tried, he was always besting me.

"Anyway," I carried on as his sharp eyes closely examined the document, "Burns supposedly wrote this poem with a diamond-tipped pen on a window of the room he was staying in at the Golden Lion Inn during this visit to Stirling."

"Writing with a diamond-tipped pen is not unheard of," Tom said. "Nathaniel Hawthorne was known to have used one to scratch notes on a window pane."

"Oh, at the House of the Seven Gables?"

"I expected that from you, DD. Glad to see you're in form tonight. No, it was at a home overlooking Concord Bridge, off the road to Lexington."

"I read today on one web site that Burns liked to scratch verses all over on windows and above fireplaces. There's some museum in Scotland that has a window preserved from the Cross Keys Inn where he scratched a verse."

"I do remember some mention of that one. History records that scratching verses with diamond-tipped pens all over Scotland was one of Burns' favorite pastimes. He also did it on a window of his home in Dumfries where he penned — scratched — a poem to

Anna Park, her of the 'golden locks.' Hand me that lighted magnifier, will you?"

I passed it over to him, and he continued his examination. Finally he said, "This definitely is not modern glass. And the inscription's not in ink, so there'll be some differences in the script, but the writing appears quite compatible with the handwriting on the document."

"So what's next?"

"Looks like this is 'a three pipe problem,' as Mr. Holmes would say. First, we check the handwriting against a known source. Next we identify the writing instrument, the paper, and note any watermarks. After that comes the hard part."

I stifled a yawn as Tom climbed a half ladder.

"I could contact one of the museums in Scotland that has Burns' Common Place Books. They were his version of a diary — full of ideas and old songs he'd heard — all in his handwriting. But since I've got a facsimile volume of the Glenriddell right here, we'll have an answer much sooner."

"What's a Glenriddell? I know I've heard of it, but . . ."

"It's a collection of poems that Burns himself redrafted in his own hand and presented to a friend, one Captain Robert

Riddell. Usually all we get to work with is an isolated signature, but this volume will give us extensive reproductions of his writing.

"By the way, DD, I hear your office building's coming down. Don't forget to give me your new address and phone number."

"Sure," I drawled, "if and when I find someplace where the rent isn't more than my bank account."

"Can't you work from your apartment?"

"No way. I come in contact with a lot of weirdoes. That's why I'm unlisted in the phone directory. I can't have them knowing my home address."

"Yeah, there's that," he grunted as he removed a calf-bound volume from a shelf about nine feet up.

"This damn thing's really heavy," he groaned, climbing down and placing it on an antique library table covered with a silk cloth embroidered with camels.

"Burns included over fifty unpublished poems in this collection. You know, some years later all hell broke loose in Scotland when an American purchased the original Glenriddell. But now it's back in Scotland at the National Library."

He ran his finger down the index. "Here it is, page 80." He located the page and pointed. "Here's the verse, but it's not in Burns handwriting."

I looked over his shoulder.

"A scribe or amanuensis wrote it," he explained. "Common practice at the time. But Burns did write a few lines underneath it. See here."

Tom the sleuth was enjoying this. I was too, but nonetheless found myself stifling another yawn. The wonderful smell of old books and the peace of the shop were having a soporific effect on me.

"You do realize, DD, how extremely collectible Burns is right now? He's an icon. He's gotten even more popular throughout the years."

"I wonder why?"

"Think about it, DD. If you've ever sung 'Auld Lang Syne,' you've quoted Robert Burns. A few years ago, a handwritten copy of 'Auld Lang Syne' sold in the States for $170,000."

"What would that sell for today?"

"Oh, in general, prices tend to double every ten years or so." He laughed and waved his arms at the floor to ceiling bookshelves. "I'm surrounded by my retirement here."

I surveyed the myriad maze of bookcases and yawned again.

"You look beat, DD. I won't ask what you've been doing. Look, since all the wassail's gone, how about a nip of something else while I work on this?"

"Yes, please," I said gratefully.

Tom took out a key and locked his front door. Then he ducked into a small kitchen, invisible to patrons behind a wall unit of antique oak barrister bookcases. I heard noises and the unmistakable clink of ice.

I sat down in one of his Queen Anne style burgundy leather chairs. The bookstore was warm and comfy. The wonderful smell of old books permeated the air. I pulled off Auntie's gloves and rested my weary feet on his coffee table.

When the bookman returned, he carried a tray with two glasses and a bottle labeled "Baker Street Blended Scotch Whisky." He poured a generous amount of the amber liquid into each glass.

"Cheers. Since we're researching Burns, Scotch is definitely in order instead of my usual Jameson's Irish. Don't worry. You won't have to nurse a hangover. It's good booze. 'Baker Street Scotch' isn't available anymore, so I keep refilling the empty bottle with Glenfiddich Special Reserve. Now relax."

The Scotch tasted great. I wanted to follow what Tom was doing as he began to compare handwriting samples, but my eyes wouldn't stay open. Everything was quiet except for the sound of pages turning.

TWENTY-ONE

"Well, I've done what I can for tonight," Tom said, breaking my reverie. "Come on over here, and I'll tell you what I've discovered so far."

I stood up, still tired but somewhat refreshed.

"Look at these letters in the manuscript," he pointed. "You can see from these capital Ss, Ts, and Ws, Burns' handwriting is what I'd call a plain, old-fashioned script. And the distinctive backward curl in the lowercase 'd' is an unmistakable trait."

"I see what you mean."

"So, I've concluded that the handwriting on your document as well as the script on the glass appear to match samples of Burns' writing. This document seems to have been written with a quill pen, not a steel nib, and that's important."

"Why?"

"Steel tips will leave a line at the outer

edge of the stroke, easily seen with a trusty magnifier. And steel pen nibs weren't introduced until the nineteenth century, so we'd know it was fake if a steel nib had been used. And did you notice this tiny residue of dark sand on the paper?"

"Yeah, I saw that. Was the manuscript buried at some time?"

"Buried? You've got a hell of an imagination, DD. No. Probably sand from a shaker was used to blot the ink on the finished page, and a few grains caught in the fold and there they have remained.

"As to paper," he went on, "this appears to be all rag, which is consistent with manually laid paper used in Burns' time. See the chain lines that run across the paper? And feel how sturdy it is." He handed it to me.

"It does have a crisp feel."

"That's a good description, DD. Rag paper like this survives much better than modern machine-made wood pulp paper developed in the mid-nineteenth century. The acid in that paper causes a slow breakdown of the cellulose fibers, and the paper just fractures.

"Now, I didn't find any visible watermarks, but watermarks are a surprisingly complicated topic, with their own reference works devoted to them, like the chain lines."

"And what's your opinion? You do have one, I hope."

"Ah, DD, you know me so well. I always have an opinion. From my personal research, I believe that date watermarks, which were common in the early nineteenth century, were fairly rare in Burns' time.

"To sum up on the document," he continued, "the handwriting, the type of pen, the paper, and the absence of a watermark all check so far. But none of them are prima facie evidence to prove that this is a forgery. If it is a forgery, then the forger was very careful and prepared."

"What about the broken glass?"

"Aahh, the infamous green glass." He picked up a piece.

"Cracks on the top here have obliterated a few of the letters in the third line."

I held up a piece in which the letter "p" in the word "reptiles" and the letter "i" in the word "line," were missing. I stood silent, remembering what I'd read about the incident at the Golden Lion Inn on the Burns Internet sites. I could easily envision the young, handsome, virile Robert Burns smashing the window with his riding crop.

"Tom, if this is the famous window pane, could this damage be from Burns hitting it with his riding crop?"

He smiled. "DD, you know that the broken pane of glass proves nothing merely because it's broken."

"You're right, Sherlock. Any smart forger would break the counterfeit glass, too."

"Certainly the sexiest cause for the breakage would be from Burns bludgeoning it with his riding crop to eliminate the evidence. History does tell us Burns was fiercely loyal to the Stuarts and wanted them back on the throne. This poem he wrote was dangerous. It was treasonous for a person to do, say, or display anything connected with the Stuart kings."

"It's probably a good thing Auntie Dragon didn't live then."

"From all you say of the Gorgon Aunt, I'd have to agree. Good thing you didn't either."

"Never mind about me. Now from what I read," I said, changing the subject, "Burns did a lot of other dangerous things, too, like publicly celebrating Bonnie Prince Charlie's birthday in 1787. That was a treasonable act, too."

"He was known for speaking his mind on almost every subject — that's partly why he was and still is so revered. And that's also why everybody suspected that he was the writer of the poem on the window pane.

The first printing of his *Poems — Chiefly in the Scottish Dialect — Kilmarnock Edition* came out in April of 1786," Tom cited from his nearly-infallible memory. "And in a few short weeks he was a national celebrity in an era before movies, TV, iPods, or YouTube. His poetry was new and fresh, and it addressed topics that had been forbidden for almost a hundred years. Remember, after the Stuart dynasty, the fortunes of Scotland declined. Scots were forbidden to speak or write their own native language, and they were forbidden to wear kilts. Burns wrote this "treasonous" poem on the window at the Inn at Stirling in 1787, only a year after his *Poems* was published. The timing is right here, and we could infer that he wrote it because his celebrity made him feel invincible."

"If this is genuine . . ."

"Then this glass would be worth its weight in diamonds, to say nothing of its historical, sentimental, and patriotic value," Tom said.

"But I can't believe any of this is genuine. Oh, I admit I got excited there for a minute. The fact is, Auntie's rolling in the hay with the guy who sold this to her."

"Hmmm." Tom looked disappointed. "That certainly adds a murky cast to the waters."

"The guy's her attorney, and he knows about Auntie's biggest weakness — Scotland and Scottish nationalism. I can't help thinking she's being conned. If I don't expose him, he'll try an even bigger scam on her next time."

"There are a few more tests I need to make, DD. I'll have to enlarge it under my binocular microscope to examine the pen strokes for irregularities and jerky movements. To authenticate the ink, I need to first see if it fluoresces under black light."

"But even I know both paper and ink can be faked."

"True, DD. Forged documents can be made on genuine, period paper, and often inks of any period can be imitated. A good example of that is the crackerjack forger, Mark Hofmann, who forged an Emily Dickinson poem that was sold at Sotheby's in 1997 for $21,000. He also imitated a number of Mormon documents, including a particularly interesting one said to be quite incriminating against their leader Joseph Smith, who . . ."

"Look, Tom, I know you know your stuff, but . . ."

"Sorry, DD. I'm rambling on. But don't worry. There's one more test. Forensic document examiners who work for the U.S.

Treasury Department now do an atomic test that can be used to measure the migration rate of certain ions in ink. Somebody discovered that these ions migrate through paper at definite rates that cannot be faked and can prove very accurately how long the ink has been on the page. That way, even if the paper is the right age, and the ink is the right formula, they can calculate conclusively how long that ink has been on that paper."

"Oh, like carbon dating for a manuscript, huh?"

"Exactly. So I can promise you an authentication, one way or the other."

"And as for the glass?"

"That's another story, and one I'm not personally familiar with. I'll ask around." Tom removed his glasses and ran his fingers through his brown hair. "You'll have to leave these things with me so I can do those tests."

"Auntie's going to be livid when she finds out I've transferred possession."

"I'm sure you'll handle her. Meanwhile, did you already check with all the known institutional collections of Burns manuscripts to confirm that nobody knows about the whereabouts of this piece and that it hasn't been stolen from any archive, public or private?"

"I'm planning to get on that as soon as I can."

"I'll do it for you. All the information's already in a database in my computer."

"Great."

"One other thing. I'll check online at Book Auction Record and the American Book Prices Current for auction records for the past twenty-five years."

"What will that do?"

"That'll ensure these things haven't appeared at some auction."

"Or maybe they have," I said.

"Good point. Oh, and I just remembered a first-rate Burns scholar I met at the London antiquarian book fair. He lives in Scotland, but I'll contact him by e-mail for his take on this."

"Thanks, Tom. Let me know your conclusions as soon as you can. Oh, and by the way, I better tell you, someone broke into the house where my aunt was staying. I think they were after these things. So you better use all the security you've got."

"Don't worry. Saving paper is my life, and I'm good at it. You already know I'm alarmed to the gills with motion detectors, magnets, and sensors because you advised me to and you got me the rebate from my insurance company for installing it all."

"Sometimes I'm quite useful," I said.

"The police station's only a block away on Racine. And as luck would have it, I'm going to be babysitting a Northern Michigan timber wolf for the next six weeks. That should settle any question of a break-in."

"Oh, God. I have this vision of a Watch-Wolf eating Auntie's valuable artifacts, and it's scaring the hell out of me."

"Better not tell her," he suggested as I grabbed my coat and walked to the door. "Oh, by the way," he said casually, "there's a store room behind the kitchen area here, DD. It's my hideout when I need to evade a customer or take a nap." He smiled broadly. "My point is, the space is yours if you need it."

I'm not good at taking anything from anybody, but I realized if I didn't find other space, my office stuff and I were going to be dumped into the street.

"Thanks, Tom. I know I'm a difficult friend sometimes."

"Sometimes?"

"You don't have to rub it in."

"Haven't you noticed DD that you abhor change? You resist it like a vacuum abhors air. I've got a healthy streak of that same outlook myself. It's only temporary till you find a place. To make you feel better, I'll even charge you more than it's worth."

I put on my coat and found my car keys. "I just might have to take you up on it, Tom."

"Remember, it's here if you want it. Oh, and a very Merry Christmas to the Cavalier Cat." Tom waved and locked the door behind me.

I shivered, and all the way to the car I watched for unknown enemies in the bitterly cold Chicago night.

TWENTY-TWO

Tom was right. I hate change. His offer of office space made me realize I'd over-procrastinated. I would try to find something tomorrow.

Home at last, I could have used a little cuddling, but Cavalier remained aloof and pretended he didn't even know I'd been gone. I settled for a shortbread cookie and a stiff dose of Wild Turkey. Although today I'd made some progress on the trainees, I still had no clue who had killed Ken. At least no cops were hassling me.

As for Auntie's "wee Burns" artifacts, tomorrow I would have to tell Phil about the break-in at Mother's. I hoped those tests Tom was making would quickly supply some definitive answers on the artifacts. As soon as we confirmed they were fake, I'd return them to Auntie's paramour, Mr. Murray. Then I'd force him to give back Auntie's money. I only hoped she wouldn't be a target for further violence. In the meantime, I had to prepare Auntie to be disappointed. Somehow I knew that would be the hardest task of all.

Last on the tomorrow list, and only because I was curious, I vowed to research those mysterious initials, KB. The name Katherine Bruce presented a good starting point.

Sunday morning I woke with a jolt, thinking of all I had to do. I ran out to pick up a *Chicago Trib* so I could check for office digs, which I did immediately after finishing the crossword puzzle. I phoned two possibles and left messages. Hopefully I'd find something right away. Meanwhile I had to work on the HI-Data comprehensives and visit a lot of people connected with the new employees. Sundays are a great time to catch people at home, so after a second cup of coffee, I hit the road.

The doorman at Marcie Ann's saluted as I pulled in. I parked in the building's parking ramp, and on the way to the elevators, paused to admire a silver Porsche Carrera 4 with a convertible top parked in the stall for 2318. It was so new it didn't have plates, just a temporary yellow cardboard sign visible through the back window with an expiration date eight weeks hence. Apparently Marcie was already taking advantage of her big-time salary at HI-Data. I guessed I'd be wildly extravagant too if I were paying taxes in her income bracket.

New wave jazz was playing in Marcie's apartment, so I was relieved I wouldn't have to return a third time. My reflection in the door's peephole made me look like the fat lady at the circus. For all the good it would do, I primped my unruly hair and rang the bell. Maybe Marcie hadn't lied to me during our first interview. But if what Sparky had said about her and Ken was true, then Marcie was, at the very least, guilty of withholding valuable information. Tucking the tidbit into my mental kit bag, I smiled into the peephole. I didn't like not being told everything. I was going to enjoy this interview.

Marcie couldn't hide her surprise at finding me on her doorstep at 11:30 on a Sunday morning. She opened the door barely wide enough to talk.

At our last meeting at HI-Data, she'd been wearing a red two-piece Chanel business suit, reflecting a sense of style not usual in twenty-two-year-old girls. That same lack of youthful informality was evident today. Her pale green and pink silk Lacoste jogging suit might be called leisure wear, but it was so strikingly trim and neat that I felt dumpy in my brand-new black Anne Klein tunic and trousers.

"Nice jazz," I opened, hoping to put the conversation on a friendly tone.

"Yes, it is. Jazz is all mathematics, and math always relaxes me." she observed with a thin-lipped smile. "Everything, Ms. McGil, comes down to math, if you're smart enough to understand it."

I don't like to show off. Usually.

"Lots of people call me smart, too," I said. "For example, I know that half the time twenty-three randomly selected people are gathered together, two or more of them will share a birthday."

Marcie's eyes widened. "So you've encountered the laws of permutations and combinations." She blinked, twice, then asked, "What exactly are you doing here? What more do you want from me? I've already spent hours filling out forms and answering your questions."

She shuffled her weight from one leg to the other, unwilling to invite me in.

"I'm sure you won't mind giving me just a minute or two of your time to confirm a few details, Marcie."

"Couldn't this have waited till Monday at

HI-Data?"

"I'm being forced to work on a tight deadline here. You were told that. So if being employed by HI-Data is important to you, then no, it can't wait."

"Oh, all right," she conceded and opened the door wide enough for me to enter. A large foyer opened into her living room, and I followed her there. The apartment, like Marcie herself, was minimalist chic. There was a black lacquer table on one wall with two computers and some books and paperwork. The golden wood parquet floors, peach walls, and clean-lined furniture could have been copied from an issue of *Architectural Digest.* Everything was neat as a pin. A few accessories provided slashes of color, but there was a noticeable lack of any clutter — no personal photos, no letters or bills, no amorphous disarray. George Vogel, my obsessive landlord, would love this girl. Her file said both parents were Methodists, and I looked around in vain for some sign of the Christmas season.

She watched me scrutinize her work-table. "I do a lot of my research here," she said, pointing me to an oversize cream chair with dark apricot piping

I sat down, she sat down, and we smiled coolly at each other. "Marcie, what have you heard about a hostile takeover of HI-Data?"

"How did you find out?"

"Just answer my question, okay?"

"Rumor. That's all it is. Just rumor."

"Well, who's supposedly involved as the second party in this rumor?"

"Oh, some European firm. I can't remember the name."

I was sure she knew more than she was telling. It was time to switch to personal data. "How long have you lived in this beautiful apartment?"

"You already know how long. It's on the form I filled out."

"What's your monthly rent?"

"That's on the form, too."

"Yes, I'm sure it is, but I wonder if you'd just confirm it."

"Twenty-nine hundred dollars a month," she said.

"Can I see your lease?"

"I'd have to go look for it. I'm not sure exactly where it is."

"Well, I'll need a copy. Now, let's review your income for last year and the year before."

"I don't know all that off the top of my head. The figures are all there on the forms I filled out."

"Yes, but I'd like to see the copies of your

last two years' tax returns, please."

"As I said, I'm not sure just where they are."

Marcie's apartment was so neat, I had trouble believing she could misplace a safety pin. I said, "Marcie, tell me, what kind of car do you drive?"

She sighed loudly. "I don't have a car. That's on the forms, too. Didn't you read anything I filled out? This is a waste of time. I'm going to let HI-Data know you're incompetent."

That did it. It was Sunday, and I knew I shouldn't swear, but I didn't have to be nice, did I? "So whose brand-new Porsche is parked downstairs in your parking spot?"

I could see the wheels turning as she stalled. "In my parking space?"

"Isn't number 2318 your space?"

"Oh, um, well," she stammered, clasping her hands together in a little ball.

I couldn't wait to hear her explanation.

"I forgot," she said. "I just bought it a few days ago. Up until last week I didn't have a car, and, it's so new that I forgot, really, that I owned it." She ended on a high note, perhaps convincing herself it was the truth.

She didn't convince me. Ken had been murdered, HI-Data was the target of industrial espionage, and someone had cut my brake line at HI-Data. Maybe Marcie was in it up to her smart neck. I needed a better read on her, so I decided to attack.

"Don't try to bullshit me, Marcie. Not if you want to go on working for HI-Data. The date on your license-applied-for sticker is from two weeks ago, which means you lied to me on the form you filled out two days ago."

She stared at me, clenched-jawed and a little pale. I was kind of enjoying this.

"So, tell me, does this have anything to do with you and Ken?" I settled deeper into her comfy chair, feeling as if we were going to finally get some answers.

"What?" she sputtered and looked down to her right.

"You know, your affair and all that. What you deliberately withheld during our interview."

Now there was no more talk about my being incompetent. She squirmed, and I wished Sparky could be here to see it.

"Well?" I coaxed. "Stop giving me crap and help me do my job, or I'm personally going to get you kicked out of HI-Data."

"I've told you everything I'm going to. My relationship with Ken was entirely personal and has nothing to do with you."

"That's where you're wrong, Marcie. This

is a top-security check. Things that normally would be personal and off-limits are grist to my mill. HI-Data hired me to find this stuff out, and as a condition of being hired, you agreed to cooperate. I wouldn't be doing my job if I didn't ask the difficult questions."

She squirmed on her beautiful sofa. "You've got to realize that there's nothing I can't ask and there's nothing you can refuse to answer, not if you want this job. Let's begin over again on that premise."

"No. No more questions." She abruptly stood up and opened her front door.

"Please leave," she demanded.

I got up from her fluffy furniture. "If you're sure that's how you want to play it, I'm heading to my office to file a report with HI-Data recommending your immediate dismissal. You don't give me any alternative."

Twenty-Three

The door slammed behind me, making a nearby wall sconce flicker. In the elevator, I pondered whether Marcie's reaction was due to lover's grief over Ken Gordon or if there were other reasons she wouldn't talk to me. It didn't matter. She had failed to cooperate and was gone. Now I was down to "two little Indians."

I stopped for lunch at the Butterfly for some Asian fusion, then for the rest of the day, I tried to forget about the little mystery of Marcie and concentrate on Ron and Joe.

My other visits turned up nothing more than a boring verification of facts. Family and friends of Ron and Joe provided the secondary confirmation I needed, so this level of fact-finding was moving along nicely. I was even a little ahead of schedule, so I could devote some time to investigating Auntie's case.

Although it was late when I got to Consolidated, I wanted to write the farewell report on Marcie and deliver it to HI-Data first thing tomorrow morning. I'd also tell Jeffrey face to face about Olson's prints. The good news was my workload for HI-Data was rapidly diminishing. First John Olson and now Marcie Ann Kent. Two down and money in the bank for me. The bad news was my curious-genes were still itching. I wanted to know what had been going on between Marcie and Ken and if their affair was connected to his death. Maybe their little romance even had some connection to why Ken had asked for me on this job. So far, all I could find Marcie guilty of was an ambitious lifestyle. Both she and Joe Tanaka had heard about takeover rumors at HI-Data. Had they learned of the rumors independently? Was the takeover linked to Ken's death? And how did all this relate to someone slashing my brake line? With every step I took in this investigation, more and more questions arose, none of which I could answer. In this job, time was money, and unfortunately I couldn't afford to spend more on Marcie.

The exterior of the Consolidated Bank building was now pockmarked all over and looked as forlorn as I felt. The beautiful marble slabs that had decorated the outside facing of the building had been removed. Each day new bits of deconstruction made it evident that this building hadn't long to live.

The wind whistled as I opened the door and stepped into the lobby. It was deserted, and after my full day of interrogatories, I was grateful for the ghostly silence. It looked so different today than it had a month ago when the eager minions of Consolidated had moved back and forth among the offices. Now it echoed to its own vacancy. It was also as cold inside as the meat section in my refrigerator.

I pressed the button to call the old elevator. As always, it shook and groaned, accompanied by unearthly echoes from its internal mechanics. Statistically speaking, it was due to break down anytime. I hoped tonight wasn't the night. It shimmied to a stop. The door opened, and a dark figure jumped out.

I screamed.

"Don't scream. I'm not going to hurt you. My name is Michael Drake. I own the company that's demolishing this building. You okay?"

"Dammit," I yelled, trying to breathe normally again. "You really startled me."

"I'm sorry," he said, taking my elbow.

I pulled away. "So you're the bozo who's going to wreck my building. I like this building. I've been happy here. Now you guys want to tear it down and build some glass and chrome monstrosity. Where am I gonna go?"

Michael Drake wore a heavy overcoat and a boyish grin, and there were red pressure lines on his forehead from the brow-band of the hard hat he doffed in my direction.

"You kind of surprised me, too." He smiled. "I didn't expect anyone here on Sunday. You're DD McGil aren't you?"

"And if I am?"

"Just that you're the last tenant left in this tower."

"I know." I stepped into the elevator.

Michael Drake ducked in too, just as the door closed.

"Look, I'm glad I ran into you, Miss McGil. I've been wanting to talk to you. We're ahead of schedule on this job, and also we've got some serious problems with this tower section."

"What does that have to do with me?"

The elevator stopped, and I stepped into the corridor. Where there used to be an expanse of highly polished marble floor providing a throughway into the main building, there now was a make-shift plywood wall that effectively separated the tower from the rest of Consolidated and cut off passage.

My stomach lurched.

"Wow, I guess I can't ignore this anymore," I said to Michael Drake as much as to myself. "If I don't find a new office soon, I'll go down with the rest of the building."

"You mean you don't have something lined up?"

I ignored the question and unlocked my office. The red light was flashing on my answering machine. I ignored that, too.

Michael Drake sat down. I wondered what he wanted from me. I turned on the portable heater and looked at him inquiringly.

"When will you be out of here?"

"I can't give you an exact time."

"Meaning . . . ?"

I didn't answer.

"Look, Miss McGil. I don't want anybody getting hurt in this demolition."

I got up and opened my door. "Thanks for your concern, Mr. Drake. There's no need to worry about me."

"This project's moving fast from now on. We'll soon be setting the charges for demolition. And this tower section you're in here is joined to the other building with some real heavy-duty steel reinforcing girders.

They weren't on the blueprints."

"And?"

"So, we've just discovered they're going to require a lot more explosives than originally anticipated."

"So," I said grouchily, "Murphy's Law applies everywhere. It's going to cost more and take more time. Happens in my business all the time."

"It will cost a little more, but it won't take more time. I told you we're ahead of schedule."

He took my arm and pulled me into the corridor. "You're an insurance investigator, right?"

"How'd you know that?"

"I made it my business to find out. You should know then that you're in danger here. Come with me. I want to show you something. You're smart enough to know you've got to get out — and I mean tomorrow."

I said nothing as we left my office and took the stairs up to the sixth floor. Michael opened the door onto a team of workers using oxy-acetylene torches on the big steel girders. The light was flickery and the air smoky. I surveyed the changing landscape of the room. The deconstruction process was happening faster than I could have imagined possible. This was my come-uppance. I knew I couldn't procrastinate any longer.

"We're weakening all the main reinforcing beams and girders to make sure that every-thing will come down in the right sequence when the charges go off."

He maneuvered us into a corner as a bobcat weaved into the adjacent wall and brought it down in a crash of plaster and white dust.

"When we're ready to bring in the explo-sives," he said, "we'll cut everything except the main computer leads. What I'm trying to tell you is, there'll be more explosives in your tower than were used in WW II. It's going to be difficult to blow, and we need to be sure it comes down on the first try. So please, I hope I've convinced you to leave."

"You have. I will." *And I meant it. I didn't like explosives.*

We took the stairs back down to my of-fice. As he left, he said, "I'm counting on you moving right away — by tomorrow hopefully. You won't have electricity after that."

I stood at the door until his footsteps faded. Discouraged, I sat down and played the phone messages. There were two long beeps from hang-ups. I decided to order caller ID tomorrow. The next message was from Marcie Ann Kent.

"Ms. McGil," she said, "I'm sorry we got off on the wrong foot today. I'd like to call a truce. I want this job, and I realize I'm going to have to answer your questions. I need your help, and I'll have the papers you requested. Meet me tomorrow in my office at HI-Data. I get in at eight. I'll tell you everything you want to know, and then some."

All was right with the world. My curiosity-gene would be satisfied, and I could go home instead of beating out Marcie's report tonight. I left with a fond farewell to the old office.

TWENTY-FOUR

Cavvy, the live-in alarm clock, woke me with a nuzzle and a meow at 5:30 a.m. I fixed a bowl of Cheerios for me and some smelly, fishy stuff for him. The *Trib*'s weather forecast for today included snowflakes and wind chill factors. I noted the weather for south Florida was a high of 80 degrees and sunny. I hate winter more every year and was giving serious thought to moving south.

I filled a few easy clues in the crossword puzzle and waited for the Cheerios to kick in. Then I phoned Phil to update him on the investigation. He picked up on the second ring.

"I can't talk now, DD. The cops are here."

"What?"

"Somebody broke in over the weekend and took apart my safe."

"I told you to buy one of those industrial safes that gets bolted to your floor. You wasted your money on that cheap model

195

from the office supply place. I warned you any tenth grader could break into that."

"It wasn't that cheap, DD. It had to be defective. Somebody used a pipe wrench and sheared off the lock. I'm suing the manufacturer."

"What'd they take?"

"That's the funny thing. Stuff's scattered all around the office, but the cash I had stashed in the safe is all here, and I can't find anything else missing. When Gilda comes in, we'll do a full inventory, but nothing seems to be gone. The cops think whoever it was didn't find what they were after."

"Even if someone was after drugs, you'd think they'd take the cash," I mused.

"Why would anybody think I have drugs in my safe? I don't handle drug cases. Hold on a sec, DD."

He didn't hit the hold button, so I overheard the cops talking to him. He came back on the line and said, "Now they want a list of dissatisfied clients. They think maybe this was some sick prank pulled by a client who didn't like what I did or what I charged."

I commiserated, then quickly filled him in on the status of my interviews at HI-Data and the upcoming meeting with Marcie. I was anxious to get off the phone. I needed to think. The word "prank" kept resounding in my head like a bell. That's exactly what the cops had called Auntie's Santa Claus robbery. Statistically speaking, two "prank" robberies were too much of a coincidence. I had a funny feeling the two incidents were connected. First Phil noticed somebody following them back from the airport. Then both Auntie and Phil were burglarized in the space of a few days. Nothing was taken from Phil, and only the red leather trunk and Ormolu casket were taken from Auntie. *Ergo* . . . what? Somebody knew about those Burns artifacts. And somebody wanted them.

"How's your beastly aunt doing with her 'wee Burns thing'?"

I'd planned on telling Phil about the break-in at Mother's, but decided he didn't have to know about that right now. "I'll fill you in on that later," I said. "You've got enough to worry about."

"By the way, DD, where's your new office? I need your new phone number and address."

"Later," I told him and hung up before we got into a discussion on that subject. True, I needed to move today, but first I needed to investigate where Auntie had got-

197

ten the Burns artifacts. That meant looking into the namesakes of the firm Murray and McSweeney, and specifically what they'd been doing for the past twenty-four hours.

A quick check of my trusty desk atlas showed Scotland was six hours ahead of Chicago, the middle of the working day for the firm of Murray and McSweeney. I searched my briefcase for the number I'd lifted from Auntie's purse and telephoned the international exchange.

"Murray and McSweeney," answered a pleasant voice with only a hint of Scots accent.

"I'd like to speak to Mr. Murray, please."

"He's in a meeting. Can I take your name and number?"

I didn't want to leave my name and number — yet, so I quickly asked for the other partner, McSweeney.

"Did you wish Mr. Gerald McSweeney or Mr. Jack McSweeney? Mr. Gerald McSweeney is now retired. Mr. Jack McSweeney is in our New York office, and won't be returning to this office for another week."

"Mr. Jack McSweeney, please." If he was in the U.S., maybe that was a lead. I asked for a number where he could be reached, and my heart was pounding so loud I suspected she could hear it on her end.

"Oh, that I can give you," she replied easily. "Two-one-two is the um, area code, and then the exchange is 555-7845."

"Thanks. You've been very helpful." I disconnected.

I called the New York number and the receptionist told me that Mr. Jack McSweeney was spending the holidays in Chicago, visiting with a client. Bells went off in my head — so loud I involuntarily covered the mouthpiece.

Thanking her, I hung up, kissed Cavvy, grabbed my briefcase and headed to HI-Data. I was planning my next move — a move in which Auntie would play a big part.

TWENTY-FIVE

The morning sky was a dirty white. It looked and felt like it might snow anytime. My breath condensed around me while I checked the car before getting in. All was well on the trip to HI-Data, and Jim Croce was almost finished singing "Workin' at the Carwash Blues" when I pulled into the parking lot. I was — for once — on time, anxious to meet Marcie.

The overweight guard was on duty again today. His nametag read "Oscar," and he wasn't very happy to see me. He gruffly consulted his palm-held computer when I informed him Marcie Ann Kent was expecting me.

"You're not on the list." He scowled. "And Marcie can't approve you because she's only a trainee. She doesn't have clearance yet."

He made me wait in the lobby while he called Personnel and told Sparky to come and escort me.

While we stood waiting, I said I was sorry about Ken Gordon and asked if he knew what had happened.

"Mr. Ken was one of the partners, and rumor is, you was involved. You got me in a lot of trouble. You're no secretary like I thought," he said accusingly. "Miss Sparky's got to sign for you and get your card. You go nowhere in HI-Data without an escort. That clear?" He turned away, not expecting an answer.

HI-Data's atrium had balconies on every floor overlooking the lobby. It reminded me of a Miami Beach hotel Frank and I had stayed in some years ago. That hotel's lobby, unlike HI-Data's, had been filled with masses of flowers and plants, a waterfall, and colorful ponds with Koi and ducks. I thought again of how happy we'd been. I spotted Sparky on one of the upper floors. I waved, but couldn't get her attention.

As a uniformed maintenance man watered the Christmas poinsettias, Oscar withdrew a Smart Card from his handheld computer. "We'll monitor you today," he said gruffly.

I reached for the card. He pulled it out of my grasp.

"No. This goes to Sparky. You have to check in with her before . . ."

A piercing scream startled us. Something

landed at Oscar's feet with a sickening thump, almost knocking us both over. A faint vibration shook the Italian marble floor, and I looked down. Marcie Ann Kent lay sprawled on her back in an unnatural position like a grotesque mannequin. Her hair was strewn round her head, and one hand still clutched her purse. Her blank eyes stared up at me, and her lipsticked mouth gaped wide open as if silently screaming.

My eyes stuttered over the rest of her body. There was blood running from her head and a few drops on her disheveled, butter-colored suit. I was sure she was dead.

Sights and sounds flickered fast-forward, like an MTV video. As I bent over Marcie's body, I heard screams and glanced up into the high atrium. On every floor, employees hung over the balconies, looking down on the scene like Romans in the Coliseum. Noise and confusion erupted all around, but the loud beat of my own heart was all I could hear.

I wanted to help, but Marcie was beyond that. She looked like the girl in my high school state gymnastics competition who'd taken a hard fall off the high rings and missed the mat. "Dead on impact," our instructor, Mrs. Soderberg, crouched over the girl, had declared. Nothing had helped then, and I couldn't think of anything that would help now.

I concentrated on the scattered X's of Marcie's gold Paloma Picasso bracelet, glittering on the floor. Maybe if I didn't look at her face again, I'd be all right. Then I noticed her Bruno Magli pumps, and I choked involuntarily. Marcie had been vulnerable, just like Frank, just like the rest of us, and she was as dead as could be.

"Ohmygod," Sparky gasped, suddenly at my side looking down at Marcie's body. "Is she . . . ?"

Oscar asked Sparky to phone for an ambulance while he kept the growing crowd under control.

"I can't," she said, clasping her hands over her mouth. "I think I'm going to be sick." As Oscar guided her toward the exit, I noticed a manila envelope with my name on it under Marcie's right arm. *Marcie must have kept her word to furnish me copies of her taxes and lease.* I picked it up and tucked it in my purse.

Oscar came back and took my arm. "Here now, you look a little pale. You're not gonna be sick on me too, are ya?"

I honestly didn't know. This was the second body I'd encountered at HI-Data, and it wasn't getting any easier. Oscar peered at me intently.

"Go call 911 for an ambulance." He pointed to a phone on the wall. "I'll punch in the code for the cops. Thanks." He looked down at Marcie, then up at the crowd. "I'll keep everybody away from here."

Overcoming numbing inertia, I found the phone, made the call, and returned.

"Is there anything I can do?" I knelt beside Oscar, coming out of the trance.

A small stream of blood trickled from the corner of Marcie's mouth, and her matted hair was wet and entangled with congealing blood.

"No sign of any pulse," Oscar said. "She's totally unresponsive. The medics'll be here any minute. Can you show them where to come? I got to stay here."

As I headed to the exit, I realized that Oscar was handling himself well in the clutch and my assessment of him had improved.

Outside, Sparky, pale and shivering, was gulping drafts of the bitter air. Icy tears traced down her cheeks. "I thought I'd wait here and direct the ambulance people." She wiped her eyes.

"Sparky, are you all right? Should I get a doctor?"

"Ohmygod, I've never seen anything like

that. Do you think she's dead?"

"Oscar does. What floor was her office on?"

"Fifth. That's a long way to fall," Sparky said dully.

Fall, I thought. According to Insurance Institute Statistics, the chance of dying from any kind of fall was 1 in 20,666. While Marcie Ann may have been smart, she was also terribly unlucky.

"Nothing like this has ever happened before at HI-Data. First Ken. Now Marcie," Sparky said, sobbing.

We heard sirens. She shivered. I put my arm around her.

"You know I didn't like her, but this is awful."

I tried to say something comforting, all the while wondering if it was the fifth floor where I'd seen Sparky just before Marcie fell. I wondered, too, how Marcie had managed to fall off that balcony. Those balcony railings were at least waist high and very sturdy. Statistically speaking, girls like Marcie aren't the suicidal type. I didn't like what I was thinking about HI-Data.

An ambulance and two cop cars arrived at the side door. Sparky wiped her eyes and motioned the paramedics to follow her. I waited with the other bystanders in the lobby, steadfastly refusing to think of the similarities to Frank's death. Instead I concentrated on figuring out what the hell was going on here at Hi-Data.

TWENTY-SIX

It was nearly one o'clock when Marcie Ann Kent left HI-Data zipped up in a dark green plastic body bag. We were all questioned as witnesses, and it was after three o'clock before they let anyone leave.

As soon as I could, I went to Jeff Fere's office. His secretary, Jennifer Brand, fussed when I showed up without an appointment, but I insisted. When he agreed to see me, I quickly filled him in on the details about John Olson aka Dan Karton.

"Excellent detective work," he said. "But I am wondering why Norman didn't uncover this information."

I suggested HI-Data revise its policies and do complete background checks, including fingerprinting, before hiring new employees. I also asked why there had been a delay in doing the full bonding check.

"We don't usually put our trainees through this type of security clearance. But Ken fast-tracked these four new employees in an accelerated training program. We realized we would be able to integrate them into our new research and development program a lot sooner than expected. Since this new R&D work is proprietary and confidential, they all had to have top level security clearances. That's why Ken contacted Universal Insurance. Again, as to why he asked for you, I don't know. HI-Data hasn't had security worries for a long time. But from what you told me about Olson, also known as Karton, my belief is that he should be suspect number one on the police list."

After saying he would take my suggestions under consideration, we shook hands and I left. I felt certain he would give Norman a hard time over this mistake. I also suspected that Norman would take revenge on me for uncovering it.

Like Jeffrey, I too considered Olson/Karton a prime suspect — not just for the murders but also for slashing my brake line. He certainly had the opportunity. So I checked the Miata for slashed tires, a broken fuel hose, and a car bomb, but nothing was wrong. Even so, when I turned the ignition key, beads of sweat collected on my forehead despite the winter chill.

There'd been no chance to be alone again

with Sparky to ask her more about the affair between Marcie and Ken, and about that file she was going to show me. Maybe something in there would shed light on why they both were now dead and why someone had sabotaged my car. Meantime, I had to finish my assignment and move my office.

I parked the Miata and bought an egg salad on wheat at the greasy spoon across from Consolidated. They serve a dose of heartburn with everything, but I was desperate. The cashier took my money and dumped mustard and mayo packets in the bag. I managed to grab it just as a day-trader in suspenders talking on his cell phone shouldered me roughly out of the way. I don't like bullies, and under other circumstances, I'd have taken action. Today, I turned and headed back to my office.

There were no messages. I made coffee and ate the sandwich, surprisingly fresh and as tasty as egg salad can manage to be. Then I hit the phone lines to finish cross-checking the data I'd gotten on Tanaka and Rivers.

The first five calls were a breeze. The more I worked, the less I thought about death and HI-Data. On the sixth call, I hit a snag. I'd gotten connected to Miss Fresher, the head librarian at the University of Michigan where they catalog dissertations from every university in the United States. She said she was unable to scan Dissertation Abstracts Outline to confirm that Joe Tanaka's Ph.D. thesis had indeed been published under the title he listed on his form. I could have connected through my local library DIALOG database on my computer like my electronics whiz friend Jerry had shown me, but that would only have given a title, and I wanted Miss Fresher to read the whole outline.

"I'm sorry, Ms. McDull, but —"

"McGil," I said.

"Well, we're on partial staff over the holidays and don't have time to do a personal search. You'll have to go through interlibrary loan or come in here personally after January tenth when we open again to the public."

"I can't wait that long. A job candidate will be out on his duff if I can't confirm this information before the first of the year. Where's your holiday spirit? Would you want it on your conscience if he lost the job?"

After a long silence, Miss Fresher sighed and agreed to get the outline. She took my number and promised to get back in a few days. I thanked her and told her to read the abstract into my answering machine if I wasn't here.

My investigation was in a way a matter of life and death for Joe Tanaka, as it had been for Marcie, and I could feel my heart double skip. I tried to relax and empty my mind. In the opposite corner, a small spider was making its careful way down a slender thread shimmering faintly in the winter sunlight. I sat back, fascinated at its jerky, steady progress. I didn't have the heart to kill it. There'd been enough death around me lately. As it made its way downward, I mentally wrestled with the eternal verities, not sure anymore of anything in this world except maybe the spider and the fly.

There was a loud knock on my door, but I wasn't in the mood to see anybody. I hunkered down near the space heater and pretended not to be in.

The knocking persisted.

"Ms. McGil? We know you're in there. Open up. Police."

TWENTY-SEVEN

Surprised, I unlocked and opened the door.

"DD McGil?"

"That's me," I said as the two detectives flashed their shields in my face.

"We need to talk to you," said the thin one in the gray overcoat. He tucked away his badge before I could focus on it and muscled in past me.

"It's important," the other one said as he pushed past me.

"Sure is a small place you got here," gray overcoat said. "Cold, too."

"What's the DD stand for?" the other detective asked.

I wasn't eager to exchange social niceties with cops, let alone tell them about Daphne December, but I forced myself.

"He's Detective Watlin," Gray overcoat pointed.

"And he's Detective Lester," Detective Watlin pointed at gray overcoat like they were some kind of professional police comedy duo. They shuffled their feet and blew on their ungloved hands.

The one called Watlin cracked a thin smile and nodded in the direction of my coffee pot. "Help yourselves."

They poured their coffees, taking plenty of my cream, all the while casing my place.

"Sugar?" Detective Watlin asked.

"I don't take sugar," I said.

"So what's a girl like you doing in a dirty business like insurance investigation?" Detective Lester asked abstractedly as he rifled through my two shelves of reference books. I winced instinctively as he grabbed one by the spine.

"Where'd you say you're from?" I asked.

"Naperville Police," Watlin said as Lester continued perusing my books.

"What do you want to see me about?"

"We understand you're the one who found Ken Gordon's body at HI-Data," Watlin said.

"And?"

"We need to ask you a few more questions, okay? Think there's enough room for all of us to sit down and get cozy?"

Lester was all cop. He didn't converse except in the interrogatory. In general, suburban cops aren't as hard-nosed as

Chicago cops, but they're more hot-doggy trying to exert control over their turf. He pulled out a chair and motioned me to sit. Ignoring his offer, I went around my desk and sat in my own chair.

"What more do you need from me? I told the other detectives everything I know."

"We've inherited the case. Did we forget to tell you we're from Homicide?" Lester flashed a lopsided grin. His front teeth were slightly crooked.

"The coroner's report says he was zapped by his computer — electrocuted by his keyboard. Jesus, this coffee tastes like mud." Lester wiped his lips.

"I like it strong." I smiled sweetly.

"We know you moved the body, Ms. McGil," Watlin said.

"What?"

"What we need to know is exactly what you saw when you first found the body," Watlin said. "Every detail."

"Yeah, you're the closest thing we got to an eye witness," Lester added.

"I already told all this to your compatriots and . . ."

"Tell us again," Watlin said.

"Yeah, humor us," Lester added.

"He had his back to me when I entered the room," I said.

214

"Was the door locked?" Detective Watlin asked.

"Yes, but my security card opened it. I heard the lock clunk. I called out to him, but he didn't answer. Then I touched his arm and he fell off the chair onto the floor."

"You notice the keyboard at all?" Watlin probed.

I didn't want to tell these guys anything more than I had that night at the station, but I couldn't evade Watlin's questions without telling a lie.

"Well, yes. It fell down with him, so I picked it up and put it back on the desk."

"That explains your fingerprints on the keyboard," Watlin said.

"Huh?"

"Your prints were on the keyboard," Lester said. His unblinking eyes did not leave me for a second. "We were beginning to think nasty thoughts about you, like maybe murder, maybe withholding evidence, maybe who knows what?"

"I thought all that was straightened out."

"Hey, look at it from our point of view, Miss DD," Detective Watlin said. "You never told us that Ken Gordon asked for you to come to HI-Data on the trainee investigations. Then we find out otherwise. You never told us you handled anything in the room. Then we find otherwise. What are we supposed to think?"

"Why didn't you tell us the truth right off?" Lester asked, circling behind my desk.

"Look, I still don't know why Ken asked for me. I told you the truth about that. And I should have told you about the keyboard, but Norman got me so upset I must have forgotten." I realized I sounded like Marcie trying to explain her new car.

"I was only there for a few minutes. I couldn't have . . ."

"Yeah. We know that," Watlin said.

It took several seconds to digest what he'd said. It was practically the only declarative sentence he'd spoken since he'd walked in.

"You know I didn't kill Ken?"

"Yeah. We know whoever did it had to have time to rig it up," Lester explained. "And they had to know how to rig it up. You wouldn't have had time, would she Watlin?"

I sighed with relief.

"But we need to know if you saw or heard anybody or anything on the third floor when you were wandering around up there. Anything more you haven't told us?" Watlin asked.

"No. Nothing. It was totally quiet. That's all I know. What I'd like to know is why you guys aren't investigating who cut the brake line on my car."

"When did this happen?" Watlin asked, peering at me while Lester rifled through some papers.

"Last week. When I left HI-Data."

"Well, I can't find a report on any incident like that. Where'd you report it?" Lester asked.

"I didn't."

They looked at each other then at me. I could tell they didn't believe me.

"So this building's coming down around your ankles and you haven't moved yet?"

I recognized the classic police tactic of abruptly changing the subject.

"What's the problem?" Lester asked. "Can't find anything this small somewhere else?"

I was in enough trouble as it was, so it wouldn't do for me to be lippy. Still I couldn't resist dropping a bomb of my own.

"I've been busy with other things. I just left HI-Data a couple hours ago. Did you know there's been another death out there?"

"What?" they asked in unison.

I'd scored a coup.

"One of the trainees fell from the fifth floor atrium balcony. Do you think this might be connected to Ken's death?" I asked, unable to resist turning the screw a little.

Lester cocked his head at Watlin and stood up.

"And did they tell you at HI-Data about the trainee named John Olson, who is really named Dan Karton, and probably an industrial spy?"

Lester wrote something in his little spiral notebook, then looked at Watlin. The two of them headed for the door.

"This is all for right now, Mzz. DD McGil," Watlin said.

"But we'll be back," Lester added. "And don't try to leave town."

"You guys really say that?"

Lester held the door for Watlin and followed him out. "I wouldn't be such a smart ass if I was you. This is serious, and you better straighten up."

I'd been hearing the same song since third grade and my Permanent Record was a mess. I waited until they turned the corner at the far end of the hallway before I closed the door.

TWENTY-EIGHT

All day I thought of Marcie lying on a slab at the morgue. I knew I should keep looking for new office space, but couldn't face dealing with it. I knew I should go see Auntie Dragon, but couldn't face that either. I locked up and headed home.

Cavvy meowed excitedly and led me straight to the bedroom. There was Scotty Stuart, back from England, naked and asleep in my bed. I blinked my eyes, but he was still there after the third time. I grinned and my heart skipped a few beats as I watched him sleep. You can learn a lot about people from the way they sleep. Ready for battle, I thought.

I jumped into bed alongside him and lightly kissed his nose.

He rubbed his eyes. "Hi there, good looking. Welcome home. I've been napping off jet-lag. Come here."

We kissed for a very long time. *Cosmopoli-*

tan magazine says men think about sex more than women do, but I think about it an awful lot, and I wonder just who they interviewed.

"Hi yourself," I said finally. "You gave me one hell of a shock, showing up unannounced like this. What if I already had a date tonight?"

"I'm real glad to see you, too," he said, his hands finding their way under my clothes. When his cool fingers slipped inside my panties, heat spread from the soles of my feet to the roots of my hair. While we made love, I forgot about Ken, Marcie, Robbie Burns, and everything else.

"God, you feel wonderful," he whispered in my left ear. "Still love me?"

"I lust you. As to whether I even like you, I'm not sure."

"Well, I love you and I lust you. It's a miracle I'm here at all. I pushed like hell to finish the first phase of the job two days early. Then I rushed to catch my flight. I was going to call your office soon as I touched ground and leave a message, but I thought you might already be home."

"I'm glad you're here," I said.

"Anyway, if you had other plans, you'd cancel them, right? You wouldn't give up these two fifty-yard line tickets I got from

Jerry, would you?" He flashed two tickets for tonight's Bears game with the Green Bay Packers.

"Wow. A chance to beat the Cheeseheads. I'm tired, but not that tired." I jumped out of bed. "Let's go."

TWENTY-NINE

After we showered, I put on two sweaters, a pair of jeans, warm socks and a down jacket. I also grabbed a roll of toilet paper. Axiom: there's never any TP in women's johns at sporting events. I jammed it into my purse on top of the envelope from Marcie. Now that she was dead, there was no urgency to go over her lease and her tax returns, but I'd follow up on them later, just to satisfy my curiosity.

We waved good-bye to Cavvy and drove to Soldier Field. The red caps flagged us toward outlying parking lots, all rapidly filling up. Scotty tipped the attendant an extra two bucks to park nearest the street so we could exit quickly after the game.

As we got out of the car, Scotty asked about the spare tire on the right front. "Where's the new Michelin?"

"I'll fill you in later." I pulled him into the crowd. "Let's not miss kick-off."

The field was lit up like Las Vegas, glowing against the backdrop of the black Midwestern night sky. A frigid wind blew off Lake Michigan. Even with our stadium blanket, it was damp and cold. Nonetheless, any Bears fan would have killed for these seats.

At halftime the score was 17 to 10, Bears. The partisan crowd was cocky, even with a wind chill factor of minus-13. While the Jessie White Tumblers performed impossible feats, Scotty told me the job he was working on in London was top-secret, and I told him about being stuck with Auntie and Robert Burns, and about the two deaths at HI-Data.

"I met some people from HI-Data at a seminar last year."

"What do you know about HI-Data?" I asked, pulling the stadium blanket tighter around us.

"Word is the CEO Jeff Fere is real innovative, but he holds the reins pretty tight and refuses to be dictated to by a board of directors. HI-Data's fighting for its life right now. The big guy in Europe, Steinmetz A.G., is trying to take them over."

"I heard something about a hostile takeover."

"It's not really a hostile takeover," Scotty

said as we stood to allow fellow fans in and out of our aisle. "HI-Data isn't a public issue, it's privately held. The company's owned by a few major investors. Jeff Fere's probably the largest shareholder."

"How is Steinmetz A.G. going to take over HI-Data if there's no public stock?"

"Over the past few years HI-Data has experienced tremendous growth."

"Yeah, Tom Joyce was telling me the same thing."

"Oh, yeah. I'll have to meet him one of these days. So he knew something about HI-Data?"

"I asked him to do a quick check on the company before I started. He was only able to give me the bare facts."

"Speaking of bare . . ."

"Cut that out. If I take that off now, I'll freeze to death."

"You're probably right. We'll wait till later. Okay, back to HI-Data. Well, he probably told you that the company financed its expansion through venture capital and lots of debt, right?"

"Yeah, he did say that."

"Well by now, all that paper has been sold several times and all his debt is probably callable on demand."

"What does that mean in terms of a take-over?"

Scotty leaned over and kissed me, his lips surprisingly warm. A surge of desire made me momentarily forget the numbing cold.

"Speaking of takeovers," he whispered, "wait till I get you in bed."

"Damn," I yelled at a guy in a dark blue furry parka who stepped on my toes.

"Sorry, lady." He burped and continued down the aisle.

"You all right?" Scotty asked, yawning again. "Sorry. Can't help myself. Not you. Jet lag."

"Tell me more about the hostile takeover."

"Technically like I said, it's not a hostile takeover. Steinmetz A.G. made an offer to purchase HI-Data, but the deal was nixed. Rumor had it that HI-Data was about to put the finishing touches on some ground-breaking software which would bring in major bucks."

"That must be the 'something big' that Tom Joyce mentioned was on the horizon."

"It's still under wraps, but everybody knew something was up when the share-holders turned down the obscenely good offer from Steinmetz. The buzz over the rejected offer sent HI-Data's profile way up. Word was that they were about to go public and offer shares so they could pay off all the debt and maintain control of the company."

"Hmm. I heard a little about that software breakthrough. I saw a portion of a sales promotion Ken Gordon made, you know, the guy who was killed."

I felt his body stiffen. He said, "Tell me what you heard."

I smiled. "Wouldn't that be considered industrial espionage?" Now at last I knew something he didn't.

"DD, you can trust me to keep it confidential."

"I don't know any details that would break client confidentiality, so don't get your hopes up. All I heard on the sales promo was what the rumors are all saying — that they've developed a revolutionary program that allows them to take apart the software of any other program."

"If they have successfully done it," Scotty said. "HI-Data will not only survive, it'll flourish."

We stood up while several fans returned to their seats in our row and the two teams came back on the field.

"I don't get it. If HI-Data refused the offer from Steinmetz A.G. — hey, what's the A.G. stand for — then why is it fighting for its life?"

"A.G. is like our Inc. or Co. It's the German abbreviation for an incorporated conglomerate. And HI-Data is in financial trouble right now because Steinmetz bought up a lot of their debt from various banks. Now Steinmetz is calling in the debt, and HI-Data needs a massive infusion of cash to meet the balloon payments. You know credit is so tight right now — nobody's giving loans, so they're stuck. Maybe this new software will be the ticket to get them back into the black."

Play action jolted us back to the game. The Pack came on strong and moved the ball at will, scoring twice, turning the score upside down, 24 to 17 in favor of Green Bay. By the end of the fourth quarter, the Bears defense had been on the field most of the game and looked tired. Under our blanket, I felt as cold and damp as an unheated medieval cathedral. Then the Bears defense intercepted a Green Bay pass and ran it in to score. The crowd went ballistic.

The extra point was good, tying the score, and the two-minute warning sounded. Green Bay had the ball. If we could keep them from scoring, the game would go into overtime.

The crowd roared as Green Bay fumbled and the Bears defense recovered at the Packers 45-yard line with under thirty seconds to play. Scotty and I jumped to our feet with the crowd. The next three plays went for short yardage gains but no first down. The Bears had to kick for a field goal or go into overtime. The kick would have to be over fifty yards with the wind right off the Lake.

I held my breath. The kicker thunked it, and it sailed dead center over the goal post into the history books just as time ran out. The crowd was on its collective feet, and no one in the packed stadium was thinking about the cold anymore.

On the way home, Scotty didn't mention the tire again, but he did ask about Ken.

"On top of his being one of the partners at HI-Data, he was Frank's half-brother," I explained. "That's why the cops think I might be involved."

We dropped the subject, but both of us were subdued the rest of the drive.

When we got back to my apartment, I uncorked the bottle of Veuve Clicquot Champagne I'd stored in the refrigerator for New Year's Eve. That lightened our mood, and I can personally attest that making love with Scotty that night gave lie to the saying that there's no thrill like beating the Cheeseheads at home.

THIRTY

It was another cold and dreary winter morning. I, however, didn't feel at all cold or dreary because I woke up next to Scotty. After we finally left our warm bed and showered, I put on the water for tea and walked around with a silly grin. I was daydreaming and didn't even try the crossword.

Auntie's homemade scones tasted good with the English Breakfast tea. Cavalier emitted a scolding meow to remind me to serve his fish stew. I realized I was going to have to shape up and come down from the clouds if I was going to get through the day.

Scotty left for a meeting, and I tried to put last night's lovemaking out of my mind. I'd promised to move out of Consolidated yesterday, but I hadn't had any calls on those available spots I'd found advertised. I knew I was in trouble. I drove to Consolidated, hoping there'd still be electric and phone, and hoping also to avoid Michael Drake. I'd pack up my stuff. Maybe that would keep Michael Drake happy.

At the Oak Street curve on Lake Shore Drive, the sun emerged from some flat morning clouds. I love this particular spot. You can see the beautiful Drake Hotel, Oak Street Beach, and Michigan Avenue all at the same time. It's the very best of Chicago, and I never tire of the view.

South on Michigan Avenue, sidewalks bustled with people around the John Hancock Center. Approaching Wacker, I passed the stately white Wrigley Building and the gray Tribune Tower, both throwbacks to an older — but never gentler — cityscape. I turned down Madison Street toward Dearborn and caught sight of the Sullivan Center, my favorite Loop landmark. For years it had housed the Carson Pirie Scott flagship operation. Now Carson's was gone, and it was filled with smaller retail stores and offices.

The same winter sun that made the rest of the Loop look so beautiful now highlighted every depression made by the demolitions team on Consolidated's exterior. The building was sadly on its last legs. I hated to see it go. Lines from an Ezra Pound poem raced through my mind:

231

Struck of the blade that no man parrieth,
Pierced of the point that toucheth lastly all.

Inside, the fog of plaster dust was so thick I didn't see George Vogel, my landlord, until he jumped into the elevator as the door was closing. I'd forgotten he'd be back this week from his holiday in Puerto Rico.

He coughed. "So it's true. You are still here. I ran over as soon as I heard you hadn't moved."

Everyone from the bank except me had relocated to temporary quarters in the Beech Building, a few blocks away. They'd be moving back into the brand-new Consolidated building after it rose, Phoenix-like, on the same ground. For successfully supervising this difficult move to temporary quarters without a hitch, the bank had rewarded George with the trip to Puerto Rico. All that was left for him to do was to straighten out any remaining problems. That meant me. At the very least I was in for a George Vogel lecture.

"You promised you'd be out of here the day after I left two weeks ago. Don't you realize the risk involved for the bank and for Drake Demolition, not to mention yourself?

"Jesus, it's cold," he complained as we got

off on my floor.

I kept quiet. I wasn't about to remind him the heating system had already been shut down.

"Haven't you found other space yet?"

I said nothing. I was grateful he'd kept my rent down these past three years, but he was annoying in so many other ways. I had hoped to find office space somewhere else and sever our relationship instead of moving into the temporary quarters.

"So I take it you haven't. Well, I've got a deal for you. I've been holding on to the last temporary office for you at the Beech Building. I'll even give it to you for the same rent as you had here. But I need to know right now if you'll take it." His sweet offer was soured by the fact that he was talking to my chest.

"Well?" He eventually looked up when I didn't reply. "Have you made up your mind?"

I smiled, relishing one of our infrequent eye-to-eyes. "George, I want to thank you for all the trouble you've gone to, but . . ."

"You can't stay here any longer," he insisted. "I'll be forced to evict you. This demolition is happening fast. Even though we're paying a bonus to the company to get it down by the first of the year, nobody expected it to really happen."

"I . . ."

"C'mon. Say yes. And you can count on me to give you a hand." He picked up a few papers from my desk. "I'll even help you pack and straighten out your stuff."

I almost screamed. Mr. Neat Freak wouldn't allow a paper clip to be out of place on his desk. The thought of him near my stuff made me shiver.

"George, I appreciate everything you've done for me. But I've already found another place. I'll be gone later today." I shooed him out the door and waved good-bye to him and his pleas to reconsider.

I surveyed my office. It wouldn't take me long to pack. But I still had some serious digging to do on the two trainees. I had to satisfy myself that their lifestyles matched their incomes; that they weren't involved with unsavories; and that they didn't have any nasty habits that could lead to their being easily blackmailed or corrupted. I had to finish what HI-Data was paying me for.

Before I dug in, I played the messages.

"Miss McGil, this is Jennifer Brand, Mr. Fere's secretary. Mr. Fere would like you to give him a progress report on the trainees at two o'clock this afternoon in his office here at HI-Data. Please call to confirm."

I was anxious to see Mr. Fere, and hoped he could shed some light on Marcie and Ken and their too coincidental deaths.

Before I could call Jennifer back, the phone rang. It was Miss Fresher calling with the Ph.D. dissertation outline on Joe Tanaka's thesis, "A New Approach to Digitally Processing Composite Signals." The outline, which I translated from science-itis into plain English, covered converting real-world sound, video, and graphics signals into binary digits — ones and zeros — then recording the binary digits into a computer. Once recorded, these signals could then be manipulated in the computer or replayed to get exactly what had been recorded. Tanaka's work involved developing algorithms or series of algorithms to break down the composite signal into its basic elements. For example, on a recording of a live performance of a symphony, if someone coughed during the performance, the composite signal would contain that cough. Tanaka's algorithm would be able to distinguish the non-music sounds such as the cough and eliminate them from the recording, allowing only the essential musical elements to remain.

Even I could see the profound impact of this technology. Tanaka was one smart boy, and it was obvious why HI-Data had hired him.

I thanked Miss Fresher and hung up to forestall her calling me Miss McDull one more time. Then I phoned Jennifer Brand to confirm the two o'clock at HI-Data. She mentioned that Mr. Fere liked punctuality.

I'd almost finished my notes on the trainees when the phone rang again. It was Greg McIntyre, the lead investigator on the Mooney Investment embezzlement case.

"I guess somebody else besides you thinks Eric Daniels might have something to do with the missing funds," he told me.

"Really? Who?"

"A Mr. Anonymous. He sent Mooney a tip in today's mail. Said we might be interested in some off-shore accounts in connection with Daniels. We got account numbers, deposit dates, the works."

"Sounds like somebody has it in for our Mr. Daniels," I said. "Gonna check it out?"

"Already in motion. Just wanted to keep you in the loop. It would be funny if that female intuition thingy of yours was right after all."

"Yeah, funny." I thanked him for the call and hung up, silently wishing Mr. Eric Daniels a very unhappy New Year.

I continued collecting and rechecking data

on the two trainees. Everything was coming out clean, but I was getting a headache. I'd had a horrendous week, starting with my stumbling over one corpse and ending with another dropping at my feet. On the other hand, Eric Daniels was in store for a heap of trouble, which made me feel really good. And Scotty was here in Chicago, which made me feel even better. Despite the headache, the plaster dust, and my need to pack, I realized I was hungry and decided to grab lunch at a Portillo's that was conveniently located on my route to HI-Data.

I locked the office and hurried out, successfully avoiding Michael Drake.

Thirty-One

Driving west out of Chicago into what used to be the great prairies, the city's gray factories and apartment buildings give way to bare trees and cookie-cutter shopping malls with vast parking lots. There are no colors left in Chicago during the winter — all the colors die or move south. I was beginning to think more and more about moving south, too.

The oldies radio station was playing "Little Darling" by The Diamonds, and a cardinal streaked past my windshield, heading for some nearby trees. Cardinals, the twins had said, mate for life and don't migrate south over the winter. I wondered why. Or why not.

I pulled into Portillo's, one of my favorite eateries, and ordered a combo Italian beef and sausage. Portillo's started with a make-shift hot dog stand and now has twenty-five restaurants across Chicagoland. The combo, a heart-buster, would fortify me against the cold as well as against HI-Data.

I took my place in a long line of cars at the drive-up windows where two workers dressed in parkas with telephone headsets conveyed orders as fast as they could to keep the line moving. Lunch was tasty and so were my daydreams about Scotty. I'd completely lost track of time and was now officially running late for my meeting with Jeff Fere. The throaty roar of the Miata's race-bred engine eased me back into traffic on the Tollway. I stepped on it, keeping an eye out for cops.

I was making great time, but had to brake suddenly to avoid a pinkish heap of gray fur that once had been an opossum. The oldies station switched to news, and I turned up the volume just in time to hear their traffic copter report an explosion.

"The DuPage County Sheriff's Office has just confirmed that a car exploded moments ago in the parking lot of the HI-Data Corporation off the Reagan Tollway. Sources are telling us that a body was found in the vehicle, a white Lincoln Town Car apparently belonging to the company's President, Jeffrey Fere. We'll keep you updated as further details come in. Back to you, Jim and Jan."

I veered onto the shoulder and turned off the engine. I took a deep breath and fogged up my windows immediately. Whatever was going on at HI-Data had apparently just claimed its CEO Jeff Fere as the latest victim. Nothing I could do there was going to help the situation. In fact, my being on the scene of a third death would not look good on my police blotter. I put the car in gear and put down my window to get rid of the fog, intending to turn around and head for home. I put the window back up, then stopped short. My client was now dead and, like it or not, whoever was responsible for these deaths had involved me. That made me mad. My prime suspect was still Olson/Karton. I wasn't going to feel better until I found out what was going on. I ditched the idea of turning around and instead checked the rearview mirror and merged back into traffic toward HI-Data.

Thirty-Two

Yellow tape cordoned off a large section of HI-Data's parking lot. Smoke from the explosion was still spiraling into the wintry air as I steered into an open spot on the far side of the lot. Cops were all over, and one of them agreed to check my status on the guest list. My name was there, but he told me I would need an escort. He pawned me off onto another uniformed cop who then called a HI-Data guard over. He immediately called Sparky to come get me.

She arrived, out of breath, somber and disheveled. "Everything's in turmoil," she said.

"I heard about what happened on the radio. I'm very sorry."

"Let's go to my office. It's private there."

We walked in silence and sat down across from one another. She shook her head. "I'm still in shock from Marcie's suicide, and now this."

I, for one, did not believe Marcie had committed suicide, but I decided not to say so. Instead, I asked, "What exactly happened?"

She frowned. "Nobody's sure. The cops are interviewing everyone. Jeff was waiting for you to show up for your appointment . . ."

"I was running late. I'm sorry."

"Don't be sorry. Your being late saved his life."

"What?"

"He had an appointment with his allergist at 2:30 this afternoon. If you'd been here on time, he'd have gone down to his car in sufficient time to warm it up. See, Jeff can't stand the cold. So when you were late, that made him run late, too. Oscar was warming up the Lincoln for him. Oscar's the one who's dead."

"So it was Oscar in the car when it exploded?"

"Unfortunately, yes."

"Oh, my God." *A dead partner, a dead trainee, and now a dead security guard.* Death times three equals . . . what?

"One of the officers told me they don't think there's enough left of him to make a formal identification. They'll have to do a DNA analysis. It's awful. Oscar's been with

HI-Data for seven years."

"Who ordered Oscar to warm up the car?"

"I don't know. Probably Jennifer Brand, Jeffrey's secretary. Jeffrey would never make that kind of call himself. Is that important?"

"Just curious," I said.

"Jeffrey's on his way to personally notify Oscar's family. He feels terrible about this, as you can imagine. He won't hold any meetings today."

"Of course," I agreed.

"Have you encountered any more problems with the other two trainees?" she asked.

"So far, things are looking good on both of them. Before I go, Sparky, I'd like to see that file about Marcie you were going to show me."

"Well that poses a problem." She stood up and walked to the window, looking out. "The file's not here anymore."

I must have been holding my breath, because I heard a big sigh and realized it came from me.

She turned from the window and went back to her desk. "Norman came in yesterday and cleaned out all the files on both Marcie and John Olson."

I'd counted on seeing that file. But if my suspicions were right, it probably didn't even exist anymore.

I mentioned the information I'd reported to Jeffrey Fere on John Olson, aka Dan Karton, and asked if they'd located him yet.

"No, he wasn't at the address listed on the master computer files — no big surprise considering what you've uncovered. But Norman's still looking."

"Do you think he was a spy, Sparky?"

"Norman certainly does. We're checking out some leads to see if he has ties to any of our competitors."

She sat down. "Norman, as head of security, doesn't look so great, and he's got to blame someone. You're the chosen candidate."

"So he's blaming me for everything."

"Norman said he told Jeffrey that it had to be more than an unlucky coincidence for you to have been there when Marcie died, too."

I wasn't worried about Jeffrey Fere. I knew he didn't suspect me. He suspected somebody inside the company. But what did Sparky think?

"I was hoping you could tell me some secrets, Sparky."

"Believe me, I would if I could. This used to be such a wonderful company. Jeffrey does so much for all his employees. He really cares. He wants everybody to succeed and make money. Do you know he takes the time to give the entire workforce lectures on investing? He gives advice on what stocks and bonds look good. If I had any money to invest, I'd probably be rich by now."

Jeffrey Fere, CEO, appeared to be a statistical outrider.

"Most corporate executives are out only for themselves," I said. "Think about Enron and Madoff and all those others."

"It wasn't like that here at HI-Data. But everything's been different since the day those trainees came aboard."

"Then I arrived and stumbled on Ken's body."

"And Marcie jumped off the balcony. Now Jeff's car has exploded. Maybe you can make some sense out of it all, because I can't," she said.

I stood up to leave. "Sparky, I seem to have walked into a viper's nest here. I think somebody from HI-Data deliberately snipped my brake line last week. Somebody wants me out of here, and given what's happened, I don't think Marcie committed suicide."

"What? My God. Wait a minute, Miss McGil. You think maybe John Olson — I mean Dan Karton might have . . . ? Maybe he and Marcie were . . . ? That file on

Marcie may not be here anymore, but I can tell you what was in it."

I sat back down. "So?" I prompted.

"We have that special phone security system that keeps track of all incoming and outgoing calls. It tells us, minute by minute, what extension is placing calls and what number they go to. And, vice versa for calls coming in. Want some coffee?"

"Thanks, no. I know about those systems. Please go on," I said.

"Well, I routinely review these detailed phone reports for Jeffrey. He insists it's good business to have two cross checks on all company data, so Norman and I both monitor these reports. I noticed that during the last several weeks, there were a bunch of calls made from Marcie's extension to an off-shore bank, and a similar number of wire transfers from the off-shore bank to local banks where Marcie had accounts. Our first-line credit check found something like ten accounts in her name. And I don't think our Marcie was by nature a saver."

I thought of Marcie's hundred thousand dollar Porsche, her expensive jewelry, and her beautifully furnished Lake Shore Drive apartment. "You're right about that," I said. "But Marcie was one very smart lady. Why would she risk making calls like this at work?"

"Maybe she didn't think there was any risk. We don't make this phone system general knowledge at HI-Data, and only me, Jeff, and Norman review the reports the system generates."

"I thought you said nobody called him 'Jeff' except the partners."

"Well, I'm careful not to do it in front of the rank and file. Longevity's got to have some perks, doesn't it? I've been with the company almost from the beginning when it was just Jeff, Ken, and Ralph. Jeff brought Norman in much later."

"About the phone system," I said, bringing us back to the point.

"Right. Well, as head of security, Norman recommended it. Jeffrey had to approve it, and then I had it installed."

"What does Norman make of these calls?"

"Norman's not what you'd call a detail person. We didn't go over the reports together, and he's never said anything to me. But he and Jeff might have discussed them. I don't . . ."

The door opened. It was the young guard I'd met yesterday. "I'm here to report, like you said. They've towed away the car, but they're still working in the lot."

When he saw me, his hand went to the gun on his hip. "You," he said.

"Miss McGil is just leaving." Sparky shrugged her shoulders and gave me a look that said we were finished. "Escort her to the elevator and sign her out."

THIRTY-THREE

All the way back to the city, I thought about what I had and what I hadn't learned from Sparky. I didn't trust anyone at HI-Data. I'd seen more than my share of dead bodies, and I didn't want to be the next one.

When I entered Consolidated, smoky chaos surrounded me. The landscape had altered considerably since this morning. Now severed masonry support columns jutted out like surreal stalactites and stalagmites. The outside walls had been hit by a wrecking ball. The rapidly fading daylight that seeped through the gaping holes was punctuated by flashes of electric blue from welders' torches. The scene was like a bombed city during wartime. Noise and workmen were everywhere. Air compressors pounded, jackhammers staccatoed, and equipment squealed and shrieked like women in distress.

It was difficult walking in my high heels.

Plaster dust and exhaust fumes from the machinery settled like a heavy fog, overlaid with the biting tang of metallic ozone from the welders.

I coughed, rubbed my eyes, and maneuvered around huge bundles of wire near the entrance to the tower.

Michael Drake suddenly appeared out of the smoke, wearing his blue hard hat stenciled with his name.

"I thought I saw you come in," he said as he thrust a similar hat, sans name, into my hands and ordered me to put it on.

"You've got to get out of here." He frowned. "I know you're under a lot of pressure, but now the explosives are here. It's not safe for you anymore." He pointed to a shed-like structure along the side of the wall peppered with red stickers reading "Danger: Hazardous Materials."

"Is it dynamite?"

"No. We use a precision-engineered specialized material — our trade secret. Today we're placing and wiring all the explosives. You can't be in the building after they're in position."

If something did go off prematurely, I'd be hamburger.

"I'm leaving later today," I assured him as another bobcat weaved around us, stirring up more plaster and white dust.

"Good. The sooner the better. Our timetable's taken a giant leap forward. We were going to do the blasting on the retaining wall between the tower and the main building in a few weeks at midnight when nobody's on the streets. But one of the big cable stations made us an offer we couldn't refuse. They want to televise the demolition on New Year's Eve, so we're going to do it then."

"But that's the day after tomorrow!"

"We've brought in extra crews. We're working twenty-four hours a day. Tomorrow we'll move the computer from the building into the trailer and run some final checks and set up the cameras."

"You mean they're going to televise this?"

"Turn on your TV — the promo ads are already running. 'Celebrate New Year's Eve With A Blast' and so on. They did it a couple of years ago to a huge hotel in Palm Beach and got ratings off the chart."

Talk about motivation. I was absolutely positively going to move out today. "Is there electric still in my office?" I asked without hope.

"We've got a make-shift electrical system going," Michael said. "That's why the light's so spotty. I told them to include your office,

251

but it's only temporary for today. At the end of today, it and your telephone are gone."

"Oh, thanks. I appreciate your trouble. I really will be gone by this evening."

"Be careful!" Michael yelled and stopped me from tripping over a pile that looked like bags of cement. He steered me away. "Watch where you put your feet. Those are the blasting agents — ammonium nitrate and diesel fuel oil mixtures."

Michael explained how they set all the explosives and how important the timing is so the building comes down in the right sequence. I felt like I was standing on ground zero.

"That custom-built computer out there controls everything. If some charges don't go off, or if they go off too early or too late, the entire building could fall the wrong way. We're right next door to the Federal Reserve Bank, and they don't want pieces of Consolidated showing up in their vault."

"So the computer sends out the signal to set off the charges? That I'd like to see." I walked away, hoping my motive of putting a comfortable distance between me and the shack with the explosives wasn't too obvious.

The control room, adjacent to the lobby, was filled with highly sophisticated computer network systems and security scanners. On the screen, a thousand tiny red dots flashed, each one representing an explosives charge.

"See this tells us exactly where to place the charges," he pointed. "As soon as a charge is wired, that light goes off. By this time tomorrow, none of the lights will be flashing, and we'll be ready to go."

Happy Oblivion, Consolidated, I silently wished the building.

THIRTY-FOUR

Michael Drake and I walked back to what wouldn't be my office after today. The bright red Eviction Notice taped to my door was visible at thirty paces.

"I didn't do it," Michael said. "I'd guess it was your friendly landlord, George Vogel."

I ripped it off and pushed open my door.

"Holy . . . ," Michael exclaimed.

My office was a mess. Even my closet had been trashed. At least I now knew what Aunt Elizabeth's vision was about.

"Damn, I can't believe this," I said, scooping up some papers from the floor.

Michael picked up and righted a chair. "Who could have done this?"

His words echoed my own thoughts. "Several possibilities do come to mind."

"Like . . . ?"

"Somebody from a case I'm working on at HI-Data." I thought of John Olson or Norman Richtor or Joe Tanaka or even Jeffrey Fere. It couldn't have been Sparky because I just left her. On the other hand, maybe it was George Vogel from the bank. Well, probably not. George would never make this kind of mess. Or could it have to do with Auntie's Burns artifacts and Mr. Jack McSweeney?

Michael snapped his fingers. "I did see a guy coming out of your office about half an hour ago. I'm sure he wasn't anybody working on this job."

"What'd he look like?"

"I only saw him from the side and back. He was, oh, I'd say about five foot nine or ten. Gray hair. On the reedy side. And he was wearing a tan overcoat. It looked expensive. Maybe cashmere."

"Let's see. The gray hair eliminates John Olson and Joe Tanaka." I said thoughtfully. "Unless the guy was wearing a wig?" I looked at Michael.

"I don't think so, but I couldn't be sure."

"Right. Well, the expensive overcoat definitely lets out George Vogel." We both laughed out loud.

"That means we're down to Jeff Fere and Norm Richtor from HI-Data. Jeffrey wears expensive clothes, but he's taller and has a bit of a paunch. Norman wears expensive clothes, and he's trim, and he's somewhere around five ten or so."

And, I promised myself, I'm going to find out A.S.A.P. what Auntie's Mr. Jack McSweeny looks like.

THIRTY-FIVE

After Michael left, I checked my computer and ran a scan. My computer wizard friend Jerry, who'd introduced me to Scotty, had insisted on showing me how to run a scan so that I could always ensure my hard disk wasn't damaged. Next I ran a virus check, again taught by Jerry. Then I read through a random mix of my HI-Data files, all of which seemed to be in order. Lucky thing, because I couldn't trouble shoot. I'd have had to call Jerry.

I straightened out what I could, sorting books and papers into boxes for the upcoming move. I'd gotten about halfway through the pile when the phone rang. I couldn't find it under the mess. Finally I spotted the cord, followed it, and unearthed the phone. Then I stopped cold. On top of the phone was the sealed brown envelope I always kept locked in my center drawer. The one envelope I've never been able to make myself look into.

I didn't want to look now, either. I answered the phone in mid-ring.

"Hi, DD. Vittoria here. I've got that information you wanted."

Vittoria was a friend from Grey Towers, a university reference librarian who'd helped me out when I was writing "Restoration Scandals." I'd phoned her earlier and talked her into doing some research for me.

"Great, Vicky. I really appreciate this."

"I didn't find out very much, but what I did find was extremely interesting. I'm e-mailing you all the citations, but in a nutshell, KB is known as Katherine Bruce of Clackmannan. The story, verified by several accounts, is that on October 4, 1787, Robert Burns and his traveling companion, Dr. James McKittrick Adair, left Stirling. This was after Burns smashed the window pane at the Golden Lion Inn. They then spent October fifth through twelfth at Harvieston, in Clackmannanshire. Dr. Adair recorded they got caught in severe storms and heavy floods that hit central Scotland. As a consequence, they stayed in the vicinity longer than anticipated. During this time they visited Katherine Bruce, sometimes spelled with a 'C,' at Clackmannan Tower."

So Katherine Bruce very well might be

the KB of the casque.

"By the way," Vittoria continued, "I did a little research on Clackmannan Tower. Seems it's fallen into decay, but it is still there today. It's part of the Bruce Clan holdings. Anyway, back to Burns. When he paid his visit to her in 1787, Katherine Bruce was over ninety. Dr. Adair writes that although she was hard of hearing and afflicted with paralytic speech, she possessed great dignity and was extremely hospitable to Burns. She and Burns shared Jacobite sympathies. She took a special liking to Burns, and Dr. Adair reported that her toast after dinner was, *Awa Uncos,* or 'Away the Strangers,' which referred undoubtedly to the Hanovers."

"I know that toast. It's one of my auntie's stand-bys."

"Your auntie?"

"Never mind. Go on."

"Well, Katherine Bruce was a direct descendant of Robert the Bruce. Even today, the family maintains an illuminated vellum genealogical history and family tree. That night, Katherine showed Burns and Adair a helmet and a two-handed sword, supposedly owned by Robert the Bruce. By the way, both of which are still owned by the Bruce family. She was quite well known as a Jacobite sympathizer. A portrait of her painted with a white rose, the sign of a good Jacobite follower, is still owned by the Bruce Clan.

"At some point during the evening Burns knelt before Katherine Bruce, and she knighted him with the sword of the Bruce. One source I checked noted that, although not well known, Burns himself was of ancient Scottish royal blood and also a descendant of Robert the Bruce through his paternal grandmother, Isabella Keith. Keith ancestry can be traced back to Lady Mary Bruce, sister of King Robert I, and it's recorded that Burns knelt to kiss the gravestone at Dunfermline Abbey."

I noted the interesting facts, thanked her, and hung up. Auntie would be thrilled to hear this. Maybe she would know someone in the Bruce family — she knows almost everybody — and we'd find out even more.

I found the brown envelope again in my hand. I put it down. I still didn't want to open it. My heart was aching. Instead, I phoned Tom Joyce.

He answered immediately, but before I could tell him about my office being trashed or about Katherine Bruce, he interrupted.

"Are you sitting down?" he asked.

"As a matter of fact, no. My office . . ."

"Listen, I've got great news for you and your aunt. That Burns material you left with me is looking good. Basically, most forgeries are not too difficult to spot. It's the genuine article that's difficult to prove. In this case, all the tests are turning out positive. I'm very excited."

"Really?"

Tom knew his job, and if he was telling me it might be genuine, I was more than surprised. I pulled over a chair and sat down.

"Really," he said. "I've done a more detailed handwriting comparison with 'The Twa Dogs,' one of the six original handwritten poems from the Kilmarnock Edition. You won't believe this, but I found it on the Burns Federation web site. Just a few years ago, before the Internet, we couldn't have done this. Technology is incredible. Anyway, other tests are confirming that the folds in the paper are original folds, and the ink test revealed the bits of brownish corrosion on the paper are due to the iron content in early ink."

"So handwriting, paper, and ink all check out as bona fide."

"Positively original. I also researched Book Auction Record and American Book Prices Current. There's no record of this poem or of the glass ever having being sold."

"Thanks for checking. That's important."

"Remember I told you about that Burns scholar in Scotland? I e-mailed him and he got back to me. He hadn't heard of anything either, and he is very excited to see if these are genuine."

"So . . . ?"

"So I'm still running the last few tests, but you must know what this means, DD."

"That these things might be genuine?"

"I think so. And I believe I can cautiously estimate a sale price of three to four million."

"Dollars or pounds?"

"Oh, good old USA dollars."

"Whoa. In a way, that's why I'm calling. I hope the Watch Wolf's doing his job, because my office just got ransacked."

"Oh, no. What happened? What'd they take? Are you okay?"

"I'm okay, but I don't know who did it, and I don't know yet what they took. I can't find anything missing. It probably has to do with one of my other cases, but somebody might be after the Burns stuff. I wanted to warn you just in case. Maximum security's in order."

"Even as we speak, all doors and windows are locked securely, the alarm is on, and

Wolfie's on the sofa."

"Good. And don't feed him too much, just in case somebody does break in. Oh, and I almost forgot to tell you, my librarian friend at Grey Towers researched Katherine Bruce for me. Burns visited her at Clackmannan Tower right after he'd broken the window. I think those initials 'KB' might be hers. I'll forward her e-mail. Oh, and one last thing, Tom."

"Yeah?"

"I'll be moving into your spare office later today if it's still okay with you."

"Let's do it."

"And I'll have my phone number call-forwarded."

"Sure. And I already made another key for you. I'll be here till about ten tonight. It's best you come while I'm here, or Wolfie might eat you. He's housebroken, but he distrusts strangers."

THIRTY-SIX

I hung up, wondering if I'd made another wrong decision. I had the feeling Tom wasn't completely joking, and I wasn't exactly looking forward to meeting the Watch Wolf.

Sighing, I picked up the dreaded brown envelope. I hoped the phone would ring again or someone would come to the door — something, anything to keep me from having to open it. I knew it held secrets, and I was afraid of the past, afraid of opening the wound that would never fully close.

I held it up, thinking and remembering. Inside were copies of the police reports on Frank's suicide, the autopsy report, and the few personal possessions he'd had on him that awful night. I had remained unwilling all this time to open it and confront the unthinkable.

But the thought of Frank's family ring had been nibbling at my subconscious. Maybe this was a sign, as Auntie would say.

I took a deep breath, opened it and reached in. The first thing I pulled out was Frank's Maurice Lacroix watch. Flares went off in my head. He'd loved that watch. The hands were stopped at 7:49. I held it a long time before I put it down and took out the file. It was labeled "Case Number 06-05-0113."

The top page was a police intake form which logged in three calls reporting a body falling from a balcony at Frank's address and recording subsequent dispatch times of patrol officers and emergency personnel to the scene.

Sitting cross-legged on the floor, I tried to keep my heart from racing as I read over the incident report signed by Detective Marvin Stamler.

"On May 13th at 19:52 hours, I was dispatched to the above address in response to reports concerning a jumper. On arrival, the lifeless body of a male Caucasian, 45–55, was on the ground, face down, with the top of the head pointing east. The body appeared to be fully dressed wearing a blue shirt, beige slacks, black socks, and one shoe on the left foot. A matching shoe, right foot, was five feet south of the body. Blood and brain matter had coagulated around the head."

Jerked back into the old nightmare, I could hear the crickets, smell the verbena in the night air, feel again the happiness in my heart as I unloaded packages from the car. Then suddenly the horror engulfed me again when I saw . . . what I saw.

I shook my head and forced myself to continue reading Detective Stamler's report. "I directed the Crime Scene Unit, under supervision of Investigator Edmond Casserly, to make a full investigation and to check whether the victim had any trace evidence under his fingernails or on his clothing. (See Report.) I asked to be immediately informed if there was any identification found on the body.

"I directed other assigned officers to canvass the apartment building while I went to obtain statements from the four individuals who had reported the incident: Doris Coker, Ted and Lucy Melton and Rebecca Rose Chamberlin. All these witnesses live at the above address and were parking their cars when they saw a body fall to the ground. None was able to identify which floor the body came from. None of them knew the victim. (See Statements.)

"The Crime Scene Unit brought to my

attention a wallet removed from the body containing a current Illinois driver's license of Frank Gordon, residing this address, Apartment 1888. The description appeared to match up with the victim. The face was unrecognizable.

"After obtaining this information, I called for a search warrant on his apartment while the Crime Scene Unit continued searching the scene, collecting evidence and making sketches and triangulations and sweepings of the area. A Miss DD McGil arrived on the scene at 20:15 hours. She stated she had been shopping at Water Tower Place and claimed she was Frank Gordon's fiancée. When asked to make a personal identification of the body, she agreed and confirmed it was Frank Gordon. She was treated by the EMT unit on site. I later got a statement from her as to Mr. Gordon's habits, present state of mind and health, as well as any business or personal dealings which might impact his sudden death. She told me he had no known enemies and was in an excellent frame of mind, as they were to be married shortly. She adamantly denied he would commit suicide. She provided a list of acquaintances and relatives of the victim. (See Statement.)

"I then asked Ms. McGil to unlock the

door to Apartment 1888 at 20:28 hours with her key. There was no sign of forcible entry. I entered alone and searched the entire unit. There was no evidence of any disturbance in any room. Sliding glass doors leading to the balcony were open. There was no sign of a struggle or any disturbance on the balcony. There were no apparent markings on the balcony balustrade. There was no suicide note in plain sight.

"Ms. McGil was then asked to accompany me through the apartment. She knows his possessions well and could check for possible robbery. She told me everything seemed to be accounted for and in its usual place.

"I next directed the Crime Scene Unit to photograph the entire apartment and balcony. I asked them to search for fingerprints due to possibility of robbery and to also search for any suicide note. (See Report.)

"I accompanied the body to the Coroner's office and met with the pathologist, Dr. Brian Pines. (See Report.)"

Something wet hit the report. I realized it was the tears trailing down my cheek. I wiped them away as I perused each of the witness reports. Then I picked up the twelve-page Crime Scene Report done by Investigator Casserly. It cataloged all the

items of evidence and scrapings and comb-
ings that had been collected and fingerprints
that had been taken to be transmitted to
the State Crime Lab.

The laboratory report from the State
Crime Lab was attached. It recorded each
piece of evidence, then listed the results of
all the examinations made on the evidence.
Much of it was too scientific for me to
understand. But some of it was easy, like
the information on Items 06-05-0113-M2
and 06-05-0113-M3 that recorded the
scrapings from under Frank's fingernails
and concluded: "No foreign material
found."

I remembered it had been that very piece
of evidence that had helped clinch a verdict
of suicide at the Coroner's Inquest. That,
and Ken's testimony. I went through the file
and located his Witness Statement, feeling
sick all over again at what he'd said. And
what he'd implied.

Ken testified that Frank had told him on
more than one occasion that he did not
want to marry me. Frank, he said, had
confided he was terrified he might become
impotent because of the prostate cancer.
According to Ken, Frank was despondent
and wanted to call off the wedding, but
didn't know how. Ken believed suicide was

Frank's way out.

The police, the coroner, the news media, all Frank's university colleagues, everybody in fact believed it. Everybody but me. I would never believe it. We'd been too close, too happy. Yes, he had prostate cancer, but I told the cops to check with Frank's doctor. His doctor had given him a clean bill of health. When the cops did check and confirmed what I told them, they insisted that, despite the good prognosis, many men harbor irrational fears of impotence. The cops also made a big deal about Frank not using his insurance to pay off his medical bills. I explained that Frank was a private person. I explained he didn't want his colleagues at the university to know about the cancer. For me, this issue of Frank's strong desire for privacy was what convinced me he could never have jumped off a balcony and smashed himself to kingdom come on the pavement in front of our building, in front of me.

At the time, I'd wondered why Frank had confided in Ken. They'd never been close. I wondered about it again now. No suicide note was ever found, and I could never accept that he wouldn't have said good-bye to me. Which, the cops said knowingly, is exactly what loved ones say in cases like this.

I removed the band around the photographs taken that night at the scene. The shot of one of his shoes on the pavement made me choke on my tears.

I gathered up the broken watch along with his key chain, comb, wallet and handkerchief and dropped them back in the envelope. His ring wasn't with the other contents. I searched through the mess on the floor, sifting through everything, but still didn't find it. Starting over, I went through every scrap of paper, every rubber band and every paper clip, careful not to overlook anything. His family ring, given to him by his father, had meant a great deal to Frank, and he'd worn it always. But when I finished my search, it was still missing.

I carefully reviewed the police report cataloging the victim's personal possessions. The ring wasn't on it.

Damn those crooked cops. One of them must have stolen it. I threw the report across the room.

Furious, I studied all the photographs again, this time focusing on Frank's hands. The large ring with its distinctive square black stone should have been visible, but I didn't spot it either on his hand or on the ground. If he wasn't wearing it, then maybe the cops hadn't stolen it. But Frank never took the ring off. So if he wasn't wearing it, what the hell had happened to it? It wasn't in the apartment. I'd gone through there personally. So where was it? That ring on Ken's hand had looked so much like Frank's. Yet Frank had told me his ring was one of a kind, handed down from his great-great grandfather through the eldest sons.

I had a terrible feeling in the pit of my stomach, but still no real answers. Only more questions.

THIRTY-SEVEN

I packed the rest of the files and books and took one last look at Frank's file before adding it to the others. That missing ring kept rankling, but right now I had to move out of Consolidated.

After getting my number call-forwarded, I unplugged everything and boxed the phone, coffeepot, and computer. Then I trudged back and forth, packing the car with boxes until there was barely enough room for me to slide into the driver's seat. I was leaving my old chair and desk, an empty file cabinet and two trash cans. Scotty, I hoped, would help me move them later tonight. I shut the door for the last time and saluted my old office good-bye with none of my previous sentimentality. I added an extra "good riddance" to my closet, feeling confident that Auntie's vision had been the terrible mess and nothing more sinister. Moving would, hopefully, effectively block any other possible problems from that quarter.

I downshifted into a U-turn out of my parking spot and realized I couldn't see out the rear-view mirror or any of the windows for that matter. For once, I'd have to drive defensively.

I nearly yelled for joy when I spotted a parking space on the street near Tom's shop. I juggled the heavy boxes of files as I approached Tom's door, and the top one tumbled off, banging into the gray steel door. A deep, throaty growl pierced my ears and stopped me in my tracks. I froze, trying not to move and not to drop everything.

The barking stopped as Tom opened the door. I peeked around the boxes. Standing next to him was a hundred-and-ten-pound wolf with yellow eyes. I thought of the Hound of the Baskervilles. The wolf was now growling, a deep, low sound. I could see its sharp front teeth. I don't mind saying it was scary as hell.

"Don't worry," Tom said, smiling and patting the wolf's head. "This is Wolfie. Wolfie, this is DD McGil. I told him you were coming."

The wolf stopped growling but still fastened on me with those yellow eyes.

"Say hello to him, DD."

"Hi, Wolfie," I murmured softly through

my teeth, careful to not upset the delicate social balance we'd apparently reached. I made no moves and kept my eyes lowered, just like they'd taught at the insurance investigator's safety class a year ago, although admittedly that had dealt with ferocious dogs, not wolves.

Wolfie picked up a stuffed dog toy between his very sharp teeth. His fierce expression didn't change, however.

"He's usually gentle as a puppy. Right now he's a little agitated because a rude customer just left. He doesn't bother anyone unless they get aggressive."

I glanced again at Wolfie and wasn't convinced. He'd look more at home carrying a ten-pound chunk of bloody meat instead of that stuffed dog toy.

I dumped the boxes near the door and stayed right there. "Is it true," I asked Tom, "that all dogs are descended from wolves?"

"It is," Tom confirmed as he shifted my boxes into the little back room cum my office. "*Canis lupus,* aka the grey wolf, the timber wolf and the tundra wolf, has been on this earth some 120 million years. The order Carnivora."

"Loosely translated — meat eaters, right?"

"Not loosely, DD. Expressly. Wolves and dogs are in the same family — Canidae.

They all have fangs or pointed canine teeth, sharp claws, and simple digestive systems."

"Simple digestive systems? Wait a minute. Didn't you tell me Wolfie ate pizza?"

Tom laughed and petted Wolfie. "Well his brain is highly developed. He's intelligent enough to make good diet choices. In fact, we're ordering pizza tonight for our dinner from Salerno's. He likes sausage, pepperoni, hamburger, and bacon — no anchovies. Let's see, what do you want on yours?"

I knew Tom liked Salerno's. Less than two blocks away, they always delivered his favorite thick crust Chicago-style pizza piping hot out of the oven because he was such a good customer. I wondered how the delivery boy was going to like Wolfie.

"Sounds like fun," I said wryly, "but I can't. Scotty arrived unexpectedly last night, so I'll take a rain check."

I was not going to be unhappy about leaving posthaste. I'd never met a wolf up close and personal before, and I wasn't sure I wanted to ever again. I was impressed that Tom and Wolfie seemed to understand each other. As to whether this was a good thing or a bad thing, I'd have to give that some more thought.

"I can't wait to meet your mystery man sometime," Tom said as we stepped around

Wolfie and stacked my boxes in the back room.

"He wants to meet you, too," I said, eyeing the wolf cautiously and hoping he wouldn't suddenly decide that he didn't like my scent or my smile or my whatever.

"I'll unpack tomorrow." My hand was on the doorknob. I was anxious to leave.

"Wait a minute," Tom called. He pulled out a chair and motioned me over to a table where the Burns artifacts were displayed next to a high-power microscope. Nervously, I inched over and sat down. Tom sat beside me. Wolfie, the stuffed dog still between his teeth, curled up on top of my feet.

"See, DD. He likes you."

Wolfie was heavy and my feet were quickly losing their feeling. I took a deep breath and tried to remain motionless. I was afraid to ask Tom what else the wolf liked to eat.

"Go ahead, pat him on the head."

"Tom, don't push it."

"Are you regretting your decision to move in?"

"Let's just say I'm having second thoughts. Wolfie's a lot to get used to. By the way, he needs a bath. He smells like the great outdoors."

"Yeah, he gets a bit gamey. Meant to do

that before you got here, but time got away from me. He likes his bath, you know.

"Now about Robbie Burns *et al.*" He lifted one of the pieces of glass and studied it with a magnifier. "I've completed all the research I can, DD, and like I told you on the phone, to me, the poem and the glass both appear genuine."

"Wow. That's absolutely incredible. I don't even know what to say. So La Dragon didn't get taken?"

"I'd say these artifacts are real treasures. I think you and your Auntie should put them in a safe deposit box and take out an insurance policy. I can't keep them here, even with Wolfie guarding the place. I don't want to be responsible for a treasure like this getting stolen or destroyed."

He carefully placed all the glass pieces into the bag and turned everything over to me along with the letter. "These truly are a marvel," he said. "Tell your Auntie it was an honor to see them."

I promised I would and put them gingerly into my briefcase.

"Do you think you could tell Wolfie to move? My feet are numb from his weight, and I've got to get going."

Tom stood up and called, "C'mon boy, treat." Wolfie got up immediately and followed Tom behind a curtain into his tiny kitchenette.

I stood up and stretched, finally relaxing with Wolfie out of sight. I was feeling a little lightheaded, looking forward to seeing Scotty.

I quickly put on my coat and gloves, picked up my briefcase and purse and called, "I'm out of here, Tom. Thanks for everything. See you tomorrow."

As I stepped out into the frosty Chicago night, someone crashed into me from the side. I collapsed onto the ground. A tall figure stood over me and pulled at my briefcase. I held tight and yanked back as hard as I could. I hate being a victim.

In response, the shadowed figure kicked me in the leg and tugged even harder. I screamed in pain and took one hand off the briefcase to grab my leg where he'd kicked it.

The tall figure stomped on my left shoulder and gave another ferocious tug on the case. I heard Wolfie's deep, throaty bark. I screamed. Suddenly one of the handles broke off the briefcase. All I was holding was the other handle and some air. "No!" I yelled and struggled to my knees.

The figure tucked the briefcase under his left arm and punched me with a mean right hook that knocked me backward so hard my head bounced off the pavement. All I saw for a second or two was stars.

Wolfie barked, this time louder and closer. The tall figure was sprinting through the parking lot across the street, nearly out of sight. Close on his heels was Wolfie who leapt out of the doorway and hotly chased the fleeing prey, leaving me with claw marks as he ran over my legs.

Tom Joyce ran from the shop and helped me to my feet.

"Are you okay? What the hell happened? Where's Wolfie?"

"Somebody grabbed my briefcase."

"OhmyGod, the Burns treasures!"

"Wolfie's after them. They went that-a-way." I pointed north.

Tom took chase, calling for Wolfie. My head was foggy, my knees weak and my left arm hurt like hell. But this was nothing to the pain I was going to feel when Auntie found out her precious things were taken.

I crept slowly back into Tom's bookshop, fell into a chair, and dropped my head between my knees. I prayed the wolf would catch the jerk and get the briefcase back.

I don't know how long it was before Tom and Wolfie reappeared. I was still queasy and foggy-headed. Wolfie appeared at my side and sat down, sans briefcase but with an even more pungent odor than earlier.

"Thanks . . . , er, Wolfie." I cast aside the impulse to call him a good boy.

"He got away with the briefcase, dammit. I ran so hard, I broke my glasses." Tom, breathing hard, held them up by the one earpiece still attached, like show and tell. "Well, are you okay, DD?"

"He got my shoulder and my knee pretty good, but I think I'll be all right." I didn't tell him how bad my arm ached or about the massive headache setting in. "He didn't happen to drop the briefcase, by any chance? Three to four million dollars of uninsured loot was in there."

"Sorry, DD, there's no sign of it. What a cock-up! We've had a lot of robberies around the shop in the past six months. The cops told me they think it might be a teen gang initiation thing."

I didn't tell him that I suspected this was not random at all. It might have something to do with HI-Data, but I suspected it was more likely the Santa robber. Right now my head hurt too much to think. What was I going to tell Auntie?

He retrieved some aspirins and a glass of water from his little kitchen nook and thrust them at me. "Take these, they'll help. You think maybe the guy was after the Burns artifacts?"

Tom was just catching up with my train of thought. I could feel my blood pressure rise another notch and my headache intensify. With Auntie's precious objects now gone, I might as well resign from life. At the very least, I'd never be able to go home.

I took a deep breath. "I don't know, Tom. I don't know."

"Wolfie nearly caught the guy, whoever he was, but he jumped into a big car and drove off. It was too dark for me to tell what make. I know what you're thinking. I'd have liked Wolfie to take a piece out of him to teach him a lesson."

"Me too. But would Wolfie have stopped at one bite?"

"Honestly, I don't know," Tom said thoughtfully.

"And how would you explain a bloody body and a wolf to the cops?"

"I didn't think of that," he admitted.

"Maybe we won't call the cops, Tom."

"You mean you didn't call the cops yet? What about the paramedics? I'll call right now. I'm sure you have a concussion and there may be some broken bones under those bruises."

"No, don't." I opened my eyes wide and

stretched out my legs and arms full length, trying to smile despite the pain. "See — everything's working. No need to call. And really, I'm clearheaded now. I'll prove it. Today is Tuesday. My name is DD McGil. My favorite color is red; my favorite food is chocolate. My favorite liquor is Wild Turkey, and my favorite pastime is sex. My . . ."

"Stop, DD. I'll never say you're normal, but you seem to be okay. You sure?"

"Yeah, I'm positive." *If I told him how truly rotten I felt, he'd have forgotten the EMTs and called the morgue instead. What difference does any of it make, anyway,* I thought. *I'm doomed.*

Wolfie thrust his head onto my lap. I jerked, surprised and a bit fearful as well. True, he'd taken my side. He even seemed to have accepted me. But his yellow eyes, staring unblinking at me, were formidable to behold.

"Tom, look. He's got something in his mouth."

"I see." Tom picked up the stuffed dog toy from the floor and traded it for what was between Wolfie's teeth.

Wolfie's yellow eyes had followed the transaction carefully, and he seemed satisfied with the trade. Tom handed me the scrap of material Wolfie had released.

I studied the torn piece of thick beige fabric. Wolfie's teeth marks were visible along the ripped edges. I'd read the startling statistic that every forty seconds someone in the United States seeks medical attention for a dog bite. What, I wondered, were the stats on wolf bites?

"Looks like cashmere." I handed it to Tom.

"And lined," he added after turning it around a few times.

Michael Drake had described a beige cashmere coat worn by my office burglar. If this was a piece of the attacker's overcoat, perhaps the attacker was the same guy who'd trashed my office and the same guy who'd . . . what, murdered Ken and Marcie and Oscar? Was I the next victim?

"This didn't come from some gang-banger, DD. I hope Wolfie didn't jump some poor passer-by. Could you describe your attacker?"

"No." I shook my head and was instantly sorry. The sharp pain nearly made me faint. It subsided quickly though, and I tried to pretend nothing was hurting. "He hit me from the side just as I was closing your door."

"Did you notice anything particular about him — his shoes maybe? His wristwatch? A ring?"

"No, I didn't see anything. I'm pretty sure he was wearing gloves. He hit me so hard, I went right down. I'm just glad he didn't break my shoulder or my leg. Probably."

"DD you have to call the cops if only to report the theft of the Burns artifacts. Those are worth big money. You have to call."

"Tom, I can't. Don't you see? Auntie has no real provenance and reporting it would really put her in hot water. They'd probably arrest her for trafficking in stolen property. I'd never hear the end of it. I've got to think."

"You'll have to tell her they were stolen, DD."

My stomach flipped and then flopped. I couldn't tell Auntie I'd failed to protect her treasures. But what else could I do?

Wolfie made a strange little mouselike noise.

"Wow," Tom said excitedly. "That's really rare. You just rated one of Wolfie's social squeaks. You're lucky. He only makes that sound for his owner and for me."

I smiled, even though it hurt. "Wolfie, your pizza's on me tonight." I reached down and gave his head a pat. His fur felt wiry, not soft. Then Wolfie cocked his head to the right and let me rub his ear. Wolfie had indeed saved the day, and I wasn't worried anymore about coming back tomorrow. That is, if I was still alive after telling Auntie the bad news.

I left with Tom still wanting to call the paramedics and/or the cops. But I was feeling better physically with every passing minute. Even if I did have a concussion, I refused to spend the night in some hospital. For one thing, Scotty was in town. And I didn't need another interrogation by another set of cops. They wouldn't find the guy who'd hit me anyway. All good reasons to avoid giving Wolfie, my new best friend, a police blotter. As to what I was going to do about the precious artifacts and Auntie, I was at a loss, except I knew I would have to beard the lion in her own lair.

THIRTY-EIGHT

With the Santa fiasco, my office break-in, and now the mugging, I had to consider that the mugger had been after the Burns artifacts and wasn't connected with HI-Data. Something had to be done and done quickly, and questions needed to be answered so I could move forward.

As I parked in front of Mother's, I felt sick to my stomach.

Auntie Dragon was there, alone. "Your mother's at one of her club meetings," she informed me.

"We need to talk, Auntie."

"Aye. I wanted to know how your investigation is coming. Want a wee drink?"

"No. No drinkies. I've had one hell of a day. Let's just get this over with. You know I'm concerned because of the Santa burglary, and . . ."

"I curse him, whoe'er he is."

I looked, but saw no evidence of the

Scotch bottle. "Have you been tippling?"

"I've not, for all that."

"Well, what I didn't tell you is that Phil's safe was burglarized the next day. And today, my office was ransacked."

"Oh. That is suspicious, isn't it?"

I handed her the phone.

"Call your Mister Murray."

"What?"

"He won't take my calls, and we need to talk to him to get to the bottom of this mess. My experts are telling me that the manuscript and the glass are genuine."

"But of course they are, DD. I ne'er doubted it. I needed you to verify that fact afore I take the next step."

"What next step?"

"Where's your briefcase, DD?"

"What does that have to do with anything?"

"Where are the precious things? Oh, my Lord. Did the louts steal them?"

"No. They're okay, Auntie," I lied through my teeth. "My experts have looked at them."

"The whole kit 'n kaboodle? They must not be out of our possession. Get them back immediately."

I wasn't about to tell her the adventures her treasures had today, or that they were now in possession of someone unknown, and we might never see them again. *I needed some bargaining power, and this was all I had.*

"All right," I told her. "I will. But first call George."

"That I cannot do. Look at the time. 'Tis nearly two o'clock in the morning in Scotland."

"Auntie, I won't bring those objects back into the house until you call him. I'm assuming you know his home number. So call him now. Do it."

"First I need a little drinkie."

I grabbed the phone from her. "No 'guid auld Scotch drink' till after you make the call."

"I approve you reciting Robbie Burns by heart."

"Never mind that. Call him. We need some answers."

Her jaw was squared. She gave me the eye, but she knew she was cornered.

After many rings, Auntie said hello to someone. Then she said no, she was all right and explained that yes, she was fully aware it was two a.m.

"Now tell him who I am," I ordered. She glared again but did as I asked.

I took the phone. "Mr. Murray? My Auntie's told me everything. We have to talk."

"Very pleased I am to make your acquaintance, even at this witching hour," he said in a deep, pleasant voice. "An' now she's told you about the twa of us, as it were, please convince her to marry me."

"What? Look, I'm not calling about that. I'm sorry it's so late, but I need to know about those Burns artifacts. Why did you want to sell them to Auntie?"

"I dinna want to."

"But she said you approached her and . . ."

"Nay, lass. I wanted to give them to her. But she wouldn't have it. She's verra stubborn. Says you are, too."

"You wanted to give them to Auntie?"

Auntie nodded in agreement.

"Aye. She's the one who'll know the right thing to be done with such precious objects."

"So you believe the artifacts are genuine. But . . ."

"Your Auntie's quite the lass. I expect you are, too. She says you're alike as like can be."

"What about the hundred thousand pounds?" I asked.

"Aye, the money she insisted to pay? Means nothing to me. 'Tis in an escrow account. I'll not touch it. After Elizabeth decides what to do with the artifacts, I'll donate that coin as well to the Burns House

290

Mauchline Museum. Now then, can you get her to agree to marry me?"

"Wait. There's something else. Did she tell you someone broke in and tried to steal the objects?"

"She did not. Is she all right, then? She's not been hurt has she? Let me speak to her again."

"She's fine," I told him. "But someone knew about these things and is after them. I understand that your partner, Mr. Jack Mc-Sweeney, is here in Chicago right now."

"Jock? That's so. As head of our American branch, he travels to America quite often. But . . ."

"Tell me, how did he feel about your selling the Burns artifacts for so little?"

"That is of no consequence whatsoever. I make the final decisions for the firm. And which in point of this case I did."

"But maybe he didn't like your final decision," I suggested.

"I regret that is true," George Murray admitted. "He strongly disagreed with my actions in the matter. An' Jock was verra angry on account I acted without consulting him. But again, that is of no matter. The decision was mine to make. A Murray has run this firm since the time of the Restoration in 1660 after the scourge of the Roundheads, and McSweeneys have been with us only for the past three generations. In any case, it was all settled by the time I informed him of what I'd done. Now tell me, what makes you believe Jock McSweeney is involved?"

"Describe him to me, please."

"Aye. He's fifty-nine, a thin man, taller than your Auntie. Grey hair, light grey eyes, and he has a distinctive hawk-like nose."

"What kind of coat does he wear?"

"Coat? He'll be wearing his camel cashmere overcoat as usual. Are we getting somewhere with this, lass?"

"What good is all this going to do, DD?" Auntie interrupted. "We don't know what Santa looked like."

"Shh," I said.

"What?" George Murray asked.

"Not you, Mr. Murray. Auntie says we don't know what the burglar looks like because he was disguised as Santa Claus."

"Santa Claus?" His voice went up an octave.

"Right. What Auntie doesn't know is that somebody trashed my office looking for the Burns objects."

"Did they get them?" George asked.

"No, but not for want of trying. Luckily an eyewitness saw him leave my office. This time, he wasn't wearing a Santa suit or a beard, so we've got a description."

"And is it Jack McSweeney?" Auntie demanded.

"Does it match what I've told you of Jack?" George asked via the phone at the same time, like a simulcast.

I glanced at Auntie and said into the phone, "Five feet ten or thereabouts, thin build, grey hair, wearing an expensive tan cashmere coat. And somebody wearing a tan cashmere coat left a piece of it as evidence when he tried to knock me out less than an hour ago. You tell me."

Auntie frowned at the rug while George swore an oath that made my toes curl.

"An' are you all right, my girl?" George asked.

"It's nothing permanent. But . . ."

"But the objects were taken, weren't they? You don't want your Auntie to know?"

"Yes, that's right."

"I'll see to it right away, my lass. I'm verra sorry. I had no idea he'd react so. This was given to my family for safekeeping, and it was up to me to decide. Jack doesna see the objects as the treasures they are. He sees them only as goods for profit. I'll make it right."

"What's he saying?" Auntie was beside

293

me, trying to listen.

"He says he'll make it right," I told her.

"If that's what he says, then that's what he'll do," she pronounced. "There's no more worry."

"What's she saying?" George asked.

"She says you'll take care of it so there's nothing more to worry about. I hope I can count on that."

"Aye. I'll book the verra first flight to Chicago. I'll let you know what time I'll be arriving. I'll handle Jack and return the objects. Elizabeth will never have to know. Now see what you can do to get her to marry me," he said.

"Have you ever been able to talk my Auntie into anything, Mr. Murray?"

"You may call me George," he said with a pleasant laugh. "And right in all, you are. Elizabeth'll do what she'll do only when she's full ready to do it."

"But I'll ask anyway," I told him warmly. "Auntie, George is down on bended knee and wants me to persuade you to accept his proposal of marriage."

"Here and now? He's daft."

"Will you think about it," I asked her.

"You may tell him that I will."

"She says you're daft, but she'll think about it," I repeated into the phone.

"That's a good start, my gel," he said. "Take care of her for me till I get there."

As I hung up, Mother arrived. Auntie said, "I'm having my wee Scotch now. Where are the treasures?"

"Somewhere safe."

Auntie stared at me. "You're more canny than I ken, lassie."

It had been a very long night.

THIRTY-NINE

It was late when I got home, and there was Scotty, lounging on the sofa, looking adorable wearing the shirt I'd sent him for Christmas. I intended to tell him about the Burns artifacts, being mugged, and about my awful suspicions concerning Frank's ring. But before the door had barely closed, he had me in his arms and we found ourselves deliciously naked. I forgot everything else, including my sore body. My bed creaked and groaned to our tender then noisy, laughing lovemaking. Just as Scotty made me scream, his beeper went off.

"Don't you dare stop what you're doing Scotty Stuart, or I'll kill you. Where'd you learn how to do that, anyway?" All my aches and pains had suddenly disappeared. Making love with Frank had been wonderful, but tame. With Scotty, sex was totally uninhibited and full of surprises.

We lay in each other's arms, drifting

languidly in and out of sleep. When I opened my eyes, he was lounging on one elbow, watching me. I could feel his body heat as I traced the blond-brown hairs along his lower abdomen.

"What are those black and blue marks from?" Scotty touched my leg where it was already turning a sickly purple.

"It happened when I left Tom Joyce's." I thought I'd start my explanation short and simple, and kind of ease into the whole Burns artifacts problem. After my conversation with George Murray, I was now convinced that all the break-ins were related to the Burns artifacts, not to HI-Data. We knew who Jack McSweeney was, and I felt certain we'd be able to stop him and get the objects back. I wouldn't need to be looking over my shoulder every minute, worried about someone from HI-Data attacking me for reasons unknown. "See, Auntie . . ."

Scotty suddenly jumped out of bed, clasping both hands over his groin.

"Mee-oww," Cavalier squawked.

"What happened Scotty? Are you okay?"

"I think so." He uncupped his hands and peered at his privates. "Yeah, everything's still there. Cavvy gave me a cat lick. That's one rough tongue he's got."

"Ohmygod." I tried not to laugh as I

thought of all the stories about pets breaking up love affairs.

"You and I are going to have a serious talk," I scolded the cat. "A good Cavalier doesn't do those things."

Scotty's beeper went off again, this time scaring Cavvy off the bed. Scotty retrieved it from his pants pocket and came back to bed. He checked the displayed numbers, and when he looked at me, I knew it wasn't good news.

"Hell, it's London. They've called twice. Better get ready for bad news."

"What bad news?" I didn't need anymore of that today.

"They probably want me back right away. God knows, I'm not ready to leave." He leaned over and kissed me as Cavalier stole back into the bed.

"Ummm . . . You are, I suspect, the best lover in the world."

"Tell your cat it's you I love, not him." He stuck out his tongue at Cavvy, who blinked and pretended not to notice. "Why don't you figure out what you want on a pizza while I make my call. That way we can order-in and stay bare-assed all night."

I jumped out of bed. "Like room service, huh?" If I wasn't going to have much time with Scotty, I'd make the best of what I had.

We laughed as Scotty touch-toned the numbers for London, and I found the phone number for Mama Rosalie's. In Chicago, pizza is the king of foods. Thin crust, deep dish or stuffed, every neighborhood, no matter what its major ethnic group, has a mom and pop pizza parlor around the corner. I liked going out to Uno's or Due's, but my favorite for delivery was Mama Rosalie's, where she and several family members turned out a fabulous thin crust cheese with homemade Italian sausage and pepperoni.

I was rustling up plates, silverware and napkins when Scotty, still in the buff, ambled in with Cavalier at his heels. I handed him a bottle of chilled Merlot and a corkscrew.

"Say, what have you got on your dirty mind?" he laughed, catching the corkscrew handily. "Is this Merlot any good?"

I giggled, setting out two wine glasses from the cupboard. "It's even better than good. It's reasonably cheap."

He uncorked the wine and poured two glasses.

"To you," he toasted, "and to Chicago."

"To us," I toasted. After a sip, I asked, "So what did London have to say?"

"They need me back right away. I'm really

sorry, DD. They've set up connections between O'Hare and Kennedy, and thence to Heathrow. I'm booked out on the next flight."

"I guess I was hoping you'd help me move into Tom's space." I tried my best to keep it light, but there was a big rock in my stomach.

"DD, the only reason I got these two days was to meet with a Treasury Department contact here in Chicago. I should have told you yesterday I wasn't going to be here long."

"I guess I expected it." *Suddenly that headache started again. Maybe I did have a concussion.* I searched for another couple of aspirins. "Why do you have to be so damn good at your job? If you were a schlep, you could stay awhile."

"If I were a schlep," he leered and lunged at me, "you wouldn't give me a second glance. Admit it. Did I hear you say you're moving into Tom's bookshop? I don't know that much about your investigator's income, but can't you find something a bit bigger?"

"I will. Soon."

He caught me round the waist, and we were in the midst of another romantic interlude when the doorbell rang.

Scotty rushed to the bedroom, grabbed

his pants and jumped into them while hopping to the door.

"Stay in the kitchen," he called as he zipped up and opened the door to Mario and our pizza.

I was hunting for salt and pepper when Scotty burst into the kitchen, his hands full of money but no pizza.

"Look. This is all I've got." He opened his fists on bills and coins all picturing the Queen of England. "I knew I wasn't going to be here long, so I didn't exchange for much American money. Have you got anything?"

Me and money is a long story. I never carry much cash. I use credit cards because my tax-man, Stan, advises me it keeps my records straight. Of course, I have to pay them off in full at the end of every month or he'll flay me alive. All this ran through one track of my mind while the other track mentally added up what cash I kept for emergencies.

"There's some in my purse," I started out to the hall when he grabbed me by the waist and pulled me back into the kitchen.

"Mario's out there. Keep your naked buns in here and tell me where your purse is. I'll get it."

I was certain he'd found it when I heard

everything fall out of it onto the hall table. I shuddered.

"Dammit, Scotty, be careful. There's valuable stuff in there."

"Yeah, like hundred dollar bills," he called from the hall.

"Right." I laughed. "I don't even know whose face is on a hundred. Ben Franklin? Bill & Hill Clinton locked in a heart shape? Obama?"

"Never mind. I found a twenty," he said.

While he settled with the delivery boy, I tried to control my pizza pangs, imagining that first bite. As soon as he closed the door, I joined him. But the pizza sat there while we both stared at a stash of hundred dollar bills spread out on my hall table, half in, half out of an envelope that had fallen from my purse.

"Where'd they come from?" I asked.

Scotty snapped one of the bills, then snapped it again.

"Where'd you get this, DD?"

"I don't . . ." I picked up the envelope that still contained a few cascading bills. "This is the envelope from Marcie at HI-Data. I thought her lease and tax returns were in it."

"There was nothing in it but this money," he said.

"Wow. Marcie must have meant to try and buy me off. I was going to go through it that night you arrived, but we went to the Bears game and then we . . . Remember?"

He unscrewed and removed a lampshade from one of the lamps in my living room. Under the exposed bulb, he scrutinized one of the bills, turning it from side to side.

"This stuff is dirty, but it's good," he said, still eyeing the bill. "I've never seen anything this good."

"Good?"

"Good counterfeit. If it weren't for the watermark and how the paper feels when you snap it, I'd never know. This paper doesn't have fiber thread in it. Watch."

He snapped the bill crisply, and it ripped cleanly in half.

"Don't do that," I shrieked.

"It's not real money, DD."

"I can't believe it." I rifled through several bills, still upset about the torn hundred. I don't see that much cash that I can feel comfortable having it destroyed before my eyes.

"Scotty, all the serial numbers are different. And look, these two are from different mints."

Scotty shook his head. "What you mean, DD, is that the bills are from different banks. The mint isn't involved. All U.S. currency is printed by the BEP, the Bureau of Engraving and Printing, and each bill has one of the twelve Federal Reserve Bank locations on it."

He checked each bill, one at a time. "You are right though, different issuing banks. As good as they look, nonetheless they're all bogus. Tell me now, you say you got this envelope from Marcie at HI-Data? Who is she? Sit down. You can fill me in while we eat."

FORTY

I picked over a slice of pizza and watched Scotty finish the rest. My appetite vanished with the torn, fake hundred-dollar bill. All my aches and pains returned with a vengeance.

What did a computer expert like Scotty know about money? And what had Marcie been doing with all those bills? Did she really believe she could bribe me? She was living like she had struck it rich with her new Porsche, expensive clothes and that expensive apartment. When Sparky told me about Marcie's off-shore calls, I'd suspected drugs or industrial espionage.

Scotty interrupted my thoughts. "I'm going to let you in on something I'm not supposed to talk about."

"I'm listening."

"All right. I've been in London doing classified work for the IMF — the International Monetary Fund — not for some multinational conglomerate like I told you. I'm working on a top secret project at the Bank of England that's part of an IMF agreement."

"Are you saying you're CIA?"

"I'm not spooky enough for that." He smiled, but I didn't.

"Go on." *This was my day for surprises.*

"This all started in the late seventies when the International Monetary Fund became concerned that new technologies would permit wide-spread duplication of major world currencies," he said. "And that's exactly what happened."

"Don't holographs and micro-printing and all that stuff make it more difficult to counterfeit?"

"Those 3-D images work for plastic credit cards, not on paper currency. And for money, the newest generation of color copiers is just the tip of the iceberg. It's now possible to make almost exact copies of just about any paper document. And all of this sophisticated technology is getting cheaper by the minute, available now in your local drug store with the cameras, watches, and deodorants."

"Sure you're not CIA?"

"I promise," he said. "You just got a peek at how good this new counterfeit currency can look. Believe me, the stuff comes out looking so real, you can't spot it except for the paper. Hardly anyone can. These copy machine counterfeit bills amount to half the bogus bills out there — and that's happened in just a few years."

"I guess that must be why every supermarket around now has one of those stubby black pens that they use to see if bills are real or not," I said.

"You bet," Scotty agreed. "They use that little black pen on all the fifties and hundreds they get. If where they touch the bill turns yellow, it's okay. If it turns brown, it's suspect and they'll investigate more. If it turns black, it's definitely counterfeit, and they get to arrest the shopper and put the groceries back on the shelf."

"What if the shopper got it from someone else?"

"You know what I mean. They get to take him in custody and grill him until they find out where the bill came from. But it's gotten that common even in grocery stores that they have a protocol to handle it. Now imagine the consequences if a lot more of this stuff got into circulation. Things are bad enough in today's world economy, but dumping a lot of counterfeit bills into it would inflate the money supply and there'd be a train wreck in the global economy. Believe me, we'd be plunged into a depression like we've never seen."

"What do you have to do with all this? Are you sure you're not CIA?"

"I've been working on a computer system to get the bogus currency out of circulation. It's based on the intelligence technology used by the military."

I didn't relax hearing that. Military Intelligence is little better than the CIA, but I smiled and said, "Computers Save the World, huh?"

"Why not? I got involved when the Pentagon had crates of satellite and aircraft intelligence photos piling up because the experts couldn't analyze them fast enough."

My headache was gone again, but my head was whirling. "All right, if you aren't CIA, are you FBI or IRS or something like that?"

"DD, I'm a computer hacker. True, I'm the best, but nothing more. Now, want to hear the rest of the story? Or we could go back to bed."

"Okay, let's get back under the covers. After all, isn't that what operatives do best? But no fooling around till you tell me everything."

We evicted the cat from the warm spot.

Snuggling close under the covers, I tried hard to concentrate on what Scotty was telling me.

"What we needed was a way to quickly figure out precisely what was happening on the surveillance photos so if necessary immediate countermeasures could be taken," he explained as his fingers began to explore and our legs entwined. "That's why surveillance photos were so important."

"Scotty, you promised we weren't going to fool around until you told me all about this."

"Want me to stop?"

"No, but . . ."

"How about if I just do this . . . real slow?"

I slapped his roving hand but moaned with pleasure at the same time.

"Where was I?"

"Surveillance."

"Right. We developed a scanning and analyzing system, both the hardware and software, to extract all the meaningful information from those bales of photos. HI-Data was a part of the project."

"Oh?"

"They were responsible for a lot of the digitized high-speed scanning technology. Suddenly we were in real-time analysis of what was happening, and that's why we were able to kick butt in Iraq and invade Baghdad so quickly."

"What does all this have to do with counterfeiting? I don't get it."

"You're going to in a minute," he laughed and kissed me.

"Scotty . . ."

"The problem is you're irresistible. Okay, okay. The point is that now we're trying to apply the same methods to scanning and analyzing paper currency. My job has been adapting this system to spot bogus money when it comes to the central bank so we can get it out of circulation."

"So that's what you've been doing."

He gently kissed and caressed the lowest curve of my stomach. I wanted more, but I knew I needed to understand what he was telling me. "You promised."

He sighed. "Getting back to the money, my dear, if we must, you see, scanning converts the signal, the light signal, off the dollar bill into digits. It digitizes it. We take this composite signal with all the little flaws there may be within the dollar bill and idealize it down to the perfect dollar bill so we can weed out the fakes."

"Like Plato's ideal," I said, realizing how Joe Tanaka's technique to clean up distortions in the digital signal might well apply here.

"This technology was developed from spy satellites. It's the source of the digitized imaging that HI-Data is working with. It's gone way beyond that now. There are improvements I can't talk about that are top secret. The jargon that's grown up around the technology sounds like gibberish to most people."

He kissed me again.

"Speaking of top secret," he whispered. This time our bodies strained against each other and desire took over. The cat jumped off the bed as we made love surrounded by visions in my head of hundred dollar bills floating around like green sugar plums.

FORTY-ONE

We left our warm bed at 3:45 a.m., an action never taken of one's own free will. After a quick shower, we pulled on heavy clothes and went out to the car. As to which of us was more cold and tired — me, Scotty, or the Miata — it was a toss-up.

"You never explained what the spare tire is doing on the right front wheel," Scotty said as I unlocked the car.

I finally told him what had happened to the new Michelin tire he'd given me for Christmas. I also told him what Dieter and I suspected.

"Now I'm worried," he said. He grabbed the flashlight from the glove compartment, got under the car and then checked under the hood and in the trunk. Satisfied, he tossed his suitcase behind the front seat, and we finally got in.

In spite of the frigid temperature, the Miata started without so much as a cough.

Traffic was almost nonexistent except for the drunks, so we sped down the Kennedy Expressway to O'Hare.

As we turned onto the airport exit ramp, I began to tell Scotty my suspicions about Ken and Frank, but he was intent on having me meet with his top-level contact Harry Marley at the Secret Service Forensics Lab. He said last night that he'd been working on a computer system based on military intelligence technology to get bogus currency out of circulation. I couldn't get over the fact that he apparently had top-level government connections. I wasn't sure I liked that.

"DD, are you listening to me?" he asked. "I'm convinced the counterfeiting is connected to HI-Data, and I insist you get help."

I wasn't eager to comply. I had no desire to be in contact with the Secret Service and maybe the IRS or ATF, all CIA surrogates. If the hundred dollar bills were counterfeit, I was sure I'd be the one the government would target when they saw them.

"I want to ask you a question about Frank," I said.

"Don't change the subject, DD. By the way, now that we know each other a lot better, when are you going to tell me what the

DD stands for?"

"It stands for DD. And I do have some important things I want to go over with you."

Scotty frowned. "I'll be in England, worried sick about you. I know you can take care of yourself. But this is urgent. Promise me you'll see Harry today."

"Scotty, even if he agrees I didn't have any part in the counterfeiting, I won't understand a thing he tells me without you to interpret. He'll just punch my name into the Big Computer as a suspect."

"What Big Computer?"

"You know, the Central Storage Computer or whatever it's called. Everybody knows the feds have one that continually updates your permanent record. What if he gets something on me? I'm the one who should be doing the investigating, not the other way around."

"DD, Harry's my friend. You'll like him, I promise. He won't think you're stupid. This technical stuff changes daily. Nobody understands it all unless they work with it every day. Even Harry has to be continuously briefed. He's not, as you delicately phrase it, a 'techno-poop' either. So don't worry. He's not going to arrest you. Why not talk to your friend Tom about counterfeiting?

He seems to know a lot of things, and I'm sure he'll advise you to see Harry, too. Now promise, or I'll stay here until you do. Wait . . . that's not a good threat."

"You'd miss your plane and have to come back to my bed?"

We were approaching the departures ramp. Scotty had barely enough time to make his flight. I was tempted to keep him here, but since the fate of civilization apparently hung in the balance, I promised to see Harry Marley, and I let him go.

"If I get in trouble or he laughs at me, I'm calling you collect. And you'll pay for it next time I see you."

"Stop worrying. Harry needs to see those bills and hear what's going on at HI-Data."

"How do I get to him? Will he even agree to see me?"

"Good point. He's in the One South Wacker Drive building, suite 2343, and he'll be expecting you tomorrow — er, today, at eleven. I'll contact his office while I'm changing planes at JFK and set up the appointment."

"What's his last name again?"

"Marley."

I pulled up in front of American Airlines and shifted into neutral. It was deserted. Scotty leaned across the gear shift and took me in his arms.

"I'm going to miss you like hell. Are you going to miss me?"

I never got the chance to answer because he kissed me, and frankly I forgot the question. Even in freezing weather, he was a terrific kisser.

"Now crawl back into your warm bed and you better be dreaming of me." He grabbed his overnight bag and waved. "I'll be thinking of you. And dammit, DD, be careful."

FORTY-TWO

I awoke from a deep, dreamless sleep, already missing Scotty. I dreaded meeting Harry Marley and wished I'd told Scotty my suspicions that Ken might have been involved in Frank's death. I needed his advice.

Luckily my headache was gone. The bruises were more noticeable this morning, but I wasn't too sore. Cavalier was cranky and even sharing some of my scrambled eggs didn't please him.

I couldn't keep my mind on the crossword. Instead, I phoned Tom Joyce to ask what he knew about counterfeiting.

"Counterfeiting money or counterfeiting goods? They're both hot right now. China's number one in faking goods, and Colombia's number one in fake money."

"Counterfeit bills. Scotty thinks someone gave me some fake hundreds. He wants me to take them to a guy he knows at the Secret

Service Forensic Lab. He says the bills are really really good."

"I'm definitely looking forward to meeting your Scotty. He's into a lot of interesting things. Is he in one of the branches — CIA or FBI or Secret Service that he would know counterfeit bills just by looking at them?"

"That's exactly what I asked."

"And?"

"He won't really say, but he's connected to some top-level investigations into fake currency. So what can you tell me?"

"Probably nothing more than Scotty did if he saw the money firsthand. I do know this isn't the first time in history that counterfeiting has been rampant. They say that nearly half of all money in circulation in the U.S. in the mid-1800s was fake. Curiously, Lincoln started the Secret Service on April 14, 1865, the day he was shot, and their first priority was to stop counterfeiting, not to guard the President."

"Scotty said that today's new wave of counterfeiting is such a hot crime because it's so easy with a good scanner, printer and color copier."

"He's right. It's easier than bigamy. And only a few get caught, like my personal favorite, the lady in Rockford, eighty miles outside Chicago, who tried to hand off a one million dollar bill."

"But everybody knows the U.S. doesn't have a one-million dollar bill."

"She apparently didn't! And even though the Feds tell the public that they catch most counterfeiters, there are still plenty out there. They log onto sites on the Internet like HowStuffWorks that tell you how to counterfeit and get away with it. So all things considered, you should probably go see Scotty's Secret Service guy."

"If I don't appear in three days, send Wolfie to find me."

"Good luck DD, and let me know what happens."

On my way to the One South Wacker building, I kept thinking of those hundred dollar bills. They looked so genuine under the harsh light of day. In spite of what Scotty and Tom had said, I didn't believe they were counterfeit. I hoped Harry Marley was as good a friend as Scotty thought.

My weekly Aikido class had been cancelled because Sensei, our leader, was traveling in Japan over the holidays. So instead, I inserted a "Karkicks" CD for some needed exercise. It began with an energetic woman alerting me to keep one hand on the wheel — as if I was going to get so involved in exercising I would forget I was driving. Then the music kicked in for shoulder rolls, tummy-tucks, and knee-knocks.

I kept trying out different scenarios about Ken and Marcie and HI-Data as I did the mouth and neck stretching exercises, ignoring the curious stares I was getting from passing cars. If the money wasn't counterfeit, Marcie had probably been into drugs. Or maybe she was being paid off for something by Ken or somebody else at HI-Data. But if the money was bogus, then HI-Data had to be involved. I was sure Marcie hadn't committed suicide. She and Ken had been murdered. And someone had tried to murder Jeffrey Fere, too. Did the cops consider John Olson/Dan Karton as the prime suspect? How did Ken, Norman, Joe Tanaka, and Sparky Groh fit into the picture? Was Jeffrey's life still in danger? And mine?

By the time I parked in the lot two blocks from One South Wacker, I'd done thirty-five pelvic pushes — which, the perky girl on the tape assured me, "were great for my sex life."

The frigid wind off the Lake was so bitter, I forgot about hundred dollar bills and HI-Data and concentrated on survival. My nose and fingers were frozen, and my feet were almost numb. Every year, I hate winter more.

One South Wacker Drive is a glossy forty-story Helmut Jahn skyscraper, built in 1982. Architecturally, it's three boxes stacked even on one end with each successive box smaller in width giving the building the look of stairs heading into the sky. The exterior is black reflective glass with colored glass in pink and blue that Jahn cleverly used to demarcate cathedral-like windows around the exterior.

A thinly clad street musician was plastered against the lobby door. I felt sorry for him and dropped a fiver in his hat, hoping his lips wouldn't freeze to the harmonica.

I pushed through the heavy revolving door, grateful to get indoors. I hope I'll never get famous enough to have a building named after me, because architects disrespect you. One nearby government building was named after Dirkson, the well-known, deep-voiced Illinois senator, and he got what he deserved. Whoever designed it had forgotten to put in a lobby. The HI-Data building did have a distinctive, all black marble lobby that was almost as impersonal and uninviting as its glass and chrome interior.

The central corridor swarmed with bureaucrats and non-bureaucrats like locusts over Utah. Before 9/11, there'd been only minimal security — a desk with one guard. And because there was no building directory, if you didn't know your way around, you would get stopped and questioned and vetted. But now their security had been revved up, and a uniformed guard shooed me to the rear of a long line where everyone passed single-file through a metal detector.

It was easy to pick out the top government guys and the lawyers waiting in line. Some wore expensive coats while others were carelessly groomed, but they all had bulging briefcases and the same darting eyes, looking for angles in every corner. And they were all talking on their cell phones or text messaging.

When it was my turn, a pasty-faced guard with lazy blue eyes opened my purse and took out a handful of objects, including Marcie's envelope containing the hundred dollar bills. Luckily it didn't open and spill out, or I'd have been arrested on the spot. He took out all my lipsticks and checked them. Then he found the emergency Playtex tampons in the zip compartment. He stuffed them back, handed me my purse, and cleared me through.

The United States Treasury Department,

Midwest Operations Center, didn't like to advertise itself, but Scotty had explained it occupied the entire twenty-third floor. There were four banks of elevators. I followed Scotty's instructions and used the south bank elevators on the far side of the lobby to reach the twenty-third floor.

Their reception room was furnished in bureaucratic regulation tasteful, falling somewhere between public aid and the White House. Medium pile carpeting of an indeterminate color covered the floor and most of the furniture was atrocious but matched.

The receptionist, an attractive Latina girl wearing a deep orange outfit with lots of clangy jewelry, cheerily checked me against a list. She said I was expected and asked me to have a seat.

After a few moments she returned with a very handsome black man who looked like Mohammed Ali in his fighting prime. At six foot four or five, he was a big man, but it was more than height that gave him dominance. He smiled slightly, exuding charisma.

"I'm Harry Marley, and you're Scotty's DD McGil, I take it." It wasn't a statement, and it wasn't a question. His rich baritone had that distinctive Caribbean accent, redolent of warm sun and James Bond adventures. I smiled, not knowing what Scotty had told him.

"Follow me," he said and led me down a maze of corridors. I covertly admired the way his tailored gray suit caressed the firm muscles in his back, buttocks, and thighs. Eventually he turned left into the Forensic Lab wing where he motioned me into a large room.

FORTY-THREE

You couldn't see the Chicago River from Harry Marley's office window. The view was obstructed by the Mercantile Exchange, but it was still a nice view by my standards. You could see the art deco Civic Opera House, a Chicago landmark and one of my particular favorites.

We were in a room dominated by a large oval table in the center, flanked on one side by glass museum cases filled with exhibits and on the other side by a myriad of instruments and specially adapted microscopes of varying sizes, shapes, and attachments. Harry Marley took my coat and got immediately down to business by asking for the money.

I removed Marcie's envelope from my purse and slid it across the highly polished table. As his long, manicured fingers reached out for it, I noticed he was wearing gold cuff links that were exact replicas of hundred dollar bills at one-eighth the size of the real McCoy. They must have been specially made. I wondered if that was legal.

"Look, Mr. Marley, I'm —"

"Harry. Please call me Harry, Ms. McGil."

He seemed friendly enough, but frankly I couldn't see myself on a first-name basis with anybody from the Treasury Department. After all, the IRS was a part of Treasury. I skipped the salutation altogether.

"I just want you to know I'm here against my better judgment. I respect the fact that Scotty thinks these are fake, but I'm hoping it's a false alarm."

"I would trust Scotty's judgment," he said, his big hands opening Marcie's envelope and withdrawing the bills.

He fanned them onto the table. "Eleven bills. All new style. Different serial numbers, all evenly spaced, all printed in the same ink color as the Treasury Seal, and with a statistically probable mix of issuing Reserve banks. One is torn in half. Interesting."

He took a marking pen and touched each bill in the upper left corner under the "100" engraving. I recognized the instrument as the same kind of stubby black pen used by retailers and banks to detect counterfeit bills — the very one Scotty and I had discussed last night.

He scooped up the stack of bills and looked at each one under the largest microscope behind his side of the table.

"Well?" I asked.

"These are definitely very good fakes, just as Scotty told you."

"How can you be so positive?"

"At this magnification, the saw-tooth points of the Federal Reserve and Treasury Seal aren't distinct and sharp like they are on real bills. With the ultra high-resolution copiers counterfeiters are using now, unless you look at one of these bills under a good microscope, you'll never spot that it's copied and not printed. Only the government prints money now."

"But color copiers won't copy money. You just get a black sheet."

His eyes fixed on mine. "I won't ask you how you know that, Miss McGil. But yes, you're right. We've er . . . persuaded the companies that manufacture the newest generation color copiers to include our special little sensor in their electronics that does not allow the machine to copy money or bearer bonds or negotiable instruments. Clever, don't you think?" Harry smiled.

I shuddered at the thought of government persuasion techniques. I pictured them waterboarding the CEO of Xerox.

"Much of this technology is, as you can well imagine, top-secret," Harry continued. "We try to stay ahead of the bad guys, and it's not easy. Desktop forgery is the fastest growing white-collar crime in America.

"We've already changed the design of our currency several times to add micro-printing and color-shifting ink. And we've embedded special polymer threads or fibers. If you look close at one of our new bills, you'll see the lines are embedded in the paper and not printed on the surface. That's one way to know it's not counterfeit."

I nodded, putting together the elements of counterfeiting, Ken and Marcie's deaths, high tech and the whole HI-Data circus.

"Right now, we're confiscating over a hundred million dollars a year."

"Wow." I mentally calculated the odds of my getting a counterfeit bill this year.

"The bad news is that some four billion dollars a year is being illegally dumped in the States through forgery and counterfeiting. With all the debt problems right now, we're bracing for even more this year. Overseas, where people aren't as familiar with U.S. currency as we are here, the problem is much worse."

"That's more than the total take from all the robberies that happened last year," I remarked, remembering statistics from a recent loss-prevention seminar I'd attended.

"Just the other day we confiscated $41 million in bogus U.S. dollars in a house in Bogota, Colombia," he said. "And while you might think that's a hell of a big seizure, I can assure you it's only a small fraction of the international counterfeiting industry.

"Now we've got to figure out exactly how this stuff was duplicated," he said. "These bills are so good, I'm thinking they came from computer technology much more sophisticated than a desktop scanner and personal computer setup. That's what we worry about here. A good computer setup could produce as much as the U.S. Mint and completely destroy international confidence in our money, especially when there's already a worldwide economic downturn."

After studying the bills in a comparison microscope, he snatched them out and inserted them under a bank of UV lights. Then he stood up and sighed.

"The boys in Washington will get us an exact answer." The furrow in his brow grew deeper. "These are so good they can defeat our best detection system and the newest system that Scotty is helping us perfect."

He didn't even notice his security gaff about Scotty's work. He pulled out a chair at the conference table and motioned me to sit down. He lit a cigar and smoke began to fill the room.

"These bills might be able to pass our new counterfeit detection system. We've got a real problem." Harry scowled as he puffed. "United States currency is used as a reserve currency by governments and businesses throughout the world. If the U.S. refuses to honor some of it, the whole system will collapse, and we'll see war and famine in less than a month."

More cigar smoke wafted across the table. I coughed but suspected it wasn't the right time for me to mention that this was a no smoking building.

FORTY-FOUR

So Scotty had been right — the money was funny. Ken was dead and Marcie was dead. Jeffrey had narrowly escaped being blown to bits, and someone might try again. HI-Data was in the middle of it all. I was certain Jeffrey Fere wasn't going to rest until he found out what was going on in his own company. Phil had often counseled me to remember that my client was the insurance company. The rule was that client confidentiality doesn't extend to protecting any illegal activity I might uncover during any given contractual arrangement. Clearly the counterfeiting was illegal, and on top of that, someone at HI-Data was trying to pull me into it. That really made me mad. Under these circumstances, I had no option except to tell Harry what Sparky had told me about Marcie's bank accounts and the offshore transactions.

Harry listened intently and made a series

of quick phone calls from the red phone in his office. When I mentioned Ken's "Safe-cracker" program and his rumored affair with Marcie, Harry's eyebrows lifted notice-ably. He asked me a lot of questions, only a few of which I could answer. Then he made another series of hurried calls.

Soon Harry Marley's printer and fax machine were spitting out pages of informa-tion on how many times Ken had been out of the country in the past two years, his destinations, the hotels he stayed in, and his credit card and phone records. Harry scanned each document faster than an Eve-lyn Wood speed-reader.

Other agents rushed in and out of Harry's office. Someone took me into an adjoining room where a chicken salad and a Diet Coke had been set out on a table. It was two thirty, and I was hungry. I ate quickly and hurried back to Harry's office but was stopped from entering by a T-woman who took my arm, escorted me nicely back to the adjoining room and told me to wait. I can't say I didn't try to hear what was going on in Harry's office, but the walls must have been soundproofed. It was after three when Harry Marley came in, alone.

"I'm taking you into my confidence for two reasons, Ms. McGil. First, you're Scotty's, er," he paused a shade too long, " 'friend,' and because of that, I trust you. Secondly, I think you are in danger. Scotty told me about your brake line being severed. You need to know a few things, but you can't repeat them. I trust I will never have cause to regret this."

He paused, expecting an affirmative answer. But I'm not so good at predicting the future, so I stayed silent, which he might have taken for assent.

"We've noticed a distinct pattern in Ken Gordon's travels. He's made repeated trips to Middle-Eastern and South American countries," Harry said. "We suspect he might be using key contacts with scientific communities in some of these countries — contacts made during the Gulf War when HI-Data helped develop some classified technology. Our best guess scenario is that Ken may have sold them some of HI-Data's export-restricted technology, the kind of sophisticated technology needed for this kind of high-level counterfeiting."

"So now these countries are using that technology to dump American currency all over the world to solve their own hard currency problems," I commented.

"Right. Using intelligence systems as distribution systems, this bogus currency will flood the international market. On top of the current economic downturn, the banking system would be destroyed and we'd have a world-wide depression."

One salient fact Harry didn't mention was that someone else at HI-Data had to be in on the plot. The someone who had killed Ken and Marcie and had tried to kill Jeffrey Fere. The same someone who had slashed my brake line and tried to kill me, too. Could John Olson/Dan Karton be involved in the counterfeiting scheme as well as industrial espionage? Norman naturally sprang to mind. As Security Chief, he would have had to know what was going on.

While Harry was telling me as much as "they" wanted me to know, other agents came in and out of the room, sharing notes, quick conversations, and cell phone calls with Harry. A female agent I'd heard Harry call Miss Gottardo came in a third time and handed Harry a paper. It was stamped "Urgent and Confidential." I leaned toward Harry to read more, but he initialed it and gave it back to Miss Gottardo so fast I wasn't able to see anything else.

When my cell phone rang, Harry's eyebrows did that up and down thing again, and he peered at me while I pulled the phone out of my purse and checked the number.

"Who is it?" he asked.

I didn't recognize the number. I shrugged my shoulders in the universal don't know sign. He grabbed the phone, jotted down the number and gave the paper to Miss Gottardo, who flew out of the room to do whatever it is they do to have it checked.

Harry handed it back to me. "Answer it."

"Hello. This is DD McGil."

"Good afternoon, Miss McGil. George Murray here."

"George, how'd you get this number?"

"Oh, lass, your Auntie told me. I am here standing at the O'Hare Airport International Terminal having arrived only a few moments ago."

Harry Marley grabbed my arm. "George who?"

I covered the mouthpiece. "It's George Murray from Scotland. He's my Auntie's um . . . putative fiancé."

Harry Marley's shoulders dropped. He slumped back in his chair, visibly relaxed. "Go ahead." He waved his right hand at me then went back to his paperwork.

"Wow. That was fast. Do you want me to pick you up?"

"Aye, that would be excellent, lass. I'm of a mind we should work as two together to get your Auntie's things back."

"I'm in a meeting, but I'll be there as soon as I can."

I hung up after he'd given me his airline details and agreed to stay put until I arrived.

After asking me a few more questions, Harry said I could leave. He handed me my coat, pursed his lips and frowned. "Miss McGil, this is important. Do not return to HI-Data under any circumstances. It's for your own protection. Remember your brake line. They've tried once already, and we don't know yet what direction this is taking."

By the time I left, it was already getting dark and the street musician was long gone. People were rushing to avoid exposure to the falling temperatures.

I struggled to comprehend what Harry Marley had told me. I didn't doubt there was a counterfeit ring at HI-Data, but I still didn't know who was behind it. Possibly Harry's cautions were more about his internal agency damage control than about my safety. I hoped so. I was determined to deliver my completed reports on the trainees by Friday. If I didn't, I wouldn't get paid. I needed that fee, so I made up my mind to finish the reports, send them over by courier, and collect it.

FORTY-FIVE

On the trip to O'Hare Airport to pick up George Murray, I sunk deeper into a black mood, thinking of Auntie's stolen treasures. She was so proud of them, and she would blame me for losing them. The world was closing in on me. I felt powerless. And like all Scots, that's the one thing I really hate. I could feel that headache coming back with a vengeance. I hoped George Murray would be able to help, otherwise he might as well forget about getting Auntie to canoodle. And I might as well forget about life itself. La Dragon would kill me.

This was, technically, my second trip to O'Hare today, and I couldn't help remembering Scotty's lingering good-bye kiss. That only sunk me deeper into the black dog blues.

I had no trouble spotting George Murray. Auntie's description of him had been ac- curate — six-foot-three, slim build, distinguished grey hair, no glasses, and an irresistible smile. Auntie must have told him to watch for my little Miata, because he was waving furiously to attract my attention.

When I pulled to the curb, he opened the passenger door and tossed a piece of Gucci luggage into the small space behind the seat. "Greetings, lassie," he said cheerily as he got in with an economy of movement that rivaled an athlete. The only trouble was, he sat right on my purse. I pulled it hastily out from under him and tossed it into the back seat, hoping it would stay closed and not spill all over.

He smiled mischievously as we formally shook hands. "You're as bonny indeed as your dear Auntie advertised. An' your little bitty of an automobile, too."

I couldn't read him yet, so I wasn't sure whether his assessment had accorded me a good grade or a bad one. He didn't look like he'd just gotten off an overseas flight — his clothing was crisp and neat and his true blue eyes twinkled madly.

"I came here straightaway. Not a one in my office knows my whereabouts. I thought t'was best to keep it secret so as to come upon Jock unexpectedly."

George Murray flashed a Cheshire Cat grin. What else could I do but like the guy?

Maybe he did have that certain *je ne sais quoi* it would take to tame La Dragon.

George said he hadn't spent much time in the United States recently, and he wanted to make up for that. But, he said, that would have to wait because he was anxious to take care of "the Jack McSweeney matter" immediately. I was happy to oblige. The sooner we tackled this, the sooner I'd be either free or dead. So I told him everything that had happened with the Burns fiasco, explaining in more detail the Santa Claus caper, Tom Joyce's involvement to authenticate the objects, the attack on me at the bookstore, and the piece of cashmere coat Wolfie had obtained as evidence.

George cocked his head to the right and listened intently. He said he was glad no one had gotten badly injured and questioned why I needed to check the authenticity of the artifacts. "Since I told your dear Auntie it was the real thing, then such it was. No doubt aboot it," he pronounced.

I guessed that in his world, his word was indeed his bond. He then asked me to call Tom on my cell phone.

I reached into the back to get it from my battered purse. The Miata unexpectedly changed a lane while I was struggling, and I was grateful for George's quick hand on the wheel. We both ignored the horn of the car behind.

Tom answered on the first ring. I told him about George and explained the connection between the bit of cashmere coat Wolfie had bitten off and George's associate, Jack McSweeney. Then I gave the phone to George who asked Tom if he and Wolfie would meet us as soon as possible at his firm's Chicago apartment in Harbor Point. He gave Tom instructions on how to get Wolfie into the building.

"I hope together we can get Jack McSweeney to settle this Burns affair today for once and all," George explained, "but I need you and Wolfie there t'a make sure it happens."

On the northern edge of Grant Park, we pulled into the underground parking for Harbor Point Condominiums. This fifty-four-floor high-rise bordered North Lake Shore Drive and East Randolph Street. I knew the building well. The firm of one of my attorney friends also kept a condo here. Almost a year ago I'd been corralled into attending a fancy cocktail party where I got a firsthand look at all the building's amenities including the hospitality rooms and hot tub. To be frank, some of us had had a bit too much to drink and proceeded to take off our clothes and get rowdy in the big hot tub. Their crackerjack security team finally tracked us down moon bathing on the outdoor sun deck and summarily evicted us. I thought that statistics were against the same security team being on duty today. Anyway, I had all my clothes on, so even if they were on duty, they probably wouldn't recognize me. I took a deep breath, played dumb about the building's layout, and was careful not to share any of these details with George.

In the elevator riding up to the 42nd floor, I fiddled awkwardly with the broken purse strap, trying to keep everything from falling out. I made a mental note to have it repaired.

As George took out his keys, he explained that their firm's unit was one edge of the building's triangle with a spectacular view of Lake Michigan that amazed him each time he visited. " 'Tis verra different from Edinburgh," he said with a suddenly strong brogue. "She's a grand city an' the capital of Scotland since 1437. Most of her structures are Medieval, some Georgian, an' we're opposed ta skyscrapers."

He turned the key in the lock, and we burst into the apartment without knocking or otherwise announcing our presence. For a moment, I imagined I could hear the faint sound of the bagpipes at Bannockburn.

FORTY-SIX

Jack McSweeney turned as we entered, spilling some liquid from the cocktail glass he was holding. For only an instant his narrow eyes got narrower, and I knew in my heart he'd been my attacker. And he knew I knew.

"George," he said and nodded to us. "What a nice surprise."

Yeah, I thought. *A nice surprise for us but not so nice for you, Mr. fake Santa Claus.*

"Aye, I'm sure 'tis," George said enigmatically as he doffed his coat in the tastefully furnished foyer. He didn't introduce me as I followed him into the enormous living room. The far wall had a curving ceiling-to-floor window bay with a magnificent view of Navy Pier.

"I did not know you were here in America," McSweeney said. A deep furrow appeared between his brows. "Why didn't you tell me? An' who's this, pray tell?"

As if you don't know, I thought but didn't

say as I felt the burning in my sore shoulder. This was George's game, and I was going to play it his way, at least for now.

"You well know who the lass is, Jock. And you know why I'm here as well. 'Tis enough trouble you've devised already. Dinna make it worse. I'm here to collect those Burns treasures you stole from her."

"I stole nothing. Are you mad? Why believe what this lassie may say. I'm your partner, an' don't forget it."

"Stop your tarradiddle and go fetch the treasures. Let's have done with it."

The two Scots faced off inches apart in the elegant apartment. George was the taller, but Jack the cockier. His chin jutted out in defiance as he walked over to the wall of windows and peered out.

In the ensuing silence, George paced the floor while I checked out the antique furnishings throughout the rooms. From watching *Antiques Roadshow,* I was able to identify a few American furniture gems thanks to the Keno brothers. In the foyer there was what looked like a Sheraton Federal mahogany card table I'm sure they would have loved to appraise. I also spotted what might be a Chippendale cherry chest-on-chest, and I'd have enjoyed their evaluation of the two pieces and whether they belonged together or were faked.

Everything was in very good taste. In another room were two roundabout chairs with pleasing yellow cushions along with an imposing Philadelphia secretaire with maple, mahogany, and white pine veneers. I was definitely impressed. A collection of portrait miniatures was arranged on one wall. Opposite was a stunning portrait of a woman by Sir Joshua Reynolds. The woman looked a bit like my Aunt Elizabeth, but I knew that couldn't be. The painter, after all, had died somewhere in the 1790s.

George Murray was opening and closing each of the drawers on a pretty walnut lowboy in the foyer. Then he pulled the piece away from the wall and walked around it. He got very red in the face and glared at Jock.

"Do ye take me for a fool, man? This is not the same William & Mary lowboy that was once here. You've done a switch, an' you know that's so on your mother's grave."

Jack McSweeney said nothing.

"This piece doesn'a have its original engraved cotter pin brasses."

McSweeney still said nothing.

"Come out with the truth, Jack. Yer taken for it."

"You're saying he switched pieces?" I

walked over to examine the lowboy, not that I would know, but I was curious. "You're saying he substituted a copy for the real William and Mary?"

"Aye, my girl. And he's aboot to reveal the whereabouts of the original."

I eyed McSweeney, who kept silent.

"What other pieces have you looted then?" George asked, as he carefully checked various pieces of furniture.

"Here, this is no the Hepplewhite table." George lifted its leaves. "Those legs look auld, but see, there's no tapered beaded edge, like the table that I myself put here."

The table was beautiful. It sure had fooled me. Apparently Jack McSweeney was guilty of more than stealing the Burns artifacts. He was suddenly no longer the trusted business partner but rather the counterfeit friend who was now the foe.

Meanwhile McSweeney said nothing. He pulled open a drawer of the Philadelphia secretaire and drew out a gun.

"George," I yelled.

McSweeney raised his arm and pointed the gun directly at me.

"Jock," George said softly, "put down that infernal weapon."

"That I cannot do," McSweeney said. "Sadly this has gone too far, an' there's no putting the genie back in the bottle."

"You're a damned fool, a coward, an ass, and a madman," George shouted and backed away toward the front door. "Don't do anything foolish."

McSweeney waved the gun at me and called to George, "Stop where you are or you force me to hurt this lass."

George had backed up against the door and could go no further.

"Why are ye doing this to me Jack Mc-Sweeney?" George asked. "I an' my family have been good to you an' yours through the years."

McSweeney turned from me and pointed the gun at George.

"If I'd not been looking after myself, I'd be nowhere today," he snarled. "Them that comes first is served first. You live in the past, George Murray. An' if I hadn't done this to you, someone else soon would have. Coin is the key, and there's money in antiques today."

"I'll let all that go, Jack. Mayhap you've been in America too long, and it's addled your brain for greed. Now tell me, where are those Burns artifacts? You'll be having to give them up."

"Not if I do away with the both of ye. I'm guessing no one knows you're here."

Ohmygod, he was right. At this moment, I could have used a wee dram of Auntie's Highland nectar. I almost said so, too. We weren't doing too well with George taking the lead. Maybe it was time for me to try my hand.

I swung my purse at McSweeney with all my strength and my Scots will. Unfortunately, the purse barely landed a glancing blow before it fell at his feet. All it did was alert him to the fact that I was on the move. He rushed me and got me in a chokehold with his left arm round my throat. What was worse, he hit my head with the gun. It hurt and caught a strand of my hair on its icy barrel. I was woozy from the blow.

"Stand still," McSweeney ordered as he shook me with great force. I lost my balance and scrambled to keep my feet under me. "Come here George. Right now, or I pull the trigger."

He pressed the gun hard against my temple and increased the pressure on the chokehold. I could barely breathe. I shut my eyes. Everything started to swirl. I saw only the colors red and black. No pictures of my life passing by, no people I had known and loved, just a big smear of red and black, like a bad Jackson Pollock abstract painting. I knew what that meant. Yes, I was scared, and I was probably about to faint. But I was also mad — Scots mad — and, like Auntie Dragon, that spells trouble. I wasn't about to go down easy, so I kicked Mc-Sweeney in the shin. He jumped back and slightly loosened his chokehold.

Just then the doorbell rang. I could feel McSweeney's body tense. I opened my eyes, gasped for air and saw George, in a lightning-quick move, yank open the apartment door. Wolfie and Tom Joyce stood in the hall. Wolfie took one look at Jack Mc-Sweeney and charged, head down, tail down, and teeth bared.

Good Wolfie, I thought. *Good boy. Eat him alive.*

Wolfie circled McSweeney, showing his big teeth and emitting a horrible deep growl.

"Get this cursed dog out of here or I'll shoot it," McSweeney ordered as Wolfie ducked his head farther, moving it from side to side like a cobra. Saliva dripped from his muzzle and his eyes were riveted on Jack McSweeney. I think Wolfie could already taste him.

"He's not a dog," Tom shouted from the doorway. "He's a wolf. And he's been waiting to meet you again. You remember my bookstore?" As Tom closed the door, Wolfie growled again menacingly, like he understood what Tom was saying.

I was ecstatic to see Tom and Wolfie, but worried that McSweeney was going to shoot us all. I could feel the clammy sweat on his arms as he pulled me closer.

"Call him off now or he's a dead wolf."

I shook myself violently, trying to get Mc-Sweeney to loosen his chokehold, but it didn't work. His grip tightened, and he yanked my hair so hard I nearly fainted. Then I realized he wasn't pulling my hair on purpose. He was trying to point the gun at Wolfie, but it had caught in my hair, and he couldn't get it free. The more he pulled, the more I screamed in pain, and the more that agitated Wolfie.

Suddenly McSweeney yowled. He jerked and lifted a leg, shifting his weight. Wolfie must have bitten him. I seized the moment and stomped McSweeney's other foot with my high heel. He yelled again and doubled over. I felt that satisfied feeling when you've hit your target, but it quickly disappeared when McSweeney ripped out a big clump of my hair as he jerked the gun free.

Wolfie sprang up and knocked the gun from McSweeney's hand. It flew across the room, and Tom Joyce picked it up.

Wolfie attacked again. His big jaws closed on McSweeney's right arm just above the hand. Blood appeared on the carpet. I watched silently as McSweeney turned a pasty white and sweat dripped from his forehead. His knees gave way, and he sunk to the floor. He was groaning and yelling for Wolfie to let go, but Wolfie held tight. It must have been very painful. I wouldn't have wanted to be Jack McSweeney right now for anything in this world.

I breathed deeply a few times to get my equilibrium, but I was weak and dizzy. I sank down onto the carpet. My eyes were watering, and the top of my head hurt something fierce. I gingerly touched my scalp and came away with blood and a handful of my hair that his damn gun had torn out at the roots.

"Look at this." I threw the clump of hair in McSweeney's direction. "See what you've done?"

"There's some blonde hairs on the barrel, too," Tom Joyce pointed out, holding up the gun.

"Shit. I'm gonna be bald!" I wanted to kick McSweeney in the groin, but things were still a bit swirly, and I couldn't seem to stand up to accomplish my desire.

"He's got to pay for this," I said. "Let Wolfie eat him." I pointed at McSweeney and yelled, "You played the evil Santa; you tossed my office; and you almost killed me by tampering with my brakes!"

"I never touched your car. I swear it," McSweeney moaned.

"Ha. As if I'd believe anything you have to say."

Tom Joyce looked at my bleeding scalp. "This looks pretty awful. Are you going to be okay?"

"What's okay?"

"Don't get existential on me, DD."

Tom didn't call off Wolfie. Instead, we watched George Murray, who'd seated himself at the Philadelphia Secretaire. He took out some paper and a pen and began furiously writing. Naturally I was curious, but I was in too much pain to get up and look over his shoulder.

The room was silent, except for McSweeney who continued to moan while George continued to write. It was a strange tableau with Wolfie playing the starring role. The only things moving were George's pen hand, the blood slowly dripping from Jack McSweeney's arm onto the rug, and Wolfie's tail.

Tom Joyce was studying various pieces of antique furniture and art throughout the apartment. I knew part of his business was valuing wealthy Chicago North Shore estates. In his work, Tom had seen a variation of just about everything beautiful and expensive there is to see in this world.

George finally stopped writing, put down his pen, and approached Jack McSweeney who was now groaning and cursing but lying very still with Wolfie's jaws tightly clasped on his arm.

"Now, tell us all where the Burns artifacts are. As soon as you do, I'll have Tom here call off the wolf."

McSweeney stopped moaning and fell silent.

"If you'll no tell, Mr. Tom will let Master Wolfie have as many bites of your hide as he wants, and I'll phone up the constables. But if you give me the treasures straightaway, then you may sign this paper. If you do, I'll not bring in the law, and there's an end to it."

"You'll call off this beast?" McSweeney managed to ask.

"Aye." George nodded at Tom.

"And you'll not turn me in?"

"Aye," George agreed.

"What paper?"

"This." He held up the paper he'd written at the desk. "It says in essence that you are herewith today selling me all your shares and interest in the firm of Murray and Mc-

Sweeney in consideration of one dollar and for other good and valuable considerations."

"What?" McSweeney sputtered. He tried to stand, but Wolfie shook his arm, growled, and reasserted his bite. I could see Wolfie's front canine disappear up to the gum into McSweeney's sleeve and the arm it contained. It must have hurt like hell. McSweeney fell back onto the rug and whimpered, "You canna strip me of my partnership in the firm."

"You were my partner, but you're a liar and a cheat. And now comes your due."

"Those artifacts are worth much more than you charged your precious Elizabeth. Anything to do with Rabbie Burns is worth a fortune. Why will you not listen to me?"

" 'Twas my decision to make, and so I told you. It's done. Now tell me where the objects are and sign this paper or go to jail and go to hell. 'Tis your own choice."

"You canna do this. It isn't legal."

" 'Twill be perfectly legal. And the lass and laddie here will witness it's not being done under duress." George smiled broadly and winked.

"I can do more than be a witness," Tom Joyce interjected. "I'm a notary." Tom reached into a pocket of his sports coat and took out his notary stamp, waving it for all to see.

"He never leaves home without it," I muttered, cracking a thin smile.

"Let's proceed," George urged. "You've already lost considerable blood, so now's the time to tell me where to find the precious objects."

"All right. You've won. They're in the safe. Let me up. I'll get them."

"No. Stay as you are. I dinna trust you a whit."

George nodded at Tom. "Stay with him," he said and walked to a library to the left of the living room where, I assumed, the safe was located.

I was curious and wondered if the firm of Murray and McSweeney had installed the newest, most up-to-date wall safe technology. Being Scots, I had no idea what model they might have chosen. Most people were funny, I'd found in my line of work. They always insisted they wanted the best, but they weren't willing to pay for it. So in most multi-million dollar homes and businesses, the security wall safe was not the Cadillac model and it was not going to do the job. With the right tools and a little time, a safecracker can usually get inside it.

George returned, interrupting my ruminations.

"It doesn't open," he announced, shaking his head.

He helped me struggle to my feet. I was still woozy and my head still throbbed where the gun had practically scalped me, but otherwise I was clearheaded. We went into the spacious library that was filled with books and interesting maps and a spectacular collection of glass paperweights.

The safe, an A-1 Quality BF Series, was in the left-hand wall. I recognized it from one of my insurance seminars. George's firm had not gone with a two-bit model that any Tom, Dick or Harry could have his way with. It was a very respectable safe, close to the top of the line, and professionally, I was glad to see they'd opted for the more expensive combination of both burglary and fire. The outside wall was undamaged, the keypad looked normal, and I saw nothing that looked suspicious. I related my conclusions to George.

"I'll try it yet again," he said and began to type in the combination.

"Stop!" I yelled and pulled his arm from the keypad. "Don't enter those numbers again. I just remembered that this model has a built-in alarm that goes off if you try the wrong combination four times or more. How many times have you already tried it?"

"Lass, I'd forgotten that feature. This last try would have set it off. Thankfully you are indeed as canny as your Aunt Elizabeth declared."

"I would guess your ex-partner changed the combination, and that's why you can't open it. That's not hard to do on this model with its electronic keypad lock."

"You're probably right. Come on, lass. We'll have Master Wolfie persuade him to give us the new numbers."

I agreed Wolfie was the key. We weren't going to be able to bypass the electronic lock unless we got the new combination through coercion. Computer hacking would take more time and more skill than I had. We'd need a lot of luck to break down Jack McSweeney. We Scots credit the ancient superstitions, so I crossed my fingers as we walked back to the living room.

Forty-Seven

Wolfie was still in the classic attack stance — back arched and legs apart, and he'd maintained a solid bite-hold on Jock's arm. More blood had pooled on the beige carpet under McSweeney's arm. I wondered how he could stand the pain.

"You've not been forthcoming. I'm heartily disappointed. Did ye think I'm not clever enough to think of the alarm?" George gave me a quick wink.

"No police'll be rushing in to save the day for you. Give me the new combination, or Wolfie here will be havin' another taste of your crooked hide. I don't know if he'll start with your face or your groin, but whichever, I'm sure he'll get to both. An' it looks like he's right ready."

"Oh. I forgot about changing the combination," McSweeney muttered. "T'was an oversight on my part."

Yeah, I thought — *a really big fat clever*

oversight that almost paid off big time for you.

Wolfie uttered a feral wolf noise and shook Jack's arm back and forth. It was primeval and gave me the goose bumps. McSweeney's eyes closed, and he whimpered.

"And the new combination 'tis . . . ?" George prompted.

"6-3-9-4-2- . . . 7. Now call off the beast."

"All in good time. First I'm going to try these numbers. If it does not work and the alarm goes off, we'll all swear we found you pilfering the safe. You and you alone will be the culprit. You pulled the gun. Wolfie here saved our lives. Can you understand the consequences to your own self if these are no the right numbers?"

McSweeney was silent. His eyes were closed. I wondered if he'd passed out. George motioned for me to accompany him back to the safe.

"Wait," McSweeney called us back. He opened his eyes but didn't otherwise move. "I — I may have given it wrong. It's 6-3-9-4-2-8."

"Och, for all our sakes it had better be," George said as we returned to the safe and entered the new digits on the keypad. We both held our breath as he turned the knob. The safe door opened and inside lay the precious red leather case.

George took it to a nearby library table and opened it. I clapped when I saw the ornate Ormolu casket inset with the initials "KB." We now knew without doubt that the evil Santa had been Jack McSweeney.

George gently removed the casket, set it down and opened it, revealing the double sheet of letter paper and under it the leather pouch. He unfolded the paper with his fingertips and then took out all the glass to see that everything was undamaged. He carefully avoided touching the glass itself. We saw again the words of Robert Burns, and I knew Auntie would be happy.

Here Stuarts once in triumph reign'd;
And laws for Scotland's weal ordain'd;
But now unroof'd their palace stands,
Their sceptre's fall'n to other hands;
Fallen indeed, and to the earth,
Whence grovelling reptiles take their birth.
The injur'd Stuart line are gone,
A Race outlandish fill their throne;
An idiot race, to honor lost;
Who know them best despise them most.

"Did Auntie tell you about the secret compartment we found?"

"Aye, that she did." George said as he felt around, opened it and extracted the paper

I'd found a few days ago. "An' to think I myself never tumbled to it."

"I'll send Tom in here to look everything over," I said, and did so.

I took the unnecessary precaution of holding the gun on McSweeney until both George and Tom returned. They were nodding and smiling, and I knew I could again face Auntie now that the treasures were safe. True, as Robert Burns wrote, things "gang aft agley," but this time I'd live to see another day. I sat down and held my head. Things were a bit blurred.

George took the gun, dumped it in his pocket and Tom called off Wolfie. Despite my fog, I did see blood drops falling from McSweeney's hand as he struggled up.

George gave him a towel to stop the bleeding, then we all gathered around the big desk. George shoved a pen at McSweeney and asked me if I had a dollar bill. I unearthed my purse from under a chair, found one and gave it to him.

"Thank yee, lass, as I have no U.S. currency yet." He handed the dollar to McSweeney. "Now sign this and here's a dollar to complete the transaction."

I witnessed the contract, and Tom notarized it and affixed his stamp.

George ordered McSweeney to hand over

his keys and wallet. McSweeney wasn't going to comply, but when Wolfie snarled, he tossed his Prada keyring on the desk. George removed the company car key, gave it back to McSweeney, then dumped the rest of the keys into a desk drawer.

"You can drive to the airport and purchase yourself a plane ticket to anywhere. Leave the car there afore midnight, and I'll have it picked up. If you don't, at midnight I'll call the police and report it stolen.

"Now your wallet, if you please." George held out his hand until McSweeney gave up his black crocodile leather wallet embossed with the Prada logo. McSweeney had a taste for expensive accessories, albeit Italian rather than Scots made. The fact Scots don't manufacture designer wallets is its own brand of irony.

George went through the wallet and removed the cards and identification associated with the firm. He returned the wallet and told McSweeney, "Afore you're out of this building, I intend to notify Edinburgh you're gone from the firm. You're under a cloud, an' if I e'er see you again, you'll be arrested. I'll be changin' the name of the firm, and under no circumstances will you ever again enter the premises."

"George, I . . ."

"Say no more. 'Tis final. An' every lock'll be changed in this apartment, too. Now leave and ne'er again show your face. You're through — here and in Scotland."

As McSweeney struggled into his cashmere coat, we all could see the missing chunk of fabric that Wolfie had removed the other night. He paused in the doorway and glared at George.

"This isn't over yet," he threatened. "You an' yours will regret doing this to me and mine."

Tom pushed him into the corridor. "If it's a blood feud you want, it'll be between you and Wolfie here. Right, Wolfie?"

Wolfie made that primeval noise deep in his throat. I think he wanted another piece of cashmere as a trophy. Again I was glad I wasn't Jack McSweeney.

FORTY-EIGHT

Tom and Wolfie left shortly thereafter with a promise to meet tomorrow night at my mother's house to celebrate New Year's Eve. Auntie still didn't know George was in Chicago, and George wanted to surprise her for the New Year. Tom and I agreed it would be fun to return her Burns artifacts at the party where he could meet Auntie and personally confirm their authenticity.

As he left, Tom whispered to me, "Perhaps this isn't the best time to say this, DD, but some pieces of George's American furniture collection in here are definitely not the genuine articles. That lowboy in the foyer, for instance, is nice, but it isn't a genuine William & Mary. I'm no expert of course, but . . ."

"Thanks, Tom. I think he already knows," I whispered back.

I was still woozy, but my spirits had lifted so much after getting the Burns artifacts back, that I wasn't feeling much pain. Probably later I would regret it, but I agreed to stay and help George accomplish all the steps to remove Jack McSweeney from the firm. While George managed the communications with Scotland and the New York office, I worked with the building manager and building security to eliminate any trace of Mr. Jack McSweeney in the building's lease and from any position of official communication from the firm. We drafted a new lease minus Mr. McSweeney, we got the locks changed, inserted a new security code, provided a revised list of persons allowed in the apartment, got new key cards, etc., etc. Due to 9/11 rules and regulations, there was more paperwork to fill out than Dr. Johnson required to create his first dictionary.

When I had done all I could do on security, George had still more work to do, despite the difference in the time zones. So I made my farewell and grabbed my purse, which fell to the floor. Frank's file spilled out. I was jolted seeing it again, but I scooped everything up, carefully put the Burns objects in it, and left for home.

FORTY-NINE

Cavalier was meowing as I unlocked the door. He sniffed me from head to toe, no doubt smelling Wolfie. I tried to explain about the wolf and teased him a bit with his favorite flying bird toy, but I knew he'd be jealous for days.

I couldn't get Frank's file out of my mind. Auntie would have said it was an omen, falling out of my purse like that. So I sat down and opened it again. Maybe this time I could bring myself to look at the autopsy report.

I took a deep breath and forced myself to open it. The autopsy protocol cataloged Frank's clothing and described the body. The details were all straightforward. His ring wasn't listed here, either. I shuddered, picturing Frank's body lying there just as it had that night he died.

The internal examination and toxicology reports indicated the uncontrolled fall had caused massive damage to Frank's heart, liver, and lungs. No drugs had been detected, and no cancer, either.

He'd suffered eggshell depressed-type fractures of the head and other numerous contusions, all described and diagrammed. It was difficult to imagine all these wounds on the body of the man I had so loved and admired.

Then I read something that made me catch my breath. It was a reference to a small surface contusion 31/2 cm. wide by 2 cm. long on the back of Frank's head on the left side, and it did not make sense. The report noted that this contusion had occurred prior to death.

As far as I knew, Frank had no bruise on the back of his head when I left him to go shopping. And he couldn't have gotten such a bruise from the fall because he'd landed on his face. I re-checked the report to verify the other bruises were on the front of his body, all clearly consistent with his fall.

I closed my eyes, and the world stopped turning for an instant. Something wasn't right. Why hadn't the coroner or the damn cops followed up on this? My hatred for them was so real I could taste it. But I hated myself even more for having lacked the courage to look at this report earlier.

The only conclusion possible was that Frank had somehow hit the back of his head before he went over the balcony. Had it been an accident, or had someone hit him? I thought of Ken's corpse wearing Frank's family ring, and I knew my suspicions that Ken was involved were right. I told myself that if I could prove Frank had not committed suicide, maybe I'd start sleeping again at night. But why would Ken have wanted to kill Frank? And how was I ever going to prove murder when Ken, my prime suspect, was already dead?

I put away the file. I had a sick feeling about what had really happened to Frank and about what was going on at HI-Data. I wanted desperately to talk things over with Scotty, but the time difference tonight made that impossible.

My head was really throbbing where McSweeney had torn out the hair, so I grabbed a couple aspirins, washed them down with some Wild Turkey and soda and jumped into bed, too tired to undress. Cavvy had forgiven me enough to climb in, too. He pressed tight against me, exuding his special brand of kitty comfort. I immediately fell into a deep sleep.

FIFTY

Something woke me. I opened my eyes.

"I've been waiting, but can wait no longer."

It was Jack McSweeney. He was holding a butcher knife.

"It's full daylight now. I admit, lass, you looked so fine lying there I was tempted to take my pleasure wi' you. But there's other business more important."

"What are you doing here? You're supposed to be on the plane to Scotland," I said stupidly.

"An' did you think all was finished wi' me? No. I have scores to settle. And above all I must have those Burns relics."

"What?"

"An' you're goin' to help me get them." He leaned closer. His eyes glistened, and he looked haggard. He hadn't shaved, and he wore the same bloody clothes from yesterday. For that matter, I was wearing what I had worn yesterday, too. Suddenly all of yesterday's bruises were screaming at me. I felt like a pinned-down butterfly. I tried to twist away and get up, but he jammed the chef's knife to my throat.

"Stay still. Don't move. I'm a bit unsteady with this arm, as you can well imagine."

I froze.

"What are you going to do to me?"

"I'm goin' to let you up, lass, but slowly. Come out this side. I don't want to use this knife unless I have to."

I lurched and rolled to the opposite side of the bed. I was on my feet in an instant. We were at a stand-off — facing each other across the expanse of the bed.

Jack McSweeney let out a yell and leaped across the bed in one jump, like Liam Neeson in that *Rob Roy* movie. I had underestimated him. I had nowhere to go except a corner. I dodged and pivoted to get leverage to toss him over my hip, an Aikido move I'd learned from Sensei. But Cavalier, in his idea of a rescue attempt, ran between my legs, and I lost my balance. Sensei's classes never included wayward cats or narrow aisles between beds and walls.

Jack McSweeney kicked Cavvy and slashed at me.

I screamed. Cavvy squealed and retreated

out of the room.

McSweeney grabbed my arm, held it behind my back, and put the knife to my throat. I could feel the sharp sting as it broke the skin. He shifted his weight so I had no chance to throw him. Now I was in real trouble.

"Leave my cat alone, dammit. How'd you get in here anyway?"

"Never mind aboot that now. I want those Burns things. I've got to sell 'em."

"You can't get away with this. George will stop any sale you try to make."

"I've no need to use the open market. I've got a buyer who'll pay a king's ransom. T'will set me up again. Otherwise my life's in a ruin. Now where are my objects?"

"I don't know."

"Has Murray got them? Has he giv'n them to your Auntie?" With each question he sliced a little deeper into my neck.

I yelled as warm blood streamed down my back.

I began to feel faint from the pain and yesterday's exertions. I found myself being dragged toward the kitchen.

"You're not gonna pass out. I dinna cut that deep." He pushed me down the corridor to my kitchen where he grabbed a dish towel hanging near the sink. He wet it and slapped me across the face with it. I grabbed the towel and held it to my slashed neck.

Clearly he knew the route to my kitchen — he must have taken in the lay of the land before he woke me. What kind of a watch-cat was Cavvy, anyway? Then I saw the empty space in my block of Henckel's knives. I briefly wondered what the statistics were of being stabbed by your own knife.

The towel stopped the bleeding, but my neck was painful and throbbing. I broke into a sweat, but determined I wasn't going to give this bastard anything. He forced me back into the living room where my coat lay on the sofa and told me to get dressed.

Cavvy, still under an adjacent chair, peeked out at the scene.

I wrapped my scarf around my neck, over the wet kitchen towel.

"We'll go see your Auntie. She won't want ta see you hurt. Mind, I'll keep you as hostage till I get what's mine."

"I'm feeling weak," I told him, which I really was, but I was also trying to buy time.

"Get into your coat and take a few deep breaths. 'Tis not my intent to kill you un-less I have to."

Somehow I didn't believe him. I figured he was going to kill me anyway. I remembered his threats of yesterday. Why involve Auntie?

I struggled into my coat and automatically picked up my purse. Too late, I remembered that the Burns artifacts were in it.

"You must know I'm desperate. Now let's be off. I know the way. I've been there afore."

I knew I couldn't let him get to Auntie. The Dragon marched to her own drummer and McSweeney would kill her for sure. She didn't even know he'd stolen the Burns artifacts from me. She'd make big trouble, and she'd get hurt for sure. I had to think, but I felt woozy again.

"Let's go," he ordered. His voice was fading as he pulled me toward the door. The pain in my neck was sharp. My knees were wobbly, and Cavvy's little shining eyes under the chair were blurring into a black mist that was rising. As he opened the door, I took a deep breath and then another, forcing myself to remember that Scots never faint.

FIFTY-ONE

McSweeney jerked open the door and was suddenly confronted by a woman just preparing to knock. It was Sparky. Dimly I wondered what she was doing here.

McSweeney's hand darted out, grabbed Sparky's coat, and he pulled her in. He kicked the door shut and raised the knife, confronting her. I watched through a haze, unable to do anything.

Suddenly the arm Sparky had been holding stiffly at her side came up. She had a gun. She fired once, then again as Jack McSweeney toppled slowly to the floor. This is some dream I'm having, I thought distantly and wondered if I was in more or less trouble now than I'd been in before.

FIFTY-TWO

"Let's go," Sparky ordered. She held the gun in my back and pushed me out the door so hard I was moving on sheer momentum. We headed toward the back door of my building.

"Hurry up," she said, opening the door and shoving me into the alley. The cold wind hit me, but it didn't help at all.

"Stop right here," she ordered as we approached a car with its motor running and the trunk open.

I wanted to run, but my legs wouldn't work. Sparky tipped me into the trunk and closed the lid before I could react. The cold wetness of the bloody towel around my neck was suffocating. I closed my eyes. The last thing I realized before I passed out was that I was lying on top of Auntie's precious treasures in my purse, and I wondered how Sparky knew I had them.

FIFTY-THREE

Off in the distance, Sparky was calling me. It got closer and louder, and I realized I was very cold and my neck was hurting.

"Come on, get out," Sparky tugged my coat. "We have some things to do, so don't try to fake a faint."

I had a flash of Sparky shooting Jack Mc-Sweeney without a word, and I sunk even deeper into the trunk. Just that movement made me dizzy. I was still not sure whether this was real or a dream.

Sparky lifted my legs over the top of the trunk then jerked me out. I stood unsteadily, the bitter wind penetrating my clothes and chilling me to the bone. As Sparky slammed down the trunk, I realized my purse with the treasures was still in there.

I began to shiver uncontrollably, but my mind was clearing. I saw we were at HI-Data and wondered why. We were standing behind a wall of yews in the "Executive

Parking Lot," according to a sign. The only visible signs of life were a few sparrows darting back and forth in the hedges. The lot was virtually empty.

My mind was working well enough that I recognized I was in shock. As Sparky hustled me toward the executive elevator, I tried to focus. It wasn't Jack McSweeney who'd fiddled with my brakes. It must have been Sparky. Something bad was going on at HI-Data. Harry Marley thought it was Ken and Norman. He was right, but he forgot to add Sparky. She really fooled me. Harry Marley figured Norman panicked when he found out Ken passed some of the funny money to Marcie. Now, after seeing Sparky in action, I wondered if we'd ever know which of them had actually killed Ken and Marcie.

As we waited for the elevator, I wondered if Jeffrey suspected it was Sparky and Norman. And I wondered if anyone else at HI-Data was involved in the counterfeiting scheme. John Olson aka Dan Karton? Rivers? Tanaka? Could Jeffrey Fere get out of this alive? I was certain he was in danger, and I hoped I wasn't going to find his body next.

"Here we are," Sparky said, her breath becoming a big white cloud in the frigid air as the elevator door opened. We entered, and the cold wind greedily followed us.

She pressed the button for the executive suite. The smooth ride was over in an instant, and when the door opened, she pushed me out — right into Norman.

FIFTY-FOUR

Just the person I didn't want to see. "Norman, please . . ."

"She was spying on us," Sparky said to Norman.

"You won't get away with spying on this company," Norman said. He took my elbow and started to walk me to his office.

"Wait. I . . ."

"Let's take her in to Jeffrey," Sparky said, and steered us toward Jeffrey's office door.

I wondered if Jeffrey was still alive. If he was, we might have some kind of a chance against these two. But Sparky had the gun, and she was dangerous. She'd already killed one person, and I feared for Jeffrey — and for myself. Why else would she bring me here to HI-Data except to kill me? No matter what else happened, she sure wasn't going to let me go after I witnessed her murder Jack McSweeney.

Norman twisted my right arm in a hammerlock and jostled me along the corridor to Jeff's office. "You must think we're amateurs here at HI-Data," he said. "I promised you'd pay for what you're doing to this company. I know that somehow those three deaths are connected to you. And now you're caught spying. I'm going to find out just what's going on."

"Norman, I . . ."

"How long have you been spying on our top secret R&D to undermine the company?" He twisted my arm even harder. I tried my best not to scream.

"You think that I . . . ?"

"Don't move," he ordered.

We stopped in front of Jeffrey's door. I wondered what I'd see behind it.

Sparky knocked softly, and the door opened.

Jeffrey Fere stood silhouetted in the doorway, looking surprised.

I exhaled, relieved, at least for the moment. We were, after all, both alive, and it would be two against two, even though our side was minus a gun. I blinked, not wanting to contemplate those odds.

"Jeffrey," I cried, "you've got to . . ."

"Shut up!" Norman tightened the hammerlock and the pain shot through my body. I almost fell to the floor, but Norman held me up inadvertently with the hammerlock.

Sparky retreated into Jeffrey's office, but Norman stayed at the doorway explaining to Jeffrey his version of what happened. "She broke in, and Sparky caught her red-handed. Sparky's calling the cops. This time they'll haul her out in cuffs."

"Call the cops?" I yelled. "Sparky just shot a man to death!"

I couldn't believe Norman said he wanted to call the cops. I couldn't figure out what he and Sparky were up to.

"Watch out Jeffrey," I warned. "They're the ones who killed Ken and Marcie."

Jeffrey frowned. "She's obviously hysterical, Norman. I'll take her into my office and find out what she knows," he announced with a tight smile. "You go home. It's New Year's Eve. I'll straighten this out."

"No, Jeff. She could be dangerous. I'm staying right here."

I saw Sparky edge behind Jeffrey and pull a putter out of his golf bag.

I screamed at Jeffrey. "Look out!"

Jeffrey looked back at his office door. All eyes turned to Sparky as she came out of his office toward us, her quick steps muffled by the plush carpet.

Without so much as a glance at me, she strode quickly to Norman and raised the putter high above her head.

I gasped.

Norman suddenly saw what was about to happen. His eyes bulged wide.

"No," I yelled as Sparky swung the putter. It slightly grazed the top of my head before it made a very solid thump as it connected with Norman's forehead.

Norman's eyes kept their surprise, but he never made another sound. He dropped like a stone and pulled me down with him.

FIFTY-FIVE

Norman's left leg twitched, and a thick trickle of blood was oozing down from the wound towards the carpeting.

Jeffrey reached for his putter and carefully inspected it as I extricated myself from Norman's lifeless grip

"I hope you haven't ruined this, Sparks," he said, cradling the club. "This is what's giving me my seven handicap."

"Sorry, Jeff," Sparky said. "I thought that would be less obtrusive than using Marley's gun."

I gaped at them both, and my innards constricted. I shook myself, unable to get my bearings.

"I wish you hadn't had to do that to such a loyal employee," Jeffrey said as he stared at Norman's crumpled form. "I'm going to miss him."

"It can't be helped," Sparky said. "He

should have gone home when you told him to."

Sherlock Holmes was wrong when he claimed it was no crime to have a cold heart. He hadn't met Sparky.

Norman had fixed me as the villain, whereas Harry Marley and I had zeroed in on him. And neither Harry nor I believed either Sparky or Jeffrey were involved. I felt trapped in a Mobius strip, a hamster turning my wheel faster and faster, going absolutely nowhere.

Jeffrey was still gazing down at Norman's body.

Sparky said, "Darling, we'll find another Norman." Her long-legged silhouette was reflected in the dark glass of the windows as she touched Jeffrey's arm and then retreated into his office.

When she re-emerged, she had a towel and was pointing the gun at me again. Fear surged through every blood vessel in my body, like water soaking into a sponge. I figured it was now my turn. Now I could see the gun was a Smith and Wesson .38, and the light glinted off the copper-colored bullets in the cylinder. Sparky put the towel under Norman's head to keep the blood off the carpet.

"It was a lot less trouble getting here than

I anticipated," Sparky said to Jeff. "Except that I had to shoot some guy. He had a knife, and it was the only thing I could do. I left him dead in her apartment, and he'll just be one more thing the cops will want her for."

"I knew I could rely on you, Sparks."

"You got me here to kill me too, didn't you?" I said. "Why didn't you just kill me in my apartment?"

"I told you, we needed you," Sparky said.

"And first we must address that issue," Jeffrey added.

"What?"

"Relax, Miss McGil." Jeffrey's smile somehow terrified me even more than Sparky and the .38. "We need your help. Come along."

Sparky jabbed me in the ribs with the gun, and I followed Jeffrey into his office.

"This is why we need your help." Jeffrey opened his office closet and pointed to the floor. Harry Marley's body was lying on the closet floor in a bundle.

FIFTY-SIX

I'd had too many shocks. I wanted to scream, tried to, but my throat closed.

"You may scream if you like, Miss McGil," Jeffrey said. "No one is here except the three of us. I gave everyone else the afternoon off for the holiday. Norman would still be alive if he'd just gone home. But he came back, and we had to do what was done. Now let's get on with this."

I wondered why they wanted my help. It didn't appear they needed any assistance killing people, and I told them so.

"Your friend Mr. Marley here was an unfortunate accident," Jeffrey said. "He tried to enlist my help to entrap Norman. He let something slip about how your investigations helped put him on to Norman and the counterfeiting. I believe he thought he was doing you a favor by giving you credit. I had a difficult few moments there forcing myself to not laugh out loud. It all fit so nicely into my plan."

"But why kill Norman? Why not just bring him in as an accomplice?"

"Norman served me well, even to being the number one suspect. But Norman could never be trusted to keep his mouth shut about the counterfeiting. He never learned how to keep quiet. Now get him into the elevator."

I stared at Jeffrey, now holding the revolver. Sparky shoved me toward the closet. She grabbed one of Harry's arms, and ordered me to take the other.

"I'm not helping. Do it yourselves."

"Do you want to die right here and right now, Miss McGil? I'll give this back to Sparky, and before the clock ticks another minute, you will be in eternity."

I had no doubt they would do it. I didn't want to die yet, so I reached down, grunted, and grabbed one of Harry Marley's arms.

Sparky was much stronger than she appeared, and together we maneuvered him into the elevator. My neck was still throbbing, but not as bad as before. That super cold air must have helped. Still I felt beaten up. And I was mad. I'd let down Sensei. How could I ever tell him that not one, but two people, had gotten the better of me today? His mind would never take that in.

He'd rip off my belt and literally throw me out the door. Maybe my next lessons should involve defensive techniques against knives, guns, and cats.

I looked around for someone who might still be in the building — a guard or a janitor — but saw no one, and we performed our grisly chore uninterrupted.

After putting Harry Marley on the elevator floor, we went back for Norman. Sparky gave Jeffrey his own coat as well as Norman's. Then she and I dragged Norman as we had Harry Marley.

"Keep his head off the rug, Miss McGil," Jeffrey ordered as he followed us to the elevator. "And let's hurry. I'm giving a big New Year's Eve party tonight, and I need time to change into evening clothes. I'll be announcing the financing package that will save HI-Data, and I can't afford any mistakes."

"If you already have the financing, why did you have to commit murder?"

"Because Ken was stupid. He gave some bills to that grasping female trainee," Sparky said as we stopped to get our breath. "I warned him that someday his skirt-chasing would be the end of him."

"So the 'Safecracker' program was used to make the counterfeit money?" I asked.

Jeffrey smiled. He handed the gun to Sparky and said, "The Safecracker software program produces almost flawless counterfeit bills. It was Ken who thought of it during one of our brainstorm sessions. Our reasoning was, quite simply, that we should not hesitate to take advantage of our ingenious software, along with the latest generation of high quality, ninety-four million color digital image copier. Stop and think about all the great unwashed out there, Miss McGil. People no better than animals who are using these color copiers to generate second-rate counterfeit gift certificates, coupons, transcripts, forged checks, passes, and tickets." He paused to put on his coat, then added, "Why shouldn't HI-Data benefit? No one else was to be involved. The bills were to be used strictly to save HI-Data."

We shoveled Norman on top of Harry Marley in the elevator and Jeffrey got in, too. With the five of us, it was a tight fit, and Sparky had to kick Harry Marley's shoe clear of the elevator door.

Jeffrey pressed the elevator button. "My scheme was beautiful, if you're smart enough to comprehend it. I used the money we created to start up a dummy, offshore finance corporation. Then we set out to buy up all HI-Data's debt before Steinmetz A.G. could get more than a fifty percent hold. A win-win situation for me personally. HI-Data continues to pay back my dummy corporation, so I'll make money there. And I keep control of HI-Data and all its assets as well."

"What I don't understand," I said, "is why Ken wanted me to do the trainee investigations."

"Don't be foolish, Miss McGil," Jeffrey said. "Ken didn't make that request. I did."

"You? Why?"

"When I realized we had to get rid of Ken," Jeffrey said, "you had to be brought in. Getting rid of you is not a spur of the moment decision. Your body will never be found. Norman and that Treasury agent were unexpected, but we've been planning your demise very carefully. You see, you're going to take all the blame because you had the motive to kill Ken."

The elevator doors opened with a blast of cold air.

"Me?"

Jeffrey pulled up his collar. "Ken became a partner in this company some years ago when he invested a huge sum of money. That money, I believe, came from his father's estate. Fighting this takeover, however, took a lot more money. Ken went to Frank to borrow it, but Frank turned him down. Ken had no choice. He needed that money, so he pushed Frank off the balcony." Jeffrey smiled at me. "Bingo. HI-Data got the cash infusion it needed to stay alive from Frank's estate."

In that moment I felt nothing but rage. I leaped at Jeffrey and grabbed his throat with both hands, squeezing with all my strength.

I heard Sparky curse, and then my world went dark.

FIFTY-SEVEN

I woke to cold and blackness. The cold was welcome. It helped numb the pain in my head. I tried to sit up but couldn't. I realized I was locked in a dark embrace with Norman's corpse. Panic flared through me like a bonfire in a high wind. I screamed and pushed and kicked against his dead coldness, desperate to distance myself. Eventually I stopped screaming and forced myself to take some deep breaths and calm down.

Painfully, I wedged myself away from Norman. We were in the trunk of a car. I turned my head every which way and spotted my purse with the Burns treasures half tucked under Norman. It must be Sparky's car. This was the second time today I was riding in her trunk.

My wrists were clamped in front of me with a plastic zip-tie restraint, the kind the cops use for mass arrests. I heard there was a way you could break them, but I wasn't having any success.

Whenever we slowed or stopped, Norman's corpse shifted and rolled against me, pushing me into the sharp edges of the spare tire holder. I could only silently plead with the gods to keep the Burns artifacts from being broken into teeny fragments under this treatment.

Tears froze on my cheeks in the deepening cold, and the panic rose again. I used all my Scots' courage to hold on. If they were going to dump the car into one of the retention ponds, I was finished. The thought jolted me into action. I gingerly reached around inside the dark trunk, stretching over Norman's body to locate the trunk lock mechanism. I found it, but it was completely enclosed, which was no help.

I lay still, listening to traffic and hoping they'd commit a traffic violation and get stopped by the cops. We were now traveling at a good pace and hadn't stopped for some time, so I guessed we were on an expressway. But going where?

I thought about Frank, treasuring the fact that he hadn't killed himself. My rage and horror at his murder were now directed at the two living accomplices, Jeffrey and Sparky.

The cold was so numbing that my own flesh began to feel like Norman's. But every time the car slowed, G-forces slammed me to one side of the trunk, and Norman rolled on top of me. If by some miracle I did get out of here alive, I was going to be one big mass of black and blue, and the pain from the slashes on my neck would be nothing in comparison.

I could now hear more traffic sounds, and soon the engine was turned off. We had stopped for good. I gritted my teeth and waited. Sweat trickled coldly down my armpits. What would they do when they opened the trunk? Would I get a chance to escape?

After a long interval, I heard a noise. It was the automatic trunk opener performing its duty.

"Get out," Sparky ordered in her efficient HI-Data voice. "Now."

Sparky didn't make the mistake of approaching the trunk directly. The trunk light was on, and Sparky could see me, but I couldn't see her. I wasn't ready to die right now. First I had to get even.

I crawled out slowly and painfully. My legs and arms were cramped. Sharp pains shot through my shoulder blades. I ached all over, and my head and neck were pounding.

Sparky's breath rose in the night air as she pointed the gun straight at my gut.

I looked around. Jeffrey was sitting in his Lincoln Town Car, parked next to Sparky's Cadillac. I didn't see Harry Marley, but I did see my battered desk and old office chair.

I shook my head to clear it. We were at Consolidated Bank, standing on the deserted street at the rear entrance to the Tower. The old furniture I'd left when I moved had been tossed out to the curb to be picked up by the junkman.

What were we doing here at my old office building? My head was spinning.

This quiet, deserted backwater where I'd so often watched the garbage pick-ups now seemed a world away from civilization. The entire area for a two-block radius was cordoned off as a safety precaution for tonight's demolition. All the action at the midnight Big Bang party would take place on the other end of the building across from Consolidated's main entrance.

Sparky's cold voice interrupted my thoughts. "Discovering you're not so smart after all?" She shoved the gun at my stomach.

"Now pull him out or I'll shoot. It's your choice."

I grabbed Norman by his lapels and pulled him out of the trunk, ripping his expensive suit in the process. I nearly passed out dragging him to the elevator. Harry Marley's body was already there. They must have moved him before opening Sparky's trunk.

Jeffrey kept his distance from me. Perhaps I'd injured him at least a little when I attacked him in the elevator.

As they walked me to the elevator, I looked for tiny cameras on the walls, but didn't see any. I wondered what they were going to do when they found out that the elevator wouldn't work. Surely Michael Drake's team had already cut off the power supply. But to my dismay, when Sparky pressed the button, it shuddered and started. The makeshift electricity was still running. I listened for signs of Michael or other workmen, but heard nothing except the elevator's usual creaks and groans.

They led me to what used to be my old office. The wrecking crew had been in to weaken the support columns and wrap them with chain-link fence and wire fabric to contain flying debris. Most of the drywall had been gouged out and removed.

My heart sank when I saw the blasting caps already in place on the columns. Then I saw the neat pile of fire mortar canisters and sticks of explosive in the center of what used to be my office floor.

Sparky said, "You're going to be blown to bits with your two victims. Your body will never be found and nothing will be connected to HI-Data. It'll be just like the Twin Towers except no one will be sifting through the rubble looking for your body." She dragged me to my old closet and pushed me to my knees, tossing my purse in with me.

Suddenly I understood exactly what Auntie's Nine of Diamonds and her black vision of my closet had presaged. Only it wasn't just me in danger, it was Auntie's precious Burns objects, too.

"No one will believe I was involved," I yelled at Sparky.

"There's a dead body in your apartment. That's a good enough reason in and of itself for you to disappear. What's so funny though, is that you don't even know what's going on in your own bank account," Sparky said. "I guess you're not such a great investigator after all."

"My bank account?" There'd been $431.42 in my account last I looked before

Christmas. Since then, I hadn't bothered to check exact pennies, knowing I wasn't going to overdraw.

"Fifty thousand dollars was deposited in your account the day you found Ken's body." Sparky looked like a she-devil in the dusky shadows of the dim emergency lighting. "You've been the perfect scapegoat."

"Fifty thousand dollars?" I never have that much money. Now even Scotty might believe I was involved. "Real money," I questioned, "or the make-believe kind?"

"A totally legitimate transaction, completely untraceable from the bank's point of view. A small enough price for HI-Data to pay for what it needed.

"The police will believe you were in on this from the beginning. I will testify that Ken asked for you in particular to do the comprehensive checks on our trainees because he wanted to ensure Marcie got the stamp of approval to access HI-Data's top secret research, thereby allowing her to steal the latest developments in digitizing and scanning technology."

"Hurry up, Sparks," Jeffrey called, suddenly appearing from the stairwell.

I felt myself come unglued. I had made what my Social Studies 101 instructor Mr. Bolos used to call a "fundamental attribution error" in not guessing the true nature of either Sparky or Jeffrey.

"The police will conclude you killed Ken because you wanted more money. And you threatened Marcie with blackmail, so she killed herself. Remember, there's no evidence to suggest she was murdered."

Sparky was enjoying the effect her fictionalized account had on me. It sounded so plausible, I knew she'd be believed. The odds of getting away with murder were a staggering two to one. The odds of being murdered, however, were eighteen thousand to one. Although those raw number odds seemed somewhat in my favor, I realized that my chances of getting out of this tonight were fading by the second.

"Poor Norman found evidence linking you to Ken's murder, but he never got a chance to tell Jeffrey what it was. He's disappeared, Mr. Marley has disappeared, and you've disappeared. If your bodies are ever found, which is highly unlikely because you'll be dust in the rubble, then it will be obvious you killed them both and didn't get out in time before the building blew. Cops are eager to clear these things off their books, and neither Jeff nor I will ever be involved."

"What about the counterfeiting?" I asked, fascinated how they'd tied up all the loose ends except that. "The Feds know something is up at HI-Data."

"Miss McGil," Jeffrey said, coming closer, "We won't get caught. But even if we do, in this country, all you have to do is say you're sorry, and they let you off with a slap on the wrist. We'll take our chances."

This was no white collar crime where he'd get a slap on the wrist. They'd left corpses strewn all over. Jeffrey was a complete megalomaniac who couldn't conceive of any of his plans going awry. But Sparky had a point. There was a good chance they would never be connected with any of this.

"We have no time to waste, Sparky. Let's go."

I waited for the shot, wondering if I'd hear it before dying. Suddenly I saw red, and sharp pain accompanied me into welling blackness.

FIFTY-EIGHT

I opened my eyes. I was face down. My head was on Harry Marley's legs. Muffled voices swam somewhere in the background. Everything hurt. Was I alive? What had happened? Were they still here?

I tried to sit up, but now my ankles were bound with a plastic zip tie, and I fell back down. I maneuvered around and sat on Harry Marley's shoulder. My head was clearing, and the voices were more distinct. They didn't sound like Sparky and Jeffrey.

Elated, I screamed. Nothing came out but a muted rasp. I was gagged. I rapidly considered my options. I might not get another chance.

The voices faded in and out. I strained to hear what they were saying about moving charges closer to the support columns and the final timing of the charges and how the structure should collapse.

My life, it now appeared, was in the hands

of Michael Drake and his demolition team. I tried again to scream. The gag was so tight that the strangled sounds that came out were almost inaudible, even to me. The voices trailed off into the distance until everything was again quiet.

I crawled over Norman and Harry until I reached the wall. I pounded on it until my arms ached and my knuckles bled. No one came. Too late.

I didn't know what time it was. Or how much time I had left.

"Four hundred sticks of explosives," Michael Drake had told me that day the deadly stuff was unloaded. "Almost two hundred pounds," he'd said, "and the ensuing chain reaction will implode Consolidated onto itself in about seven seconds."

Like Mary, Queen of Scots, awaiting the executioner, I churned over all the other details I could remember. The hundred fire mortars which would be set off about ten seconds before midnight; the final computer systems check; Michael personally pressing the detonator at midnight. Then the entire building reduced to a twenty foot pile of rubble in the time it took to blink your eyes. It had all the elements of good drama, including the fact that Michael Drake himself would kill me. They do say that nine out of ten times, you know your own killer. Nice to know that at the end, statistics would be on my side.

My end would come quickly, but waiting in this dark closet was terrifying. I already felt dead and gone. I wondered if being blown apart was going to be any less painful than being crushed by the rubble. According to a recent public health survey the number one fear most people have is public speaking. My number one fear is dying, with explosions under Subset A.

I thought about Frank. If I died today, maybe I'd see him again. I thought about Scotty, Tom, Cavalier, my mother, Auntie and the twins. And the Burns Artifacts. Auntie was never going to forgive me. Somehow I knew she'd haunt me through whatever eternity awaited me to take her Scot's vengeance.

I'd long since stopped trying to find a position where I wasn't putting my heel into Harry Marley's face or my elbow into Norman's stomach. I sank down onto the bodies and thought about what Michael had said about that final computer check. It was supposed to happen just before the plunger was pressed. If I could break a wire connection to the detonator, the faulty connection would show up on the computer check. One light would still flash, signaling a broken connection. Maybe, just maybe, Michael would see the flashing light and save me. But would they stop the detonation and the show for one flashing light? I didn't know, but I had to try.

I had absolutely no idea which wire to cut. If I picked the wrong one, I might send myself to another dimension ahead of schedule. At least having a plan made me feel alive again. I wanted to — needed to — avenge Frank and keep the treasures safe.

I slipped off my left shoe and had to twist like a pretzel to grab hold of it. That was the easy part. Then I pulled myself up to a standing position and balanced on Harry's torso. My legs shook unsteadily as I reached up and felt for the wires.

I chose one at random and pounded it with the heel of my shoe to break the connection. I hit it again and again, but it wouldn't break. My coat was hampering my ability to hit, but I couldn't take it off.

My arms ached. My whole body was shaking. I couldn't stand up anymore. How much time was left?

I tried again, but lost my footing. I sank down, stabbing myself as I landed on the sharp end of one of Harry's hundred dollar bill cuff links.

I grabbed Harry's arm and pulled off one of the cuff links, cutting my finger in the process. If this razor-edged cuff link couldn't sever the connection, nothing would.

I stood up again. Racing against an unknown time clock, I balanced on unsteady tip toes on the two bodies. The wire was just out of reach. Stretching till I ached, I succeeded only in nearly wrenching my arms out of their sockets.

I was ready to give up when, without warning, red and orange lights streaked into the murky darkness. Loud booms made me flinch like a bird on the wing ducking shots. These were the fire mortars being exploded for the crowd. If I correctly remembered Michael's timetable, I had ten seconds left.

I tried one more time to cut the wire with Harry's cuff link. I stretched and strained, knowing the end was coming any second. Suddenly Harry Marley's corpse moaned, and I distinctly felt it move under my feet. I screamed and jumped. The jolt propelled me that extra millimeter, and I felt the cuff link slice through the wire.

The adrenaline boost dissipated as quickly as it had come. I sank back down on top of Harry and Norman.

The corpse moaned again.

I screamed into the gag. How long could ten seconds be? Was Harry really alive, or were we already dead, and I just didn't know it yet, like in the Topper movies?

Harry moaned, louder this time. I felt his warm breath on my arm. I sobbed softly through my gag and tried to call his name, but I doubted he could hear. We were both alive, and he and I and Auntie's Burns treasures were headed for eternity together.

FIFTY-NINE

The next thing I knew, Michael Drake was holding me in his arms, calling my name over and over. He removed the gag. I looked at him, puzzled, wondering why he too had died.

"DD McGil, can you hear me? It's me, Michael. Michael Drake. And this is my father, Michael Senior."

"Michael, the archangel?" I gazed at a small, wizened man with a shock of white, unruly hair bending over me.

"So this is the one you told me wouldn't move out," his father said, frowning. "Girlie, you must really love this office." He then proceeded to tell me how his son had noticed the flashing light on the computer screen at the last possible second. "He ordered a final walk-thru on this floor," he added. "Otherwise — poof. You wouldda been gone."

"Yeah, but I really had to insist," Michael

Jr. added. "The Mayor's undies are in a bundle because of the TV cameras running and the time frame. He was ready to walk out, mad as a wet hen that one trip wire connection made us go off line. Especially after all the fireworks went off."

"Lucky my boy didn't cave in though," Michael's father said and thumped his son's shoulder. "He disconnected the plunger with his master key."

They helped me up, then Michael lifted me out of the closet. I was too weak to move on my own. I flung my arms around him and dropped my head onto his chest, clinging to a warmth I never thought I'd feel again.

"You're going to be all right. Do you understand? Tell us what happened. Why were you in the closet? Who was with you?"

"What happened?" I repeated like a parrot.

I was tense, waiting for the onset of my eternal torment. Then I had to pee real bad, and that's when I realized I wasn't dead. And I knew I had something very important to tell, but I couldn't remember what.

"Get those other two out," Michel barked at a swarm of men who pulled out Harry, then Norman.

"This is a crime scene, DD. Do you

understand what I'm saying? As soon as I saw you in that closet on top of two other bodies, I had one of my men call a captain I know. He should be here any second. Come on, I'll carry you outside to the shed where you can warm up and talk to him before they take you to the hospital."

I told him I didn't need to go to any hospital. "I want Jeff Fere and that bitch Sparky to get what's coming to them," I repeated several times as he took me to the shed.

Captain Fisher arrived, worried about the mayor and all the commotion. But he patiently took down everything I told him about Jeffrey Fere and HI-Data and Sparky Groh.

He asked if I knew the other two victims, and I told him who they were. At the mention of a Treasury Agent, Captain Fisher turned a funny color and swallowed hard. I heard him tell one of the cops to get the mayor away from the site and seal off the area. Then he conferred in a huddle with all the other cops.

"They've killed others, too," I shouted to the captain. He emerged from the huddle, and I related what Sparky did to Jack Mc-Sweeney in my apartment.

Michael Drake listened, then told the

captain he wanted to check why none of the cameras had picked up anything that had happened on the feed. He returned, shaking his head and explained that someone had cut the camera wires in all the tower cameras. His father approached and interrupted.

"Son," I heard them talking at the outer edge of my fog, "The mayor has pushed that fake detonator button so many times by now it's worn out. He wants to get this show on the road right now. We better do it, or we'll be completely finished in this town."

"We can't just blow it up, even on the mayor's personal okay," Michael said. "Anyway, I think the mayor's being escorted home right now. We're going to have to wait for the cops to give us the go ahead, and it's not going to be any time soon. This is a crime scene now."

They moved away with Michael's father complaining about how dangerous it was having all the explosives ready to go. I felt bad that their company might lose out on the bonus they'd been promised. But right at this moment, all I could think of was that I had to pee, and it felt so good to be alive.

Then I heard Auntie. I thought I was hallucinating.

She was rushing toward me, pushing

through a throng of cops and workmen, shooing them aside like children in her way. George Murray was right behind her. I couldn't believe she'd gotten past the Mayor and all the security.

"DD, what's happened?" Auntie asked, out of breath. "Are you hurt, lass?" She ran her hands gently over my head and arms.

"We went to your apartment when you didn't show up for the party," Auntie said, "and you know what we found. A . . ." She made a face, not willing to say "dead body" aloud.

"I told the cops what happened . . ." I tried to say, but George interrupted.

"Your Auntie then was seized with one of her dire feelings about your office closet, and she'd have nothing but to come here and see for herself that things are well."

"I ken something bad was happening," Auntie said, looking me in the eyes. "I had more than one flash that was warning me clear and loud that you and the precious objects were involved. What's going on DD?"

Ohmygod, my purse with the Burns artifacts. Where was it? And in what condition were the treasures? I couldn't bear to think.

I took a deep breath and called Michael. I introduced him to Auntie and George and then asked him to go rescue my purse, still in the closet. As soon as he was out of earshot, I asked if they'd called the cops and reported McSweeney's death.

"O' course we did," Auntie said. "We were worried about you. There's a general look out for you or whatever they call it."

"I'm afraid you're a suspect in Jack Mc-Sweeney's murder," George explained. "O' course I am as well. Sorry, lass."

"Auntie, you were absolutely right when you said something bad was going to happen. Something real bad did happen. But everything's fine now." I smiled at them both. "Auntie, your job is to get me to a ladies room at once. And George, please go find Michael and get my purse from him. I'd like you to examine it and tell me if anything inside's been damaged."

I winked at him, hoping he'd fathom that I wanted him to look in there and find the treasures. I didn't want to spring anything on Auntie and panic her. She was fully capable of making a scene over the artifacts that would make the rape of the Sabine women look tame.

Two cops escorted us to the john, which Auntie didn't like but tolerated. They had to hold me up between them as my legs were still weak and my motor skills weren't working very well. Auntie did tell me that Cavalier was at Mother's house and not to worry about him.

"Not to worry," I repeated vacuously over and over, hoping that George would deftly handle the problem of the Burns artifacts because I could not.

SIXTY

Two days later, they released me from the hospital. They were all glad to see me go. Scots do not make good patients. The word "patient" is not in our vocabulary.

The soft-spoken Indian doctor completed his examination. He had liquid brown eyes that seemed to hold the secrets of the universe. He muttered something, then made some notes. I still wasn't feeling very good, but I didn't want to say anything to prevent him from releasing me.

Finally he looked up and said, "I am agreeing to sign these release papers today, Miss McGrill, but only upon condition you go home and rest."

"McGil. It's McGil," I said. His name was Callugulagula, and this was payback for my calling him Dr. Caligula.

"The concussion you are sustaining," he continued in his clipped Indian accent as he flipped through my chart, "may well continue to give you small side effects, such as headache, blurred vision, ringing in the ears, or slight nausea."

I'd been feeling all of that, plus more he hadn't mentioned to do with the pain in my neck.

"And I hope you realize how extremely lucky you are that the slash on your neck was not deeper. It could have injured your vocal chords or severed a major blood vessel," he said in a tone that inferred I'd brought all this on myself. Then he snapped my chart closed and cautioned me not to operate an automobile for another week. His parting instructions as he shut the door were to "take things slow and easy."

Yesterday they told me that Norman had died instantly from the blow to his head. Harry Marley had been luckier. He'd survived Sparky's assault, and his prognosis was excellent. That cold Chicago west wind had been good to him. Hypothermia had saved him from bleeding to death. He'd been transferred to Northwestern University Research Hospital.

Mother wanted to come pick me up and have me stay with her for a few days, but I refused as gently as I could. I promised to come pick up Cavvy as soon as I got released, but then I wanted to be alone. I needed to go back to my apartment and check things out. They'd long ago removed McSweeney's body, but I had to come to terms with what had happened — not just McSweeney's murder but also Frank's death, and I knew it was going to take a little more time before I could put it all to rest.

Mother did make me promise to take a cab, but I would have anyway. I was having the vertigo Dr. Caligula had so cheerfully predicted.

The nurses put me in a wheelchair, and a candy striper escorted me to a waiting cab. She warned me that the temperature was minus two. I climbed as quickly as I could into the back seat, feeling cold and a bit woozy, but very glad to be alive.

On the way to Mother's, I played the messages that had accumulated on my cell phone. The first was from Phil.

"I can't believe what happened," he said. "I'm sorry I got you involved with HI-Data. What a mess. Are you okay? I know you're in the hospital, but call me when you can. I have news for you. I went to Jeff Fere's New Year's Eve bash. Everybody was there, and then, wow, all of a sudden an army of law enforcement types stormed in and arrested him. Cuffed him right in his own living room. And that tall girl, Sparky Groh, too. Talk about shock. You should have been there. Well, I mean you should have seen the look on Jeff's wife's face when Sparky threw herself into Jeff's arms. The whole place went up for grabs. Anyway, call me as soon as you can. I want to hear all the details. And, by the way, where's your new office? I need your new address."

I looked forward to talking to Phil again soon, but not today. And as for sharing the grisly details, I was still trying to remember things. Even after my two-hour meeting yesterday in the hospital with the Feds there were some gaps. Sparky had hit me hard on the head with that revolver, and needless to say, I hated guns more now than ever before. For all they'd done, and especially for Frank, I was going to enjoy the trial of Jeff and Sparky and their public disgrace.

Then I heard the next voice. "DD, this is Scotty. If you're hearing this message, I love you, and I'm glad you're okay. I hope you're resting. I'm calling from somewhere high above the Atlantic en route to your bedside. I took a week's leave, so expect me momentarily. Oh, and by the way, I talked to Harry in the hospital. He's embarrassed all to hell about what happened and you having to save him. So do me a favor. Don't go visit him. And, oh, would you have any idea what might have happened to one of his gold cuff links? He says they're his lucky charm, and he's really upset one's missing. Now get into bed and wait for me."

Yes, I knew where Harry Marley's lucky gold cuff link was all right. Somewhere under the pile of debris where my old office once stood.

When the cab pulled up at Mother's, Tom Joyce and George Murray rushed out to greet me and help me up the stairs. I was surprised at the attention and told them I could manage myself, but they insisted.

Mother threw her arms around me as did Auntie, and Cavalier wanted to be picked up and cuddled. For once he was glad to see me.

"I know you don't like any fuss over you, DD. That's why I didn't tell you everyone was here," Mother said, taking my coat and scarf and staring at the bandages Dr. Caligula had placed on my neck and on my head where they'd shaved my hair.

I looked around for Scotty, but didn't see him.

"Scotty'll be arriving shortly," Mother said. "He's delayed at Kennedy. They've had nine inches of snow in the last few hours, and all the takeoffs were cancelled. He sounds like such a nice man."

"Aye, an' important, too, coming all the way from London," Auntie nodded her approval. "Now come sit down, lass. I'll give you a wee glass of your mother's sherry. It'll do wonders for a concussion, an' we must celebrate the safe return of the artifacts."

I stared at her as she smiled and poured a small sherry for me.

"I know what all happened, my girl," she said and went to fetch a bottle of Macallan "1876 Replica" Highland Single Malt Scotch Whisky. She announced proudly that a friend in Scotland had given it to her and that she'd smuggled it in past customs. Some Scots traits have a monotonous predictability.

We enjoyed several toasts — to me the detective niece, to Tom Joyce, to Rabbie Burns and the precious artifacts, to Scotland, and to the Stuarts. I was careful not to take more than a sip for each, and was glad for the interruption when my cell phone rang.

I answered, thinking it might be Scotty. It wasn't.

"Hi, DD. Special Agent Greg McIntyre here. Are you out of the hospital yet?"

"Hi, Greg. I just got out. What's up?"

"The whole team's dying to hear what

happened at HI-Data. We understand you're quite the heroine."

"Yeah, yeah, that's what they all say, but I sure don't feel like one. I feel more like a pin cushion."

"No, really, that's the word going around. And on top of that — which I hate to admit — you were right all along about Eric Daniels. Thanks to that tip we got from Mr. Anonymous, we recovered most of the Mooney Investment funds. I wanted to let you know that we got ahold of Eric-boy just in time, too. He was about to bail with a ticket for Las Vegas and a fake passport when we cuffed him. Old Mr. Mooney's so happy he's pushing us to identify the tipster so he can personally deliver the $10,000 reward. Well, take it easy, and we'll talk later when you feel better."

I chuckled as I hit the off button, thinking that's me, DD McGil, Tipster. But I could never collect, because I'd never let anyone know about a certain B & E caper that produced the information for the team to get Mr. Daniels. Oh well, good-bye ten thousand lovely dollars.

"So," Tom said, eyeing me closely. "I heard that about Eric Daniels and the tipster. Methinks the tipster was DD McGil. And I think Agent McIntyre guessed, too."

"A girl has to be a Jill of many trades in this world," I replied, staring into space, fighting a damn headache that may have been from either the concussion or the sherry.

My ears were ringing and I was experiencing another bout of that intermittent nausea Dr. Caligula told me to expect. But the mention of the reward triggered something. I smiled. Suddenly the headache and the nausea disappeared. I remembered the fifty thousand dollars. Sparky said they'd deposited fifty thousand dollars in my bank account hoping to frame me and convince everyone I'd been involved. Real money, she'd said, not counterfeit. "A Bank Error In My Favor," as the Monopoly game cards so nicely put it.

Maybe the fates weren't so impersonal after all. Maybe HI-Data was going to end up paying me for my work. All I had to do was print out an invoice for services rendered on the trainees in the amount of fifty thousand dollars, mark it paid, and send it to HI-Data.

I grinned and relaxed.

"DD, are you sure you're all right?" Tom asked, his voice fading in and out. "You've got an awful silly grin on your face."

As I drifted off, I saw George Murray on

one knee, proposing to Auntie Elizabeth. I hoped Scotty would get here soon.

ACKNOWLEDGMENTS

People do make a difference. Thanks to Grace Morgan, agent and friend, who worked long and hard, and to Molly Weston of Meritorious Mysteries for her early interest and suggestions. Also thanks to Midnight Ink's great staff and especially Senior Editor Connie Hill.

Thanks to the gods for Enid Perll, whose editing always challenges and improves. And many thanks to Stuart Kaminsky for his contributions and stimulating friendship.

Thanks to all my readers, including Velma and Fred Roberts and Richard Sumner, and especially to Gordon Drawer for Chicago-related continuity; to Albert and Shirley Gilbert for extraordinary encouragement and champagne; and to my Mom, Alice Lemke Gilbert, and brother Wayne Gilbert for their unwavering support.

Thanks aye to my dear friend and Burns scholar, Frank Campbell, President of the

North American Burns Association, for his advice and help. And many thanks to friends in Scotland: David Sibbald, Past President of the Glasgow and District Association of Burns Clubs and Past President of Glasgow Haggis Club, and Peter Westwood, director of the Robert Burns World Federation and editor of the Burns Chronicle, for their ever generous help in Burns research. Special thanks also to Lord Bruce and his family for sharing information on Katherine Bruce.

The quick wit, enthusiasm, suggestions, and involvement of Thomas J. Joyce contributed greatly to this work, as did his invaluable advice on manuscripts and bibliophilia.

And ever to Tom Madsen, continuity expert, plot boiler, friend, and husband extraordinaire — let's put time in that bottle and see the pyramids along the Nile for eighty-eight more years.

ABOUT THE AUTHOR

Chicago native **Diane Gilbert Madsen** brings a real feel for the Windy City to her DD McGil Literati Mystery series. Madsen attended the University of Chicago and earned an M.A. in seventeenth-century English Literature from Roosevelt University. She was Director of Economic Development for the State of Illinois and oversaw the Tourism and Illinois Film Office during the time *The Blues Brothers* was filmed. She also ran her own consulting busines and is listed in *Who's Who in Finance and Industry* and the *World Who's Who of Women.*

Fascinated by crime, history, and business, her interest in writing murder mysteries was sparked when she met the suspect in a murder that occurred near her home. The suspect was convicted, then later exonerated of the crime, and the encounter caused her to rethink how people form their first impressions of murder suspects. Her Scots heritage and membership in Robert Burns, St. Andrews, and Caledonian Societies contributed to writing this book.

Recently Diane and her husband Tom moved to Florida where they live at Twin Ponds, a five-acre wildlife sanctuary. Check the latest news at http//dianegilbertmadsen .com

We hope you have enjoyed this Large Print book. Other Thorndike, Wheeler, Kennebec, and Chivers Press Large Print books are available at your library or directly from the publishers.

For information about current and upcoming titles, please call or write, without obligation, to:

Publisher
Thorndike Press
295 Kennedy Memorial Drive
Waterville, ME 04901
Tel. (800) 223-1244

or visit our Web site at:

http://gale.cengage.com/thorndike

OR

Chivers Large Print
published by BBC Audiobooks Ltd
St James House, The Square
Lower Bristol Road
Bath BA2 3SB
England
Tel. +44(0) 800 136919
email: bbcaudiobooks@bbc.co.uk
www.bbcaudiobooks.co.uk

All our Large Print titles are designed for easy reading, and all our books are made to last.